THE FAVORITE GIRL

MONICA ARYA

To my favorite girl, Mila. You are every bit of sunshine and light that the world needs. I love you, my little butterfly.

To those that are in the middle of a storm—I hope you remember that it's just a chapter and not your whole story. You are strong enough to weather it and the sun always comes out. I pinky promise. This is our now.

AUTHOR'S NOTE / CONTENT WARNING

Dear reader,

I am honored that you chose my novel to read. The Favorite Girl is my ninth book and sixth thriller. It is the *darkest* of my thrillers with horror elements and contains **MANY** content warnings. Please note, they are all listed on my website www.monicaarya.com and if you have any concerns you can contact me at moni caaryaauthor@gmail.com or on social media @moni-caaryaauthor. There are many topics, descriptions and scenes that may be troubling to some and I urge you to protect your peace by checking out the list. Those of you who choose to continue, I hope you enjoy meeting The Favorite Girl. Those of you who read the content warning list and turned back, I have many other books that aren't *as* unhinged as this one. Key word, as.

Sending my best wishes and good vibes always,
Monica Arya

AUTHOR'S SECOND NOTE

Are you absolutely sure you don't want to double check the trigger warning list?

There's still time.

Okay then, you've got this. I've got this. Here we go.

Happy reading, my little birds…

PROLOGUE

DARKNESS. It's interesting how, as humans, we are conditioned to be fearful of the dark. As children, we fear what could be lurking. What if there's a monster under our bed? What if the boogeyman is hiding in the crevice of our closet between our winter coat and rain jacket? What if the squeaking floors and doors are due to an intruder? But now, I've learned I'm more afraid of the dark when I know what's really waiting for me.

As women, we are conditioned to be in a constant state of fear. Leaving a place and it's dark out? You must check your surroundings. Home alone? That creaking must be someone breaking in. About to get into an Uber? Double check the license plate and ask the driver their name. Is someone following you for far too long while you're driving? Don't you dare think about turning onto your street; you've got to loop

around until you lose them. Going to the bathroom...
well, you already know we're already taking a friend
or two. It's as if the universe sets the stage for us to be
frightened.

Yet, even with the precedent of an innate need to be
hypervigilant, we also occasionally have a fatal flaw.
We are too trusting. We trust that humans aren't
capable of heinous activities. We trust that our lives
have the potential to be smooth and stable. We trust
that someone will love us, protect us, and save us.

Except, there's a reason we are conditioned to be in
a constant state of fear.

Because humans *are* capable of committing atro-
cious crimes, wrecking lives, and making sure the
dreams we hoped for never comes true. The biggest
mistake we make is to believe that our lives are solely
ours to control. We are often mere puppets even in our
own stories and I'm positive there is nothing more
terrifying than that.

CHAPTER
ONE

IF THERE IS one thing in life that I know with absolute certainty, it's that there is a vast difference between surviving and thriving. When two cars crash, you'd think that the only ones with repercussions are the two cars involved, but that's not true. When they collide, traffic piles up and nosey drivers rubberneck. The crash causes chaos all because one person may not have been paying attention, or someone was texting while driving; maybe a drunk driver was involved... or simply Murphy's Law was in effect. That's how I felt about my life. My life was a series of things going wrong because of decisions made for me. Or honestly, just terrible luck.

People who don't believe in luck are lucky, while those of us who believe in it are unquestionably unlucky.

Same with fate. If you have an amazing life, you're not crediting fate to be on your side, you're just crediting yourself and the wonderful job you did to make it all happen.

Now, here I was, holed up in a shitty, Super 7 Motel, ingesting a line-up of vending machine junk food and praying that I could maybe alter my fate. Maybe, just maybe, luck would actually work in my favor.

I took an obnoxious bite of the Twinkie in front of me, the cream splattering against the corners of my mouth. I tilted my head as I lifted the small, spongy cake.

"You little bastard, you should have stayed discontinued. You're far too delicious for this world." I sighed.

Go ahead, mark this as an all-time new low. Demi Rao, nineteen-year-old female, is speaking to a Twinkie.

Please, luck, I need you to change... *now.*

Propping my feet up on the cheap vinyl table, I stared at the yellowing wallpaper that was clearly put up in the 1970s. Shuddering, I looked down at the green shag carpet and nodded in confirmation.

Blowing out a breath, I knew I needed to stop pretending I was some interior designer and look for an actual source of income. All things considered, I was talking to a Twinkie and had only about two hundred dollars hidden inside my sock.

"Nanny? No way." I tapped the neon green highlighter against my chin while I flipped through the classifieds section of the *Charlotte Observer*.

The scent of bleach and cigarette smoke felt suffocating to me, but I knew I was just looking for any distraction.

"Does everyone need a nanny?" I drew my finger in a straight line down as the word repeated down the column. Why do people have so many kids if they can't watch them? As I continued to scan the section, I saw there were some positions open as gas station clerks, front desk receptionists, and my personal favorite, used car model.

"Yea, no thanks, pedophile." I shook my head and was about to toss the paper away when a listing that seemed a bit more promising caught my eye.

Live-in housekeeper for prominent Dr. Ivory and family. Gated community. Wonderful stipend. E-mail your resume and information to ivorysurgery@gmail.com.

"Well, hello lucky stars…" I highlighted the listing excitedly and pushed the cap back on. My fingers were stained neon green, junk food crumbs were scattered across my black leggings, and I knew I probably looked like I hadn't showered in days. Because I hadn't. I spent most days on park benches or walking aimlessly until I collapse under a tree. Getting to stay in a motel was a luxury.

But this… this was going to be amazing.

I needed a place to stay, I needed a steady income, and I needed a job that wasn't going to require learning new skills. My educational background was… missing, to say the least. Not to say I wasn't naturally smart, and honestly, I loved to read to the point where I devoured books. I always dreamed of going to school, maybe becoming a psychologist and helping girls, especially girls like me. The ones whose fate had been altered and tainted; the girls who didn't even get a chance to dream. Maybe that's why I loved to read so much. I could escape my reality and live a thousand lives through the pages and words of others. Thanks to the library, I could actually have a warm place to read.

I could be anyone and anything.

I could be loved. I could explore. *I could feel…*

Looking back down at the worn table, I tilted my head and licked my bottom lip while staring at the tarnished scissors. Spinning it around and around, it scratched against the surface, making the thin plastic layer of the table indent slightly.

"Don't," I whispered to myself. But that's when

depression and anxiety like to rear their ugly heads—when you're at your weakest. Even though you fall to your knees and tears line your eyes as you pray to a God you don't even know exists, because truthfully, how could a superpower allow the brutalities that have happened in the world—especially when you lived through some of them before you had even lived at all.

That's when all the pain surfaces, when the anxious thoughts overtake any rationale and suddenly, it's easier to lift the metal between your fingers and peel down the fitted leggings.

It's easy to spread your legs and squeeze your inner thigh, hoping you'll be able to find a place that hasn't been marked so heavily, and that's when it's easy to slice the scissors into your skin until the blood seeps out and you can remember…

I'm actually alive.

Because I feel the fucking pain that I'm inflicting on myself, but at least… at least, I'm the one inflicting it this time.

CHAPTER
TWO

THE SUNLIGHT SEEPED IN, and my head was pounding. Clenching my eyes shut, I cursed the heat of the malodorous motel room. It was the middle of summer in North Carolina, and between the sticky humidity and suffocating heat, the room had essentially become a hot box with complimentary flies buzzing around my sweat-covered body the entire night.

Sliding up, I reached for my water bottle and shook it. Nothing.

"Damn it!" Crushing it in my palm, I threw it to the ground. The floral, thin comforter—that definitely had never been washed—was piled on the floor, and when I glanced down at the sheets, I saw a giant puddle of blood by my thighs.

I passed out after playing a game of operation on

my legs and decided an entire bottle of three-dollar wine would take the edge off. A bottle I was able to steal by sliding into my tote bag and using a gas station bathroom. The clerk was Indian so he didn't think twice when he saw me. He didn't think a well-raised Indian girl would steal from one of her own. Sadly, I wasn't raised right. I was barely raised at all. I just existed.

But this was a milestone moment for me. I was officially no longer going to be this girl.

Today was the day I was going to prepare for my interview with the Ivory family that was to be held tomorrow.

After using the computer from the dial-up days, I finally created a new email address and messaged Dr. Ivory from the newspaper listing. His assistant, Carla, replied immediately and gave me detailed information on the interview. I thought it was a bit dramatic considering I was applying to be a housekeeper and not a nurse, but beggars can't be choosers.

The e-mail was peculiar because she listed things I needed to do before coming in tomorrow. Luckily, I was able to convince the sleazy front-desk clerk here at the motel to print it out for me, even though the cheap bastard made me give him a dime.

Sliding it off of the nightstand, I studied the list once more.

. . .

Dear Miss Rao,

We are pleased with your interest in the position available with the Ivory family. Dr. Ivory asks that you arrive tomorrow, at 6207 Knights Place, promptly at noon. Lunch will be served. As per the Ivory family policy, please dress accordingly:

Simple white dress, or white slacks and a white blouse.

Hair must be neatly pinned up, no jewelry, and minimal makeup preferably a nude lipstick.

Nails must be trimmed and unpainted.

Thank you for respecting the aesthetic of the home and family.

Best wishes,

Carla Cross

After reading it at least ten times, I dug the crumpled newspaper from the trash bin, which was covered in sticky ketchup and grease from the McDonald's French fries that had been split to become both my lunch and dinner. I ran through the classifieds one more time and even scoured multiple online listings. The number one most requested job that didn't require an education was either a nanny or a house-keeper. I'd rather scrub toilets and potentially splash bleach in my eyes than have to care for young children.

"The aesthetic of the home and family? What does that even mean?" I wondered out loud. *Bougie-ass rich people.*

Stretching my arms over my head, I sighed. I really needed to stop over-analyzing everything. Truthfully, the live-in aspect had me sold; I just had to hope I, somehow, was the most appealing to the family.

But then again, who was lining up and pleading to be a housekeeper?

————

I quickly showered, feeling grateful even though most would consider it a shower from hell—the water never heated up properly, and I was using a small bar of soap from my scalp to my toes that was left behind by the last tenant of this room.

Standing in front of the mirror, I swiped away the layer of steam. Blowing out a breath of air, I felt defeated at what a mess I was. My skin was dull and lackluster, my long, thick black hair was in terrible knots. Brushing one of my eyebrows with my index finger, I clenched my teeth at how overgrown they were.

I wasn't near presentable to go to Charlotte's most

prestigious country club neighborhood and plead my case for a job.

But after paying for one more night in the motel, and setting aside the rest for some food and clothes, I didn't have anything left for anything more.

A banging on the door sounded, and my thoughts shattered as I clutched the towel tighter around me.

"Demi! We know you're in there!" A wicked laughter echoed.

"Demi, baby... come on. We need you to come back. You know your job isn't done," another voice mocked.

My palms grew moist and my legs shook violently as my breathing hitched. The banging grew rhythmic, and the voices muffled together as spots clouded my vision. My head was light, and before I knew it, I was on my knees having a panic attack that I couldn't get out from.

Panic attacks were a whole different form of cruelty. You often know you're having them—you feel them mentally and physically—but no matter how much you hope to get through it, you just have to ride it out.

Except, I didn't ride it out. I scrambled across the stained, shaggy green carpet on all-fours like a wild animal and grabbed the scissors that were coated in my dried blood.

"Ah!" I screamed as I jammed them into my thigh,

but I quickly slapped my hand across my mouth. Blinking repeatedly, I looked at the door and realized the noise was gone. *I'm okay.*

Sweat dribbled down my temples as blood trickled down my leg and I stood naked, and slowly walked to the window. Sliding the thick curtain to the side by less than an inch, I let out a long breath of relief.

No one was there. The parking lot was mostly empty, except for a woman smoking by the vending machines.

"You're okay, Demi." I clutched my arms and rubbed them. I had to pull myself together. I had to... *for her.*

CHAPTER
THREE

I HAD SPENT the rest of the day stuffing my limited belongings into a trash bag and tying it up. Grabbing the thinned-out stack of cash from underneath the mattress, I made my way to a thrift store on the wealthier side of town. Rich people throw the nicest, barely worn designer things in their local Goodwill collection bins. It was worth the two-dollar bus ride.

The dusty scent of Goodwill slapped me in the face as soon as I walked in, but within seconds, I was padding through hangers that had beautiful designer pieces I had only learned about through fashion magazines I'd dig out of retail trash bins.

I needed an all-white outfit, but wasn't having any luck until I turned, about to leave, and noticed a stunning jumpsuit. Pinching my lips to the side, I lifted it off the rack. The material was smooth like butter, and I was certain I could fit into it. All I needed now were some white shoes, a few hair clips and ties, and maybe pop into a drugstore for tweezers, powder, and mascara. Brushing the tag of the outfit, I saw someone had scribbled their name on the back: *Navy Mian.* Shrugging, I walked to check out.

The teenage boy behind the register was too busy texting and didn't acknowledge me, not even when I placed my items on the counter. Clearing my throat, he huffed as if I was such an inconvenience for shopping at the store.

"There's a small rip on the leg of the jumpsuit. I'd like twenty percent off." I pointed out the tear—the one I had created by jamming my nail into the delicate threading, knowing it would be a sure-fire way to have some more money knocked off it.

"Ten is the best I can do, sis." He took a long slurp of his gas station soda before lifting his phone again.

"Fifteen, and I don't tell your store manager that you're looking at porn on your phone." I shrugged as his mouth dropped.

"Fine." He rang up my items and sure enough, when he told me the total, he had given me the twenty percent off I had initially asked for.

Clutching my bag, I pushed through the doors and scrunched my nose. The scent of something delicious was floating around, and my stomach rumbled. I didn't have enough money left over for food, so I'd have to stick to the vending machine fare tonight.

Sulking, I walked to the drugstore and quickly grabbed some powder, lipstick, and mascara from a clearance bin. The powder was two shades too dark for my skin, and the lipstick would definitely look orange on me. Sliding the mascara and lipstick into my Goodwill grocery bag and glancing around nervously, I went to the cashier and quickly checked out the powder.

"Havin' a good day, sweetie?" The older woman behind the counter smiled brightly.

"Mm-hmm..." I averted my gaze. Something about her made me feel nervous. Maybe it was the way her wrinkles sunk in by her eyes when she smiled, or the Southern drawl... or maybe it was the pearls around her neck.

Maybe it was the way she was a stranger, but also completely familiar.

My heart began pounding against my chest. "You live around here, honey?" she asked as she slowly bagged the small powder compact.

"Why?" I looked up at her with rage pooling inside me.

She was immediately taken aback by my tone. "I'm... I'm sorry, sweetie. I didn't mean to pry." She ripped the receipt and handed it to me.

"Southern hospitality doesn't excuse you from

being a nosey old hag," I spat out before rushing out of the store.

The day was disappearing quickly, and I was thankful. Having a job interview tomorrow gave me something to look forward to and a sliver of hope that I wouldn't be bound to park benches, an occasional night in a cheap motel or fearful of when my next meal would be.

I walked as much as I physically could, and the sun was setting. I knew I'd have to call a car, but I only had a twenty left. Looking around, I stood by the side of the road and stuck my thumb out.

Did this really work to hitch hike? It was worth a try, considering I didn't want to spend the last dollars I had on a bus ride.

An hour flew by, and no one stopped. Some idiot guys hollered at me with their heads hanging out of the window, and I couldn't help but roll my eyes and hum the lyrics to "No Scrub" by TLC. That made me smile—something I rarely did. It was the first song I had ever heard in America. The entire time I thought the singer was talking about a dish sponge.

Finally, a car did stop, and it was a woman. That didn't put me at ease, considering it was a woman with a trusting face that ultimately aided in wrecking my life.

"Hey, are you okay?" She had her emergency lights

on, and when I cautiously walked closer, I got a better look at her.

She couldn't be more than thirty, and when I peeked in the backseat, I saw a toddler in a car seat, giggling at their tablet.

"I lost my wallet and phone, and really need to get back to east Charlotte... I'm staying at the Super 7 Motel." I looked down at my worn-out dollar Old Navy flip-flops.

The cold air conditioning blasting in her car provided a moment of solace as the summer heat still beat down, even though the sun had already set.

"It's a little out of my way, but I'd feel terrible if I didn't help. Come on in." She looked slightly uneasy and glanced back at the sleepy child in the backseat.

"Thank you." I quickly opened the door and slid in. The soft beige leather interior was stunning, and the scent of jasmine floated inside.

"I'm Raina, and that's my son, Kai." She offered a small smile at me.

"I'm Demi." I nodded and wiggled my fingers at the uninterested toddler. She didn't begin to drive and just sat there looking at me. Furrowing my brows, I opened my hands and asked, "Is something wrong?" I tried to conceal the irritation churning through me. Here this young mom was, wearing her expensive

Lululemon athleisure, probably second-guessing why she let me in her luxury car.

"Buckle up, please." She pointed at my seatbelt. I couldn't help but laugh.

I shook my head and bit back the overly large grin that was surfacing on my face.

She let out a loud laugh and nodded. "I am such a mom. I'm only twenty-nine, but once I had this little guy… it's like I aged a few decades, and now being a mom is all I know. Well, that, and I'm a pretty good dermatologist." She brushed her hand against her smooth cheek.

"Isn't that like a skin doctor?" I asked curiously as I clipped my buckle.

"Sure is." She looked over her shoulder, checked her mirrors, and carefully pulled back into traffic.

"I have a job interview tomorrow. Any tips of how I can magically look less like, oh, I dunno, a girl who stays at Motel 7 and more like… well, *you*?" I asked softly while I fidgeted my fingers, feeling embarrassed.

She took a quick look at me but kept her hands at ten and two while driving.

"You know what…? Do you want to come over to our place for dinner?" She rolled her lips together and kept driving.

"Hot food?" I asked excitedly.

She smiled. "Yes, hot food."

And just like that, she turned her car onto the highway and headed in the opposite direction of the shitty motel I was staying at and back toward the richer side of Charlotte.

"You're not like a suburban serial killer mommy, right?" I let out a small, nervous laugh.

Once we took the exit and got to a stoplight, she reached into the side pocket of her door and tugged out her wallet. Opening it, she showed me her driver's license and a business card.

Raina Kumar, M.D.
  South Charlotte Dermatology

"I promise, I'm not a suburban serial killer mommy." She patted my hand and I looked back at her before looking over my shoulder over at Kai, the little boy who was drifting to sleep.

"Sorry, I'm just…" I started to speak as she made another turn.

"Demi, you absolutely should ask those questions. It's a dangerous world."

Before I knew it, we pulled up to a giant, intricately carved gate and my lips parted in shock. Raina punched in a code and suddenly, they creaked open, somewhat scratching against the smooth pavement. The sound sending chills across my arms.

We drove through a canopy of trees that lined neatly trimmed lawns with elaborate floral displays framing the most stunning houses I'd ever seen in my life.

"Holy..." I breathed as I took in the massive mansions. It was a world of its own. A minute later, Raina turned into the driveway of a gorgeous stucco house that was lit up by floodlights.

"This is your house?" I looked over at Raina, who was getting Kai out of his carseat.

"I mean, just until the real owners come back from their trip to London," Raina replied, her face completely stoic.

Freezing in the driveway, I looked at her until she broke out into laughter.

"Demi, I'm joking. We live here. Full time, I promise."

CHAPTER
FOUR

WHEN WE GOT INSIDE, I felt like I was visiting the Biltmore Estate—a place I dreamed of visiting after finding a brochure. That brochure got me through the hardest moments of my life because I would pretend one day I'd go there, and that, maybe one day I could live a life as lavish as that one. Stupid me. But now, here I was, twirling around in the foyer of a complete stranger's house, in awe.

The interior was even more stunning than the exterior, if that was even possible. The ceiling had this gold-encrusted design, the walls were a stunning shade of navy blue, and one wall had built-in shelves, meticulously decorated with gorgeous knick-knacks and picture frames. A stunning, velvet emerald couch sat atop a lavish rug, the accent chairs were a deep golden mustard color, and everything had this bohemian peacock yet rich vibe to it.

"Your home is stunning." I looked over at Raina, who had her sleeping son on her shoulder. She was beautiful. Her eyes were a lighter brown, but her hair was a deep raven like mine, except shiny and well taken care of. Her skin was a creamy tan, and her makeup was applied to perfection.

"Are you Indian?" I asked as she kicked off her shoes and gently put her bag down.

"I was born here in Charlotte, but yes, I am. My mom is actually Persian, and my dad is Indian, so half, but we really grew up immersed in the culture. I'm going to take Kai up to his bed, but please, make yourself at home. I'll be there in just a minute." Raina smiled at me and made her way up the curved marble staircase.

Tugging my dirty flip-flops off, I neatly placed them next to her Golden Goose sneakers.

For a moment, I felt bad that someone as dirty as me was in a place so beautiful. Here I was, in a house that easily had to cost five million dollars with a Goodwill bag in my hand.

Sighing, I let my calloused, rough feet glide against the gorgeous smooth floors. They weren't wood or carpet; they were marble, just like the stairs.

I'd never seen, let alone been inside a home with

marble floors. I walked toward the built-in shelves and began looking at the golden framed photos—mostly black-and-white, professional images of Kai and Raina —and when I went to the other side, I lifted a large wedding portrait.

"It's been ten years, but it feels like yesterday." A voice startled me from behind and as I jerked around, the frame slipped and crashed to the floor.

"Oh, no!" the tall, handsome man, who was now crouched on the floor by my feet, called out.

Stumbling back, I avoided the glass and gripped the edge of the built-ins. "I'm so sorry!" I winced as he shook the shards off and lifted the now broken frame.

"Demi, are you alright?" Raina was at the bottom of the stairs, glancing between the two of us.

"I didn't hear him coming and I... I'm so sorry. I'll buy you a new frame," I stammered, even though I only had five dollars to my name and, by the looks of that frame, I'd need to add two more zeros at the end in order to match what it was.

"No, no... it's okay. I always joke that Jax is abnormally light on his feet." Raina grinned.

"This is my husband, Jax Roberts. Jax, this is my new friend Demi." She widened her eyes slightly at him as he stood with a pile of glass stacked on their wedding photo.

"It's so nice to meet you, Demi. Do you live around here?" he asked politely.

"No. I'm kinda new to town." I looked back down at my feet. Suddenly horrified that her husband was inches away from my chipped-up toenails and feet that were stained with dirt and grime.

"Well, Raina is what we call a people collector. She loves new friends, and I'm sure you'll find her to be quite useful in getting to know the city." He paused, but then did a quick sweep of my body before lifting his eyes back to mine again.

"Are you working somewhere?" Raina cleared her throat and looked at him with repulsion.

"Actually, I have an interview tomorrow with this surgeon, Dr. Ivory." I chewed on my bottom lip nervously.

Jax's demeanor changed. "Dr. Ivory?"

"Yeah, do you guys know him?"

"Demi, he lives right down the street from us." Raina squinted at me. "Why don't you come sit down? I'll order some food for us; there's this great Chinese restaurant, and I'm sure you're hungry since it's past dinnertime." She waved me over to the velvet couch. My stomach rumbled loudly as I sunk into the seat, and Raina quickly tugged her phone out to place the order.

Jax finished cleaning up the mess and began walking. But I didn't hear him. Peering over my shoulder, I looked at his feet.

He was wearing these strange looking white foam slippers. *No wonder I couldn't hear him walking.*

"What kind of shoes are those?" I asked Raina, who was finishing up the takeout order on her phone.

"These? Do you like them? They are my favorite slippers," she replied with a smile. I glanced down at her well-manicured feet covered in pink fluffy slippers.

"No, your husband's," I said quietly.

She tilted her head and looked deep in thought. "Jax is intense about his feet staying all soft and clean. He got those from some... podiatrist, I think." She shrugged and placed her phone on the sleek coffee table in front of us.

Nodding, I put my small grocery bag down on the floor by my feet, even more embarrassed that the man who clearly had a foot fetish saw my nasty feet.

"So, Demi, tell me more about this interview with Ian?"

"Ian?"

"Dr. Ivory." Raina pulled her legs up on the sofa and crossed them.

"Oh, right. Ian Ivory. I'm interviewing for—" I stopped mid-sentence. Here I was, sitting in front of a gorgeous, successful dermatologist, who was only a decade older than me. Her entire life was a complete contrast to mine. I couldn't tell her I was going to essentially be pleading for the position of lead toilet scrubber at the mansion down the road.

So, I lied.

"I'm interviewing to be his new assistant. Like medical billing stuff, I guess." My shoulders were stiff, my chest was tight, and I felt stupid for lying. "Are you guys good friends?" I quickly realized I had just lied about someone who lives only houses away and could potentially be one of their close friends.

"No, no... not at all. They are a bit... eccentric. But I do know Ian and Daphne are very particular with who they keep on their staff, both in their home and at their practice. Do you really want this job?" She laced her fingers together.

"I don't want this job; I *need* this job." I exhaled and just as she parted her lips to say something, the door-bell rang.

CHAPTER
FIVE

JAX, Raina, and I sat around the dining table. Jax had put each item into gorgeous, blue bowls with intricately carved serving spoons.

I'd have been fine eating straight out of the white cardboard cartons, but I guess rich people didn't do that. I took a sip of my sweet tea and shoveled another oversized bite of veggie lo-mein into my mouth.

"This is delicious," I said with a noodle dangling from my lip. Jax smiled while Raina watched me happily. Lifting more noodles up with my fingers, I slurped them with no shame. I couldn't remember the last real meal I had, and this was phenomenal. I also couldn't remember the last time I had silverware, so it wasn't something I was accustomed to.

"You know, I was thinking... why don't you just stay the night here, Demi? I could give you a quick little makeover, we could set out your clothes for your interview, and you could get a good night's sleep in our guest room. You'd be right on time for your interview with the Ivory family." She glanced over at Jax, who dropped his eyes back to his plate.

"I don't want to impose. Besides, my last day at the motel is tomorrow morning, and I have my clothes there." Raina passed me a napkin. My cheeks felt warm as I looked at my already-cleaned plate. There was plenty of food left in the bowls, considering Raina and Jax both took the smallest portions humanly possible, instead of filling their plates like I had.

"Please take more." Jax handed me a serving spoon. As much as I wanted to show them I had some form of manners, I also remembered I only had a few bucks to my name left, and if I didn't get this job tomorrow, I'd be off on another starvation stretch and vending machine meals.

"Well, I'm sure I have plenty of clothes you could sort through. Honestly, I needed to purge anyway, and if nothing is… irreplaceable, then we'd love for you to stay somewhere… safer?" Raina narrowed her eyes as I took a fistful of noodles and shoveled them into my mouth, not even breathing before taking a hefty bite of the spring roll.

I'm sure any other human would have the common decency to wipe their mouth, spread a napkin across their lap, or maybe deny third servings, but when you've faced a life I had—one in which hunger was used as a violent way to get you to do things... horrid things for someone—then you don't think twice.

Closing my eyes, I thought back to the moments in the darkness... when my stomach would be in knots and I'd pray that something, anything edible would magically appear.

But it rarely did.

"Demi?" Raina's hand shook mine. Her forehead was slightly creased, and she kept looking between her husband and me.

"Okay. I just... I need to go back and get one thing from the motel before check-out time and house-keeping trashes my things. It'd have to be before the interview." I knew it was foolish, but it was the one thing that helped me survive.

"Well, how about Jax can swing by and get it tomorrow before work and anything else you'd like from... from the motel." Raina took a long sip of water before offering a tight-lipped smile.

"Okay." I nodded as I reached for another spring roll.

"Ladies, I'm off to get some more work done, but let me know if either of you need anything. Goodnight, sweetheart." Jax stood and planted a kiss on his wife's face. She smiled up at him and brushed his face with her hand. "Night, Demi." His lips were pursed but somewhat curved, as if he couldn't force out the smile he knew Raina would want him to.

"Goodnight." As he walked, I tilted my head to look at his feet. The thick white sandals literally concealed all sound from his steps. I couldn't even tell if he was up the stairs or not, but after counting two minutes in my mind, I turned to Raina.

"I don't think he wants me to stay." I swallowed the lump in my throat, quickly grabbing my water and chugging it as droplets trickled out of my lips.

Raina rested her chin on her palm and watched me intently.

"No, no, don't mind Jax. He's just... He's a bit of an introvert, and ever since we had Kai, he's more on edge with anyone we don't know well." She paused and passed me a napkin.

"Demi, where did you move from?" She hesitated for a moment. Looking at her, I wiped my face and leaned back in the chair, clutching my overstuffed stomach.

"Um... well, it's a long story, but Tennessee." I shuddered at the simple state name.

"Oh wow. What part?" Raina stood and began to clear the table. My stomach started to churn, and I didn't know if it was from the nerves or the fact that I had inhaled an entire family's worth of a meal after sustaining myself on Twinkies or fries here and there.

"Nashville." I reached for the pitcher of water with trembling hands and began to pour more into my empty glass.

Watching the clear liquid slosh into the glass had my heart pounding even harder. There was a day where I was drinking water out of a dropper. Forcing myself to steady my hand, I clutched the glass and took a long sip.

"I love Nashville!" Raina exclaimed, with a pile of dishes stacked in her hands. I quickly stood to help her.

Following behind, we walked into her stunning kitchen. The entire kitchen was a deep navy blue, with gold accessories and meticulously decorated. The stove was immaculate—showing that this family probably never cooked.

"What made you leave Nashville for Charlotte?"

I looked over at Raina as I placed some of the plates down and she began rinsing them.

"I got tired of the music," I replied without hesitation. It was true, but not in the sense that most people would think.

Raina's lips twitched as she looked at me curiously. "Really? How does one become tired of music?" She flipped the water off and dried her manicured hands.

"When the noise is used to conceal your thoughts, and you no longer can hear the one voice that will help you survive." I shuddered as I thought back to the small window that shook and vibrated as music rose from the bars below.

They couldn't hear our screams, they couldn't hear our cries... they couldn't hear the pain in our prayers.

All because the music concealed the truth. Because that's what music does; it removes us from reality and loses us into the melodies and words that resonate with us, or don't, but either way, we hope to find some form of truth in the songs.

I never found truth in the often-melodramatic country songs—I hated it all. I hated the optimism, the way the musician would take heartbreak or pain and guarantee a positive outcome. Meanwhile, we were right there, hovered in the dark—shaking, bleeding, aching...

Aching for them to stop singing. So maybe then, someone, anyone, could hear us.

But they never did...

CHAPTER
SIX

"THE BATHROOM IS COMPLETELY STOCKED and here are a few outfits for you. Pajamas for tonight, and an interview outfit for tomorrow."

Raina had set out a stack of clothes that were all neatly hung on black velvet hangers.

I was standing in the middle of their beautifully decorated guest room—which was essentially bigger than a studio apartment.

Catching a glimpse at the labels, I immediately stumbled back. "Oh, no, I can't possibly borrow these." Dolce & Gabbana, Chanel, Marc Jacobs, and others I couldn't even pronounce.

"Demi, you can keep these. I wouldn't ask for them back." Raina smiled as she lifted white blazer and slacks, beaming as she held it closer to my frame. "This would be perfect for your interview."

I felt an overwhelming rush of nerves cutting through me. "Why are you being so nice to me?" My words shook and suddenly, I felt dazed with fear. Walking away backward, my palms grew moist and my eyes narrowed on the blush- and cream-colored room as I felt sweat beads build at my hairline. Tripping over my own feet, I collapsed onto the plush carpet and pushed back into the corner as I refused to blink.

What was this?

How stupid could I have been? Raina's face dropped as she set the clothes down and watched me until I gripped my knees and tugged them to my face. My breathing grew unsteady, and I was asphyxiating on the air around me.

"Demi..." Clenching my eyes shut, I shook my head as tears streamed out. Grinding my teeth, the sound sent chills up my spine, but I stayed focused on it until a searing pain grew in my own jaw.

A soft hand brushed against my arm, and I sobbed harder.

"Demi, please, just breathe. I need you to take a deep breath in and then exhale. Let's do that together." Raina tried to breathe in and out loud enough for my body to mimic hers.

Suddenly, I could hear the strumming of a guitar, the hum of a piano, and… It was all too much.

"I'm choking." I slammed my hands around my throat, tightening my grip, further cutting off the oxygen from my body.

"Demi!" Raina cried out and dug her nails into my hands, peeling them off my throat.

Sobbing hysterically, I collapsed onto my side. Raina lifted my head into her lap and brushed my hair from my face. "Shh, shh… It's okay, honey. It's okay."

I couldn't stop crying as the snot dribbled down and intertwined with the tears. My body was convulsing from the extreme high of emotions, and all I wanted was to cut my own flesh. I *needed* to cut.

I needed to numb myself and the noise.

"It'll be okay. I promise." And suddenly, Raina kissed my forehead in this maternal, reassuring way that made me cry even harder.

———

I don't know how much time had passed, but eventually, I took a shower. A long, hot shower, rubbing my body with actual body wash, and using shampoo and conditioner on my hair. I couldn't tell if it was water or tears, but I stayed in there until I felt dizzy from the steam.

Wrapping myself in a towel that resembled a cloud, I slowly wiped the condensation from the mirror, and within a moment, I felt a cool breeze brush against my arms.

No, no, no. She's here.

She was behind me, staring at me with blood dripping down her face from the whites of her eyes.

"No!" I screeched, flinging around with my arms flailing. "I'm sorry, I'm sorry!" I sunk to my knees.

She looked down at me, slowly shaking her head. Her once thick brown hair was shriveled. Her frame was thinner and slowly, she bent down to grow closer to me.

Opening her mouth, it was a darkened black hole and…

"Demi?" A knock on the door sounded. I instinctively glanced that way, but quickly looked back.

She's gone.

"Demi? Demi, please open the door." Pressing my palms against the counter, I tugged myself up and tied my towel back in place. Taking a deep breath, I gradually opened the door.

"I've never experienced a rain shower." I shrugged as the concern melted off Raina's face and was replaced with a trifling grin.

"I'll give you privacy and let you get some sleep, but Demi, please let me know if you need me. I'm right down the hall on the right side; Kai's room is on the left." She deliberated for a moment. "Do you want me to stay?" she added delicately.

"No, I'm fine. Thanks. I'm sure you're wondering why the hell you let a mentally insane girl into your house." I dug my index finger into the softened flesh around my thumb. "I promise, I won't leave my room until the morning." I reassured her.

Raina tilted her head and paused. "No, Demi... I'm wondering how someone could have hurt a girl as sweet as you. And I want you to know, if you ever need to talk about the music from Nashville... I'm here to listen."

My chest tightened, but this time it wasn't from fear; it was from the fact that I could tell she really cared.

About me.

CHAPTER
SEVEN

THE NEXT MORNING, I woke up peacefully. Not
with an aching back or dizziness from blood loss, not
with trepidation and dread. I woke up because the
sunlight was trickling in through the curtains and
shining blissfully against my face, warming my cheeks.

I didn't want to move. I was under the most
comfortable goose-down comforter and laying on
sheets that had to be three-thousand thread count. Was
that even a count for sheets?

I didn't have a phone, so I had no clue what time it
was. My interview was promptly at noon, and I needed
to do some damage control, considering I looked like
well, a girl who had lived in a motel, under bridges, on
park benches and city buses. I was sure after last
night's nervous breakdown, my eyes had to be
swollen.

Quickly peeling myself out of bed, the plush carpet felt luscious against my rough feet.

I was wearing silk, navy blue pajamas that Raina had given me. I had only been to hell before, so I was positive this had to be heaven. What most people don't understand is that poverty and fear are two of the worst things a human has to live with. When combined that means they are in the lowest and darkest parts of a valley that is killing them every single day.

I brushed my teeth, washed my face with some fancy dermatology skin care line, and changed into the black leggings and oversized sweater that was folded inside of the bathroom.

Everything felt like butter against my skin as I went back into the bedroom. My goodwill bag was sitting on the small corner desk. I could just wear what I bought and not take Raina's clothes, or...

I could embrace this once-in-a-lifetime kindness and just pray the outfit from a rich doctor could persuade another rich doctor to hire me to scrub his toilets.

Leaving the guest room, I looked from side-to-side. The hallway seemed never-ending, and I figured no one was awake yet.

Tiptoeing down the stairs, I froze mid-way.

Jax was wearing a white painter-style jumpsuit with the same strange white sandals, and he was on his hands and knees, slowly painting the banister with white paint.

Clearing my throat, I stood awkwardly.

"Demi, good morning." He was taken aback, and quickly began cleaning up his paint supplies.

"Good morning. Please don't stop; I'll just go back to my room." I felt flustered and immediately uncomfortable.

"No, no. I'm done. Kai loves to take crayons…" He pointed to a spot. What's strange is that the banister was black, but he had begun to repaint it white.

It didn't even match with the aesthetic of the home, which was mostly jewel tones and deeper colors.

I forced out a small laugh, as if I knew what a toddler was like, though I had no experience with children at all.

Honestly, I actually couldn't stand them. I didn't find them cute, cuddly, or sweet; I just thought they were kind of annoying and perhaps the thought of their guiltlessness frightened me.

"I grabbed your stuff from the… motel." Jax stood and smiled at me. He was probably six foot four, buff, with dark brown hair and deep green eyes.

I felt embarrassment build inside me as I pictured this really handsome man walking into the Super 7 motel where my Twinkie wrappers and wine bottles were lingering shamelessly. And the blood. I cringed as I thought of the blood stains all over my sheets.

"Thanks." I looked down and walked behind him down the stairs.

"No problem," he replied and quietly disappeared. I made my way to the kitchen and glanced at the time.

It was 7:10 a.m. A moment later, Jax reappeared but again, I noted how I didn't hear him coming with those thick-padded shoes. He began washing his hands, the white paint dripping off into the sink, pooling into a milky mess until the water ran clear. He obsessively cleaned under his nails with a sponge before turning the water off.

"I ordered everyone some egg white sandwiches. I hope that's fine with you; it's usually our go-to."

Yep, they never cooked.

"That sounds good." I tapped my fingers nervously against the marble countertop and looked around, feeling awkward.

As if he could sense my uneasiness, he said, "Raina will be back soon. She's dropping Kai off at his grandparents for a visit, but she said she'll come help you get ready for your interview before heading to work."

Nodding, I rolled my lips. I wondered what Jax did for work.

"You really want to work for the Ivory family?" He

came around and sunk into the kitchen island stool farthest from the one I stood by.

"I really need a job and a live-in position… beggars can't be choosers and all that. Truth be told, I don't really know anything about them." I pulled the chair out and took a seat.

"They are…"

"Good morning!" Raina appeared with a bright smile on her face. "DoorDash left this." She lifted the bag of food and placed it on the counter before she hurried to the other side for plates.

"How'd you sleep, Demi?" She slid a plate toward me and looked back at her husband. I couldn't tell what that look was, but it was something that had me feeling guilty even when nothing had happened.

"I slept better than I have in my life. Thank you so much." I lifted the egg white sandwich with avocado and spinach.

"So glad to hear that." Raina handed me a cup of coffee and took a sip of her own. "So, what were you both talking about?" she asked curiously.

"About the Ivor—" I began, but Jax cut me off quickly.

"Kai," he filled in.

That was strange. Why couldn't Raina know we were about to talk about the family she knew I had an interview with?

"Aw, Demi, I wish you could have spent more time with him. He'd have loved you." Raina continued to drink her coffee. "So, I took the morning off to help you get ready for your interview."

"Oh, you didn't need to do that." I looked up at her after eating my entire sandwich. Raina passed me her untouched meal and nodded.

"I'm full." She lifted her coffee up. "And, Demi, I know I didn't need to, but I really wanted to." She smiled and walked toward her husband. Leaning down, she kissed him before coming toward me.

"After you finish up, we can go to my office. We have a medi-spa, so you can get a facial, and I'll have my wax and nail lady meet us there to do the works."

I didn't know how to react, so instead, as usual, I just said what was on my mind without thinking. "Do you think that's all necessary for a housekeeper interview?" I added an awkward laugh.

"Demi, you have to dress for the job you eventually want, not the job you're qualified for." Raina's face shifted.

"Don't let anyone put a barrier on you. Who knows, maybe you start there as a housekeeper and could land a significantly better job, eventually. Dr. Ivory has multiple practices and businesses, so he could easily promote you. Just for the record, you didn't have to lie about interviewing for an assistant role."

My cheeks warmed with embarrassment as I realized my own mistake.

"Okay," I replied under my breath. I mean, she was right, but I highly doubted a girl like me, with zero education beyond high school, could magically break out and become like Raina.

Successful and rich people always assumed poor, unsuccessful people were unmotivated or not driven, but that wasn't the truth. The majority of us would never have the same resources they did. That's why the rags-to-riches stories are special; if it was the common occurrence, we'd never see it as a headline.

They didn't get it, because they never lived it and would never have to. But damn, did they love acting as motivational speakers to the lowlives like me.

Loosening my shoulders, I finished my meal and drank two giant cups of water.

Raina didn't know what it was like to drink water out of a dropper for days. Raina didn't know what it was like to cut up a Twinkie into fourths to make enough meals to last you two days.

But I wasn't going to say that; instead, I was going to smile and take her up on her fairy godmother role.

Because I desperately needed this job, and just like everything else in my life, all odds were stacked against me.

CHAPTER
EIGHT

YOU KNOW that part in all the chick flicks where some catchy song starts playing and the girl comes down the long staircase and everyone gasps at how she went from abnormally unattractive to breathtakingly beautiful?

I honestly laughed at those moments, until now. Now I was living it. All I was missing was a jock at the end of the stairs and a dad gushing with his camera— and maybe the theme song from *She's All That*.

After spending the morning getting a HydraFacial, my entire face waxed, a manicure, pedicure, and even a blow out, I wasn't the same Demi from a few hours ago.

Talk about a confidence boost as I walked down the stairs in Raina's stunning, white two-piece Dolce and Gabana blazer and pants, feeling worthy of her clothes.

Raina was waiting at the end of the stairs with Jax, her hands on her cheeks as she stood excitedly with the proudest smile I'd ever seen in my life.

Kai was a lucky kid. I'm sure she'd be the mom who threw him a party over a participation award.

Feeling slightly awkward, I averted my eyes, and so did Jax. "Demi! You look like a goddess." Raina tugged my hand and spun me around. "Jax, doesn't she look gorgeous?" she squealed.

"Mm-hmm… you look nice, Demi." I could tell he was uncomfortable with how he cleared his throat mid-sentence.

Looking down at my bare feet, I turned them in and whispered, "Thank you."

"Well, let's find you some shoes. We don't want you to be late." Raina tugged me toward a long hallway lined with vibrant and colorful photographs of their family.

"Here, I had Jax pick these up for you." She handed me a box as we entered the mudroom.

Curiously sliding the top off, I squinted at the contents. They were solid white shoes with thick-padded bottoms. Almost like the shoes Jax wore.

"Um… thanks?" I didn't mean to sound ungrateful, but here I was, feeling bad bitch vibes and staring down at shoes that belonged to retirement home Bertha.

"I know, I know; they aren't cute. Listen, Demi, I wish I had a job I could offer you with the whole live-in aspect, but I don't. The Ivory family is a great opportunity for you, but they are very… particular people, and…" Raina paused and looked up at the oversized wall clock. "You've got to get going. Put these on and just answer their questions in short sentences. Don't give too much background, and don't tell them we met you. They are ridiculously private people, and that may hurt your chances. Good luck."

I had no idea how to even interpret everything she just said, but begrudgingly, I tugged the shoes on and thanked Raina as she waved me outside through the garage. Once on her driveway, she shielded her eyes with her hand and pointed with the other.

"The house on the secluded hill at the opposite end of the neighborhood; the all-white one. That's the Ivory house. Just hit the buzzer and they'll let you in. Good luck, honey. Swing on back when you're done; I want to hear how it went."

"I don't want to keep taking up your time." I squinted at Raina with the sun directly above us.

"No, it's okay. I took the day off, and honestly, if you get the job, I'll know you have a safe place to live and if you don't… Well, we can help you find a temporary place." She rolled her lips together and smiled. "Now get going, Dr. Ivory is extremely punctual." She nodded at me.

Taking a deep breath in and releasing it slowly, I began to walk down the smoothly paved driveway, making my way down the sidewalk that ran by the exceptionally manicured lawns.

Vibrant flowers, bright green grass, and stucco homes all neatly lined the street. It made me laugh that many had gates in front of their homes when the neighborhood was already gated. *Talk about being paranoid.* But then again, I suppose I'd be paranoid too, if I lived in an enormous mansion amongst diamonds and gold, and never had been tied up in a disgusting crack house. It's ironic that the most guarded people are the most terrified. They are the most terrified because they have the most to lose.

Looking down at my shoes, I realized they didn't make any noise against the concrete. It was as if I was walking on air.

Rich people things. My nerves were completely shot, and I was thankful Raina insisted that I pin my thick black hair up into a neat bun or else it would have been sticking to the back of my neck where sweat began to build.

It wasn't even as hot of a day. Fall was officially trickling in, and the trees were beginning to shift with splashes of rich reds and warm shades of yellow. There was a trickle of crisp, cooler air lingering, teasing the otherwise sticky humidity.

The sun shimmered through the canopy of trees that lined the street. I couldn't help but wonder what it must be like living with this kind of wealth and prestige?

How it must be to go to sleep in a plush bed, knowing you'll never have to worry about food or water. You'll never have to run and hide. You'll never be taken—or sold or beaten.

You just get to exist and be happy. You don't have to fight for the life you were forced into.

And if you're not happy, well, you have the wealth to do whatever it takes to find it.

I arrived in front of the massive gate that was wrapped around the largest home on the street—one that left my mouth parted in actual bewilderment. It was like the White House. Literally. The gate was white, and the house was an all-white stucco. The yard was in immaculate condition, with vivid green grass and blooming white flowers.

Peeling my eyes off the mansion in front of me, I looked down at my outfit. This was weird, right? I mean, this family had a serious fetish with the color white.

"Welcome to the Ivory House," a voice called out, startling me, and I quickly glanced around with my heart pounding.

"Miss, are you here by appointment?" the voice echoed.

Looking around, I glanced up at the cameras pointed down at me and a small box with a speaker built in.

"Oh… um, yea. I mean, *yes*. I'm Demi Rao." My words sounded just as uncertain as I felt.

No other words were exchanged, and at least three minutes had to have passed, but just as I narrowed my eyes and considered leaving, the gates slowly began to open. Unlike most gates, there was no sound—no squeaking or scratching—just the slight shift in the air around the heavy metal cutting through it.

In life there are moments, crossroads, really, in which we stand there and look side-to-side and know one path is the one we need, and the other is the one we want.

The problem is, sometimes the path we need, is the one that hurts us the most. It's unfair really, how life works against us, and we don't even realize it's happening until we're thrown into situations we are forced to be in. Situations that wrap us up in a wrath like a deadly tornado and then when we're finally out of it, all we are left with is immense destruction. The worst part of it all is knowing had we listened to our inner sirens, perhaps we could have avoided the storm and its aftermath.

Walking down the smooth pavement, my entire body felt cold, even though it was warm out. I was nervous, I knew. But it wasn't just because this was my last chance at having a steady income and place to live; it was also because my intuition kept telling me to turn around and leave.

Something was off, the feeling was palpable. Four years ago, when I was taken and held in the small room, I developed a very strong sense of intuition. It was the way I could finally fall asleep without being terrified; it was the way I knew what was coming.

Today, everything felt the way it does before a storm and you've left your umbrella at home.

You know something bad is coming and you also know you're unprepared, but you still go. I stood in front of the enormous stark white doors and before my finger could even meet the small doorbell, a man opened the doors.

"Miss Rao, come in. The Ivorys are waiting for you." He waved his gloved hand at me with the other tucked behind his back.

Turn around, a whisper grazed my ear, but I didn't. I couldn't. I had no other choice.

The worst position to be in is a person without choices, because that means others can make decisions for you.

CHAPTER
NINE

"MISS RAO, I'm Bradley. Dr. and Mrs. Ivory are seated in the Orchid Room." The man in front of me eyed me carefully with his bright green eyes and neatly brushed platinum blond hair.

"Thanks." I nodded. *The Orchid Room? What the hell was that? Who named rooms in their homes?*

I picked up my pace as Bradley moved swiftly down a long hallway. My eyes kept darting around in every direction. I didn't get to absorb it all, but the one thing I noticed was everything I had seen so far were in shades of white—cream, white, ivory, and the lightest beige. It was the strangest house I'd ever seen, though still gorgeous in an off-setting way. Taking a quick right turn down a narrow hall, the walls felt as if they were closing in on me. Both sides were lined with perfectly placed picture frames containing black-and-white images that weren't clear faces or people, but rather blurred images I couldn't make out. I slowed down in order to study one.

"What is—"

"It will be in your best interest to come now," Bradley fired at me with irritation as he halted in front of a closed door.

"I'm sorry, I just… What is…?" I pointed at the image in front of me. It looked like a person running away, with light hair flying around their face, but I couldn't be certain.

"Listen, Miss Rao, there are no questions to be asked. Dr. and Mrs. Ivory will ask you what they need to, but beyond that, you mustn't be a meddlesome nuisance." He shook his head and widened his eyes at me.

"Okay." Who was this guy? What was his role here? Some butler who thought we were all in a game of Clue or something?

I had to bite back the smile that was growing on my face. With two hands, Bradley gripped the door handles and slowly opened them.

"After you." His eyes ran down my entire body in this creepy way that made me really want to gouge his eyes out.

Right as I walked in front of him, he let out this satisfied sigh that made my entire body tense. *Asshole.*

I squinted as soon as I walked into the room. The sun was beaming brightly through the vast windows directly in front of me. But it was the couple in front of me that made me stumble back slightly.

They stood from the couch they had been seated on and smiled simultaneously. The woman's eyes drifted to Bradley, who was still hovering too close to me.

"Bradley, you aren't needed," the woman said softly with a small nod. He immediately turned away, but something caught my eye and I turned to look at him.

His shoes… They were the same thick-soled white shoes that Jax wore. Completely silent.

"Miss Rao…" The woman's voice in front of me broke through my thoughts and I slowly turned back and looked at the couple in front of me.

They could have been on a cover of Architects Digest. Both of them were completely, unnaturally beautiful.

Mrs. Ivory was wearing a cream-colored dress, light pink lipstick, and her blond hair was cut in a short, neat bob; while Dr. Ivory was tall, with broad shoulders, and blond, almost white, hair. He was slightly more tanned than Mrs. Ivory, which wasn't a challenge considering the woman looked like she never saw direct sunlight. They could easily be Edward Cullen's biological parents.

"Hi." I licked my dried lips and rubbed them together nervously.

"Come, take a seat, dear," she said with a smile that showed no movement on her face.

Walking slower than imaginable, I took a seat in the accent chair across from the sofa the couple sat back in. A porcelain teapot and assorted baked goods were neatly lined in front of me.

"Miss Rao, I'm Daphne Ivory and this is my husband, Ian Ivory—" Her husband cleared his throat and she fidgeted her hands. "*Dr.* Ian Ivory," she corrected.

"It's really nice to meet you both. You can just call me Demi, though." I clasped my hands together to help buffer the shaking.

"And you can just call me Daphne." She smiled and poured a cup of tea, lifting it toward me.

"This is a beautiful blend our chef Margot makes right here with herbs from our garden." Daphne let go of the delicate teacup once I gripped it. I really didn't want to drink the dark tea while wearing all white and sitting on an all white chair, but they were watching me intently, so I said a quick prayer and took a sip.

"Mmm… wow. This is actually really good." I was surprised how sweet the tea was.

"I'm so thrilled you like it." Daphne smiled over at her husband, who kept his face mostly stoic.

"Demi, we'd like to ask you a few questions." Dr. Ivory straightened his back and brushed the light beige pants he wore. I was grateful for the hints of color in their clothing or else I'd have thought I was in the middle of some kind of cult.

Sometimes I would catch those six-episode crime series on the motel T.V., so my mind would always jump to worst-case scenario, and because, well, my life always became the worst-case scenario.

"Of course." I crossed my leg over the other and carefully placed the teacup on the mini plate.

"Please state your full name and birth month." The question seemed so strange to me, especially how it was presented.

"Demi Rao and my birth month is June."

Nodding, he looked at the stack of papers in his hands. What was on them? I had no records. I mean, for the past four years, I wasn't even Demi.

"Where were you born?" Dr. Ivory asked with zero emotion.

"Well, I was actually born in India, but we moved here when I was young, so I really don't even remember much." I shrugged.

"Where is *here*?" Dr. Ivory furrowed his brows as his piercing green eyes seared into me. I always thought green eyes were rare. But Bradley, Daphne and Ian all possessed them.

"I grew up in Gatlinburg, Tennessee."

"Oh, we adore Gatlinburg. Such a scenic mountain town." Daphne offered a smile in my direction.

"Yeah…" I added before looking back at Dr. Ivory, who was still staring at me as if he was trying to figure out a puzzle.

I'm here for the position of a housekeeper; I'm not trying to be your surgical partner.

"What brought you to Charlotte?" He set the stack of papers down and laced his fingers together.

"Tennessee didn't feel like home anymore," I answered honestly. Well, somewhat honestly. Truthfully, it hadn't been home for four years. Instead of providing the comfort of home, it was the place that held the most treacherous memories for me.

It was the place where I fought for my life and barely survived. Hell, survive may not even be the right word since I didn't even feel alive most days.

"Tell us about your family…" Daphne glanced at her husband before looking back at me.

"Oh…" I didn't know how any of this was relevant to this job position, but then again, I'd be living here, in this colossal mansion with them, so I suppose I'd be careful with who I allowed inside, too.

"My parents are… Well, they both died. And I don't have any siblings." I bit my tongue, feeling a sting in my eyes that had my stomach tumble.

"Oh dear, we are so sorry to hear that." Daphne slapped her hand across her heart, as if she physically felt the pain of a stranger's past she just met.

"Thanks." I began peeling at my thumbnail and kept my eyes down. I couldn't sit here, crying in front of my literal last hope.

"Demi, we run a tight ship here at The Ivory House." Dr. Ivory spoke crassly. "Privacy is the number one most important aspect of this position. You will be expected to clean certain areas of our home, which are never seen by anyone besides our immediate family. You would live with us, be given a room, a private bathroom, and food, along with a stipend. You'll be asked to sign a document and an NDA. If you share anything, and I mean *anything,* we will take legal action. Do you understand?" Dr. Ivory and Daphne were both staring at me intently.

"Yes, of course." I nodded eagerly.

"Do you have experience in housekeeping?" Daphne interjected as her husband was opening his mouth.

I swallowed the lump in my throat. "Y-yes."

It was somewhat true. I was forced to clean and cook and do things according to someone else. "Any-thing else, I can learn. I'm a quick learner, and…" I stammered anxiously.

"Demi." Dr. Ivory held his hand up. "You must

learn to speak lower. And you'll be given a uniform, along with… Well, you are a bit…"

"*Different* from who we'd normally hire," Daphne filled in and lifted a plate of cookies.

Were they implying that because I was Indian or had brown-skin that stuck out abnormally in their safe haven of all-white?

"I'm sorry… I don't understand?" I questioned.

"Demi, how badly do you want this job?" Dr. Ivory asked as his eyes darkened.

"Dr. and Mrs. Ivory, I will do anything you ask of me… because I need this job. I *really* need it."

"Well, it's settled. You're hired, Miss Rao," Dr. Ivory said quickly, which completely surprised me.

"Wait? Really?" I titled my head and glanced between the couple in front of me.

Daphne stood and opened her arms. "Dear, Dr. Ivory and I never joke. Bradley will escort you to the drawing room to go over our non-disclosure agreement, and then he will take you to obtain your belongings. We'd like for you to move in right away so you can begin work in two days. You may tour the estate tomorrow."

Non-disclosure agreement? What was that? I looked around the room and back at the couple in front of me. Their eyes felt piercing as I began peeling at the chipped black nail polish I had stolen from a drugstore.

I had forgotten that they expected bare nails. Suddenly, Dr. Ivory's eyes fell to the light wood floors beneath us. His cheeks began to fill with red, and Daphne's eyes darted between him and the ground.

What's happening?

"Bradley!" he shrieked so loudly, I stumbled back.

"Ian…" Daphne grabbed his arm as the door behind me opened, and Bradley rushed inside.

He shot me an angry look before he turned to his employer. "Yes, sir?"

Ian swallowed and let out a hard exhale. "Fix it," he gritted, pointing to the floor by my feet. His face was bright red as he shook with clenched fists.

Bradley looked at me and then the floor by my feet. Within a moment, he dropped onto his hands and knees and began crawling. *Crawling.* A grown man began crawling toward me like a fast predator in the woods. My heart was pounding and my ears started to buzz. I didn't know what was going on. I clutched my hands together and took a few steps back until my legs crashed into the accent chair.

Bradley hurriedly began to pick up the shreds of nail polish off the floor and piled them into the palm of his hand. My eyes felt like they'd swell out of my face.

His platinum blond hair didn't move—obviously, it was carefully coiffed in place with a hefty amount of gel. His fingers were trembling after he rubbed them repeatedly across the floor to make sure there were no remnants of my polish.

In that moment, I felt like I should have run through the doors from sheer embarrassment. But I couldn't.

So instead, I stood there until Bradley got back up, clasped his hands together, and spun on his feet to face the Ivorys.

"Anything else, Dr. Ivory?" He bowed his head slightly.

Dr. Ivory's face was beet red, and Daphne lifted her hand and patted at her head.

"No," Dr. Ivory hissed and wafted his hand at Bradley as if he were a peasant.

Bradley nodded and sped out of the room. Releasing the breath from my puffed cheeks, I licked my lips, feeling so uncomfortable.

"Dr. Ivory, Mrs. Ivory… I'm so sorry. It's a nervous habit—"

"Nails must be kept clean. *You* must be kept clean." Dr. Ivory cinched his brows and looked at his wife.

"I hope you're right about her." He shook his head and began to walk away. Except he didn't leave through the main door, he went through a side door and when the door shut, I saw him cut through a meticulously maintained backyard.

"He's going to the serenity garden. You must learn

quickly, Demi. You absolutely must learn the rules of the Ivory Estate quickly… as if your life depended on it." Daphne pursed her lips and just as I processed the words that left her mouth, her lips tipped upright into a smile.

"Welcome home, darling." She opened her arms wide, and at that moment, I wasn't sure what the hell I just signed up for.

But my life quite literally did depend on it.

I just didn't know the magnitude of it all yet.

CHAPTER
TEN

AFTER LEAVING the expansive room I had met Dr. and Mrs. Ivory in, Bradley guided me down a different hallway until we reached another room. This room was completely different aesthetically from the rest of the house. The walls were painted a deep, haunting red, and behind a massive black desk was an off-white wall that was the most unusual thing I'd ever seen.

"What is that?" I looked at Bradley, who was lining up stacks of papers quietly while I pointed at the elaborate wall.

Clearing my throat and feeling uneasy with the silence, I sunk into the chair across from the desk that separated me from the massive, curved black leather chair with metal pieces outlining it. I couldn't take my eyes off the wall, which consisted of textured shards of off-white objects pieced together with a slight gloss over it.

It was oddly beautiful.

"Conrad will be in shortly to discuss the details of the paperwork." Bradley finally looked up at me. His eyes were such a pale shade of green, they almost blurred into the whites of his eyes. "I really hope you're better than the last girl." He clicked his tongue and let out a long, dramatic sigh as he studied me once more before he left. I watched his feet as they glided across the floor, the thick platform shoes literally making no sound as he walked.

"Who is Conrad?" I called out behind him, but half of his body was already out the door. He paused and slowly shut the door behind him, and as he did, all I could see was a sliver of his icy eyes.

I swallowed the lump in my throat and stood from my seat. Rows and rows of medical textbooks were neatly lined on the shelves on the other side of the room. Brushing my finger against the spines, I tilted my head and squinted at the gold words.

"Orthopedic Surgery Essentials: Spine," I read out loud and began to tug it out.

"Hey," a voice right over my shoulder echoed. Flinging around, the giant textbook that was half off the shelf dropped loudly to the floor as I froze and stared at the man in front of me.

He was tall, broad-shouldered, with light brown hair and whiskey-colored eyes that stood out against his skin.

Unlike everyone else in the house, he wasn't wearing white from head to toe; he was wearing a fitted, forest-green V-neck and worn denim. He looked like one of those men who posed on a yacht with a bottle of Armani cologne in an ad.

"I'm Conrad Ivory." He stuck his hand out and his jaw ticked slightly as I continued to stand there frozen.

Clearing his throat, he took a deep breath. "You're Demi, right? The new housekeeper?"

"Yes." I quickly shoved my hand into his and shook it. Unlike my trembling one, his was steady and warm.

"Are you sure you want this job? You don't seem like..." he began, gripping my hand a moment longer than needed.

Tugging my hand away, I laced my fingers together. "I don't seem like, what?" I peered at him. He couldn't be much older than me.

Shrugging, he did a quick swoop of my body. Crossing my arms across my chest, I scrunched my nose.

Once he was making eye contact again, he let out a light laugh, one that made me bite back my own smile.

"I'm not checking you out, really. I'm just not sure why a girl like you, in designer clothes, wants to scrub toilets and wash clothes, *especially here*..." It didn't go past me that the last two words of his sentence were full of hesitation.

"I..." Embarrassment pooled through my body. "These clothes aren't mine." Although Conrad was wearing a pretty basic outfit, I could tell it had to cost more than a month's rent for the majority of America.

He nodded slowly as a small smile peeked out between his knitted lips. "That's actually really good to know, because honestly, it looks like you robbed a designer ghost..." He lifted his eyebrows, and I couldn't help but laugh as I looked down at my entirely white outfit that really didn't match me at all.

Conrad's face lit up in a bigger smile as he watched me unable to suppress my laughter.

"That... that was really funny." I coughed as I choked on my spit, mid-laughter.

"Wow, thanks... Most girls make me wine and dine them, and then they'll feel bad and just fake a laugh at my jokes." He shoved his hands into his pockets with his shoulders slightly lifted.

Rubbing my arms, I tried my best to compose myself. Suddenly, my eyes caught a glimpse of the

THE FAVORITE GIRL   69

surgery textbook splayed on the ground. Dropping down, I carefully picked it up, attempting to smooth out the pages before closing it. Furrowing my brows, I noticed that Conrad was also wearing the thick padded shoes. While his resembled sneakers, they were the same shade of white, with the same thick, amplified soles.

Slowly standing, I carefully placed the textbook in the gap on the shelf and turned back to Conrad.

"Do you want to become a doctor, too?" I asked, only to prevent me from asking all the wild questions that were circulating through my mind.

"I have to." Conrad shrugged and pushed his hair from his forehead.

"Have to?" My eyebrows lifted. What a peculiar way to answer a question about something you have complete control over.

"Yeah, I mean, I'm my dad's prodigal son. Have to take over his—" Conrad stopped mid-sentence, pinching his lips to the side. I was guessing he meant his dad's private practice? One look around this massive estate, and I didn't blame him.

"What about you? You never really answered me. Why would a girl like you want to do a shitty job like this?"

I let my eyes wander around the space as I thought about my answer. I didn't know how to lie very well. I mean, a girl like me—who had been living in a tiny closet for years, with another girl; a girl who was my sister that I watched get attacked daily so it wouldn't have to be me; a girl like me, who hid crumbs in a tiny tissue in case there wasn't another meal for a while...

"I'm saving up for college." I lied, feeling my cheeks heat up as soon as the lie left my lips.

"Oh, yeah?" Conrad smiled at me. "I go to UNC. I'm just home for an extended summer. You should apply there. Maybe, if you want a tour or something..." He ran his hand through the back of his hair anxiously, and I couldn't help but roll my lips together to hide the stupid grin that was tempting to come out.

Suddenly, a buzzing sounded, startling me. "Conrad. Your father wants to make sure you have the documents signed and brought to him promptly. He's growing impatient. He said to bring the book she dropped as well. He needs to replace it since it's probably damaged and has touched the dirtied floor."

My eyes shot around the room. How did Dr. Ivory know I dropped his book? How...

Hugging myself, I realized something.

We are being watched.

CHAPTER
ELEVEN

I SAT across the desk from Conrad as he shifted his voice and mannerisms. His eyes locked onto something in the corner of the room, but I was too uncomfortable to follow his line of vision, especially when he looked at me for a moment longer before clearing his throat.

"Working for the Ivory family comes with the understanding that confidentiality is the number one priority. Anything you may hear or see within these walls may not be shared with anyone. Know that if you do, the repercussions are severe." He straightened his spine and kept his eyes down on the hefty stack of papers in front of him.

"There are a few guidelines that you must agree to in order to obtain this job. I'll let you read them, unless you'd like me—"

"No, it's fine. I can…" I felt embarrassed that he even assumed I couldn't read a simple document.

IVORY ESTATE RULES

- Confidentiality. Anything you witness may not be repeated in or outside of the home.
- You must not wear any form of fragrance, makeup, or accessories unless approved.

- You must wear all white.
- You must be willing to get an IUD.

Wait. *What?* I squinted as I re-read the first four rules. I mean, I could somewhat understand fragrance and makeup, because maybe someone in the family had allergies or sensitivities to certain chemicals? Or maybe, in an all-white house, they didn't want to risk makeup getting on anything. Even accessories were understandable since I was going to be cleaning.

Wearing all-white seemed strange, but employers had uniforms. But why would an IUD be mandatory?

I glanced up at Conrad, who immediately looked at the pen in his hand. "Can you explain…"

"Rule number four?" he immediately filled in painfully.

"Mmm-hm." I cleared my throat, looking down at the glass of water in front of me.

"Can I drink that?"

"Oh, yeah. Of course. It's for you." My hand shook as I grabbed the glass and quickly took a long sip, hyperaware of the way the water sounded sloshing down my throat. Placing it back on the marble coaster, I glanced at Conrad.

"It's so you… I guess… Well, so you don't get pregnant and stop working, basically. My parents like to keep their staff around long-term." He nodded, as if he was trying to convince himself of the strange explanation. But was it strange? I mean, this family was clearly insanely wealthy and private. I'm sure there'd be a line of desperate, jobless individuals who would happily sign the line below to dust some fancy frames in exchange for a hefty paycheck and a beautiful estate to live in.

Not to mention, the son of your boss being quite the eye-candy. My cheeks grew warm as I realized I'd been dazed out. "That makes sense." I rolled my lips together and continued to read the rest of the rules.

- **You must not speak or make any bodily noises while in the Orchid section of the Estate.**

Bodily noises? "What if I need to sneeze?" I pointed at the fifth rule and looked up at Conrad, while stifling my impending laughter.

"You don't. You can't make a single sound in the Orchid section, Demi. It would cost you *everything*." Conrad didn't smile, he didn't blink; he just stared at me blankly. But then I realized something. He wasn't looking at me... he was looking behind me. Following his line of vision, I turned slowly and slapped my hand against my chest.

Dr. Ivory.

He was dressed in white scrubs, with a small white surgical cap and white gloves that reached his elbows. The lines across his forehead creased as he stared at his son. "What is taking so long, Conrad?" His voice was unnervingly low. "We actually need her to begin today."

It was very uncomfortable how he was talking about me but avoiding eye contact with me at all costs.

"Okay, Dr. Ivory." My eyes shot between both of them. *Did he just call his dad Dr. Ivory?*

Dr. Ivory took a quick glance at me before turning away. I couldn't help but watch as he left. Not a single sound came from his movements, and when he opened and closed the door, it made no noise.

What kind of house was this?

CHAPTER
TWELVE

THE REST of the rules were abnormal, but nothing compared to the IUD requirement. One of the rules was that I would not be allowed to bring my gifted phone out from my room. I wasn't allowed to take photos inside the house or on the sprawling property. I wasn't allowed to text or call anyone until after eight p.m. when my shift ended. I had never had a phone before so I was stunned they'd even be offering one to me.

Conrad handed me a lifestyle section of the hefty contract. "So, this part they'll want you to read out loud." His eyes flicked behind me to the corner of the room. Chills shot up my spine as his face flushed. I didn't dare turn around to see where his eyes were.

"Um… okay." I shrugged. Clearing my throat, I felt like a student in a full classroom, when the teacher tells you to read a passage out loud and you didn't have a chance to read it through and prepare.

Feeling winded, I hesitated and skimmed across the paragraph which seemed to jumble together. Granted, I stopped attending school by the time I was fifteen—though not by choice, but due to the fact that I was abducted and forced to...

"Demi?" Conrad tapped my hand and I looked up at him. It was as if he could hear the racing thoughts coursing wildly through my mind.

"Sorry." Loosening my shoulders, I began, "The Ivory House requires a lifestyle agreement. We prefer to keep our environment healthy, nourishing, and positive. In addition, we cannot allow for illnesses to invade our space. You will be weighed once a week; you will consume only whole food, with absolutely no processed food. You will drink a designated green juice every single morning alongside your breakfast. All meals will be prepared for you by The Ivory House chef. You will take two vitamins and one probiotic that will be provided for you as well. You must consume one gallon of water a day. Before your working hours, which will begin promptly at seven a.m., you will go on a walk on the estate grounds, and we will monitor your daily step count. You must drink the peony-infused tea for its vast-health benefits. As long as you're employed here, you must wear the bracelet presented to you."

Okay, maybe I could work at a fast-food restaurant. But then again, I had about three dollars left to my name, so sleeping on a bench for a few months until I saved enough for a roach-infested apartment versus staying at a stunning estate with a steady paycheck seemed like an easy decision. After all, they were essentially asking me to eat clean and be healthy. People paid big money for whole food programs and workout routines. This wasn't a bad thing. Pursing my lips, I thought of the countless Twinkies and vending machine snacks I'd consumed this last week alone—not to mention the half-eaten burgers I scored from the dumpster behind the McDonald's near the motel.

My stomach twisted as I thought of peeling trash and dirtied napkins away from French fries before swallowing them down from sheer starvation.

"This sounds good." I placed the paper down and reached for the pen.

Conrad's eyes widened in shock. "Really?" He sounded stunned and then he reached and held my hand in place so I couldn't sign. His nails digging crescents into my flesh.

Again, he looked up in the back corner, and I understood. Someone was watching us. Taking the pen from my hand, he scribbled on a blank sheet of paper.

'Are you sure, Demi? There is no turning back from this job.' He pushed the sheet toward me with trembling hands as his pleading eyes locked onto mine.

Clenching my jaw, I couldn't tell Conrad all the reasons why I didn't over-analyze this job. I couldn't tell him about my past; I couldn't tell him that staying in the four walls of a stunning estate sounded far safer than the prison of my own mind. It was safer than being out there and them finding me. Lifting the pen from his hand, I offered a somewhat sad smile and nodded once.

"I have to be sure." And with that, I signed my name in cursive that resembled a second grader's.

CHAPTER THIRTEEN

MY HAND WAS CRAMPING by the time I signed every single document, and Conrad had stamped it with some fancy gold ink. About an hour later, he stood and neatly put the papers into a large manila envelope. He slid a white box to me and tapped it. "Put this on and never take it off."

Opening it, I looked at the pearl bracelet.

"Welcome to the Ivory family, Demi." He reached his hand out.

Smiling, I took it, shaking it slowly. "Thanks...I hope I don't screw it up."

"You can't, Demi. You cannot screw this up. Please, don't." He took his hand back quickly and walked toward the door. "I really like you, and I don't want you to get..." He paused as his eyes seemed to darken. He helped me slide the bracelet onto my wrist.

. . .

I didn't know what to say. He doesn't want me to get, what? I hoped he'd finish the sentence, but as soon as he opened the door, I jerked back.

It was Bradley, dressed in a pristine white suit with a long coat and matching white bowtie.

Rich people were bizarre. This family ensured their staff matched their aesthetic.

"I'll lead her to her quarters, Mr. Ivory." He bowed his head to Conrad, and something in the small gesture had the hair on the back of my neck stand straight.

"Bye, Conrad," I whispered as Bradley spun around on his heels and waved me to follow him.

"Don't say bye, Demi. Say see you later." He furrowed his brows and watched as I walked away. I didn't want to look forward at Bradley; I wanted to stay with Conrad. Something about him felt safe and normal compared to the eeriness that radiated from everywhere in this house. In my entire life, I don't think I had ever been in a house that was even middle-class, let alone something that would be a mansion like this.

Bradley kept walking so quickly, I basically had to jog in order to keep up with him. His sharp cuts around the corners had my head spinning. Every wall we passed began to get less and less decorated. After what felt like miles later, we paused in front of a strangely narrow door. Punching a code into the keypad, the automatic door opened quietly.

"After you." Bradley had one hand behind his back while the other waved me forward. I really didn't want this creepy man walking behind me, but something told me that was going to be the least of my concerns.

Once through the door, I froze. It was a long, constricted hall, with one single light dangling from the ceiling in the middle.

"This is your room. You need to take those off, and place those on before entering. Main house shoes are not permitted in bedrooms. You must bathe, then report back outside your room in precisely sixty minutes before I collect you for dinner with the family. They are hosting your welcome meal."

"So, I'm officially hired?"

"You begin work tomorrow. They preferred today but realize that would be rushed."

I supposed that meant yes. I couldn't help but do a little dance and excitedly cheer out loud.

Bradley slapped his hand across my mouth, shocking me completely. My eyes protruded with the pressure he placed.

"Are you insane?" he seethed. "You must not have read the contract properly. We do not speak above a hushed tone."

Peeling his fingers off of my mouth, I looked at him and pointed my finger in his face.

"If you touch me like that again, I'll bite your fingers off," I gritted out in a whisper. "I hope you heard me, because I won't repeat myself."

I pulled my shoes off as Bradley backed away and dropped his eyes to the floor. Neatly lining the shoes Raina gave me by the door, I slid on the thick, padded slippers.

Without another word, I walked through the door and it automatically closed behind me. This time my shoes made no sound, the door didn't, and suddenly I began blending in. Finally, alone, I looked around the room. It resembled one of those cruise ship rooms—extremely small with a circular window. I walked closer to the window and saw nothing but dense trees for miles. I must have had a room on the side of the estate or perhaps the back. The bed was a twin, and of course, in all white. And above the bed was one framed image of a pale pink peony flower, which brought me some kind of happiness. Walking into the bathroom, I glanced around. I didn't know how they let the hint of pink slide in from the peony without a full-blown panic attack, but I started to laugh as I looked at my reflection in the mirror.

"They let a brown girl in with jet black hair." I chuckled.

'I miss you, sissy.' The smile on my face melted as I heard her voice and flung around.

She's not here. She's gone. She's dead. Because of you. You didn't protect her, Demi. It's all your fault.

"I didn't mean to. I couldn't save us both." Tears streamed down my cheeks as I clenched my eyes shut.

"I'm sorry. I'm so sorry." My heart ached as I pictured my beautiful sister. She was older than me, but it was still my job to protect her. Our parents said they'd come get us when the loan was paid off. They said they'd save us. But they didn't. Years passed and they never came. I had to do what I needed to in order to escape.

I had to stop this. If I showed the Ivory family signs of being mentally ill or unstable, they'd definitely fire me. I couldn't lose this job. I could do it for a few years, save up every penny, and then maybe I'd really go to college. I could get a degree and then make a life for myself. Maybe, I could get married. And while I never wanted to have kids, marriage seemed nice. A companion to be with every day. Someone to drain out the racing thoughts and suffocating solitude I pretended I was fine with.

Quivering, I realized that I really needed to get ready, but I didn't have anything to wear. I didn't bring a bag or a suitcase—and the little amount of stuff I had was with Raina. Speaking of, would I get to leave tonight to see her? I mean, this wasn't a prison; this was my employer's home, and I could leave when I wanted to.

The shower was narrow but pristine. Bottles with small labels were drilled into the wall—shampoo, conditioner, soap. This was like a luxury hotel. There was a toothbrush, and a tube of toothpaste on the vanity, but none of it had flashy brand labels, not even the toothpaste. It was all in matching cream-colored tubes and bottles with tiny labels of what the product was.

Damn, to have this level of money and time. I smiled and quickly tugged off Raina's outfit, hanging it on the hook behind the door. Turning the shower on, I opened my palm to wait until it warmed for me to get inside.

"Ah," I groaned as the hot water pellets beat against my fatigued body. Sleeping on benches, shitty motel mattresses, and under bridges had taken a toll on my body. I didn't feel nineteen; I felt eighty. Cracking my neck on both sides, I savored the fact that I didn't have to worry about how much this shower would cost me. I didn't have to worry about washing my body in some gas station sink or using a water bottle to splash under my armpits. I could just bathe myself.

Pumping shampoo into my hand, I took a sniff of it

—not scented. Rubbing it into my thick, unruly hair, I thought about how Dr. and Mrs. Ivory were probably those people who knew fragrances caused illness and whatnot.

It made sense. It all made sense. Or at least desperation had me colorblind to any red flags.

The thing about everything fitting too perfectly together is that it really means jagged pieces were shaved down to fit so perfectly. It means the rough edges were smoothed down and hidden away.

Because there is no such thing as perfect. And sometimes the more perfect something seems; the more secrets are hidden away.

CHAPTER
FOURTEEN

I TOOK the longest shower of my life. Once wrapped up and out of the bathroom, I put lotion on and dabbed the steam away from the bathroom mirror.

I looked and felt clean. A simple human state that most people never really even give a second thought about. For me, I think the last time I was this clean was when I was fourteen—before I was taken, before I escaped and became homeless. A glaze of grime always seemed to plague me and dirt under my nails that couldn't be washed away. The worst was when I was on my period. It was comical to think I'd ever be able to afford sanitary pads or tampons. No, instead I'd have to stuff my hoodie pockets with enough toilet paper and rip up my shirts to make into makeshift pads. I always wondered in those moments that if men were the ones getting periods, we'd definitely have free supplies. Women, no, we were inferior.

Just to stay sanitary, I was expected to shell out ten dollars for a small box of pads that would only last me a month. Poverty is a bitch, but I was born into it and not knowing what I didn't have actually protected me.

But now I'm going to turn my life around. I'm going to fight for a future and make sure I don't mess up this golden opportunity. I pumped some face cream onto my face and combed my hair before brushing my teeth. Widening my mouth, I cringed at the yellow tint and chips that lined each tooth. Conrad must have been repulsed. Sometimes I forgot that this— who I was—wasn't normal.

I shook my head in disbelief that I even allowed myself to flirt with him. How could I embarrass myself like that? How could I disrespect him that way?

Walking back through the small doorway, I glanced around and opened the small armoire. It was empty, except for one stunning, silk white gown, and in a small basket on a shelf, there was a pair of matching gloves.

Wasn't the dinner just at the house with the family? I looked around the room but had no one to ask. I definitely didn't know my way around and couldn't risk getting lost, and in return, be late for creepy Bradley to 'collect' me. My hair was wrapped in a towel, and I decided I probably should get dressed. I didn't see a blow dryer or anything to help tame my hair beyond a brush—I didn't even have a hair tie. This wasn't good. My thick, black hair would air dry into what would resemble a lion's mane.

"Fuck." I chewed my bottom lip while carefully sliding the dress off the hanger when suddenly, something occurred to me. Stepping into it, I shimmied the fabric up my body. It was a perfect fit. Tilting my head to the side, I admired the gorgeous material. Sure, the excess bloat on my midsection was showing a bit more through the thin material, but this was the most stunning dress I'd ever put on. Pulling on the gloves, they reached to my elbows, and I felt like a princess. If this is what they did for their new housekeeper as a welcome dinner, then I was already excited to see my holiday bonuses.

This job is going to change my life. Towel drying my hair, I began to hum softly, but I stopped with the realization of something making my stomach flip.

How did someone have this dress in my size already hung in the closet...? Especially when I signed the contract only an hour ago? Suddenly, the room felt colder and smaller. Looking around, I wrapped my arms across my chest and shuddered.

"Miss Rao, it's time," a whisper echoed through the

small room. My mouth dropped, and I jolted as the pulse in my neck thumped rapidly.

"Who's there?" I screeched, spinning in a circle.

"Shh! Hush, Demi, it's Bradley. I'm outside your door. It's time for dinner."

My eyes danced around the room as I looked for the speaker, but everything was seamless.

Opening the door slowly, I kept my hand on the wall and the other on the door.

"Dear God, you look ratchet," he hissed. He was wearing a white tuxedo, with matching shoes and gloves. This man was intolerable. Shutting the door carefully, he pushed past me and walked straight into my bathroom, but if I hadn't seen him do it, I wouldn't have known—not with his bizarre, soundproof shoes.

"Um, excuse me! You can't just barge in here. This is now my room!" My voice sounded even louder than it was.

Holding a small bag, his jaw clenched. "Your hair is...." He shuddered as if it physically repulsed him to see my hair.

Disgusted, I licked my lips and pointed at him. "I'm so sorry I don't have tacky, bleached hair like yours." I stuck out my tongue and instantly regretted it as a small smile grew on his lips.

"Yet." Bradley snickered.

What did he mean by yet?

"Look, this bag is kept under the sink. We don't have much time. Just tie your hair up in a bun and put some Chapstick on. Your lips look like shriveled prunes. And why are they so dark?" He scrunched his nose.

"Melanin, maybe?" I cocked my head to the side in sheer disbelief. "I'm sure that's hard for you to understand, seeing that you're an Edward Cullen-wannabe." I grinded my teeth together, proud of my comeback.

Rolling his lips together, I swore he was about to potentially murder me, right here, right now.

But he didn't. Instead, he let out a dry laugh and a defeated nod.

Checkmate.

"You're not as dark as most Indian people. I mean you are actually kind of pale compared to the ones I've met. You could be one of us." He shrugged his shoulders.

Rolling my eyes, "I didn't know every Indian person had to be a specific shade in order to be Indian. Besides, how many Indian people have you actually met?"

"One of those Jonas Brothers married one of your kind."

"You mean to say, Priyanka Chopra, a former Miss World, actress and humanitarian married some Jonas Brothers guy." I shot at him.

A small smirk grew on his face. "You're feisty, Demi Rao. I like it."

Tugging the bag from his hands, I turned my back toward him because I didn't want him to see the stupid smile on my face.

This might actually be the best job ever.

CHAPTER
FIFTEEN

BRADLEY and I walked down the cold hallway in complete silence. Looking down at my feet, I couldn't help but watch myself walk. My shoes were just like his—padded, with some kind of foam-like material. When I rubbed my finger against the bottom, I could tell it was coated with something...

Something to make sure it emitted no noise.

"Why is everything so quiet here?" I breathed out in a hushed whisper as we turned into yet another constricted hallway. I noticed it was warmer as we moved closer to the main area of the estate.

"What do you mean?" Bradley looked at me as if I asked the most ridiculous question on earth.

"The shoes, the doors... I mean, you keep quieting me." I stopped and crossed my arms. "You basically only talk in a whisper, as did the rest of the Ivory family."

"Miss Rao, I urge you to understand one simple rule in this house: you must never question anything the Ivory family does. You must never ask questions, you must never even think twice about the way things are managed here. You don't come from anything, so this," he paused and waved his arms around us, "this must all feel abnormal to you, but darling, this is absolutely customary for the wealthy. Truthfully, the only anomalous aspect about this now, is *you*." He bopped my nose and I swear, if I didn't have this new job lined up, I'd have slit his damn throat.

'Sissy!' As soon as the thought came through my mind, I heard her voice and flinched.

"What did you call me?" I gasped and looked at Bradley. He didn't look scared or nervous; he just smiled again. A smile that had chills running down my arm.

"Oh, they really did find the perfect fit for this job." He grew so close to me that his minty breath brushed against my face. "Don't ever show them that you're insane." He winked at me.

"I'm… I'm not…" I began to ramble, but Bradley didn't even look at me.

I rushed to follow after him as he walked. "Don't

mess this up," Bradley whispered as he pushed open enormous, intricately designed doors.

They had a stunning shine to them, unlike most of the rest of the home, which mostly had an unnerving matte finish. Once the doors were flung open, I couldn't even believe what my eyes were taking in. The table had at least twelve stunning, velvet emerald chairs, a glossy black table—which was the first non-white piece of furniture I'd seen in the house. The room had gold walls, and it almost reminded me of Raina's house. Speaking of, I really hoped I'd be able to make my way back to her house to tell her I got the job and to thank her for her kindness. If she hadn't picked me up and loaned me the clothes, I may not have been here. I may have been piling grocery bags together to craft a makeshift pillow for a wet park bench.

No one was here yet, besides four women dressed in matching knee-length, white dresses holding silver platters.

"You sit here." Bradley pointed to a seat. I sank into the plush chair, and he walked to the other end of the table. As maddening as he was, I really didn't want him to leave me alone at the opposite side of the table. Who was going to sit next to me? I looked down at the silverware as immense anxiety filled me.

There were three forks, two knives, and two spoons. I didn't even know how to eat. Swallowing the lump in my throat, I looked at the largest knife. Brushing my index finger against it, I felt moisture build in my eyes.

'Sissy!'

I puffed out a breath of air and slammed my eyes shut.

"Miss Rao?"

Turning slowly, I looked into Mrs. Ivory's light-green eyes. Her blonde hair was down in shiny loose curls. I didn't realize her hair was that long when it was pinned up earlier. Pearls were strung around her neck, and the pale pink gown she wore looked like it belonged on the red carpet, not in their dining room. "Hello," I let out, feeling relieved. They had a stunning, color-filled room, and Mrs. Ivory was wearing pink. Who cares if they had some strangely, sterile preference in how their employees and house looked?

And then, Mrs. Ivory leaned down, held my head between her gloved hands, and kissed the top of my head.

"We are thrilled to have you join our family. Our employees are not just employees; they are truly family to us. Isn't that right, Conrad?" She didn't turn—and we didn't hear him come in—but there he was, dressed in a stunning navy-blue tuxedo, approaching us.

Unlike my sister, my skin was lighter and showed when I blushed. His mother glanced between us with a lifted brow. "Conrad, your seat is right beside Demi." Mrs. Ivory gave me a small grin, which caused me to drop my eyes out of sheer embarrassment.

Was it that obvious I was drooling over her son? This wasn't good. She may think it's precious at this moment, but it'll all change as soon as I'm dressed in a maid's uniform with my hands in her toilet bowl.

I cleared my throat. "Thank you, Mrs. Ivory, for hiring me. I promise I'll do anything you need me to do."

"Well, we will remember those famous words, won't we, dear?" Dr. Ivory's hands planted on his wife's as he looked down at me. I should have stood, especially since this was such an awkward angle.

Conrad took the seat next to me as his parents cradled one another and stared down at me. "I'm so happy you're here, Demi. Truly." Mrs. Ivory leaned down once more and kissed the top of my head.

I know most people would have found this peculiar, but I don't think someone had ever kissed me lovingly like that... The small gesture was so powerful, it terrified me. I couldn't afford to be vulnerable; I couldn't afford to think my employer would actually care about me.

No, I wouldn't set myself up for heartbreak and disappointment. This was a job and a safe place to live, nothing more.

"Thank you for this opportunity, Dr. and Mrs. Ivory; I am really grateful."

Dr. Ivory scoffed in a way that made me feel humiliated. "Excited to clean up feces and urine," he said under his breath as he walked away. Turning slowly back around, I kept my eyes on the plate in front of me.

"I'm sorry about him," Conrad murmured so low I could barely hear him. I didn't dare lift my eyes at him. My cheeks were now warm, not because I felt some kind of crush on my new employers' son, but because he was consoling me after his dad just humiliated me.

The worst part was he wasn't degrading me; he was speaking the truth. I was about to scrub a bunch of rich people's toilets. Here I was, sitting in a gown after taking the first real shower with real bath products in ages, thinking I was some beauty queen.

Racing thoughts replaying those embarrassing moments ran through my mind, and I paused. A door on the opposing wall that blended into the dark, navy walls swung open and, one by one, women came out wearing short, white sheath dresses, carrying platters of food. My blood froze as I stared at them gliding in sync. They were all thin, Caucasian, with short, neatly brushed blonde hair and green eyes. None of them had any ounce of makeup on, but they all looked meticulously... clean. Their collarbones and jaws all protruded enough to make me think twice, but not enough to say they were being starved or something irrational like that.

But wasn't this crazy? Wasn't this family kind of outrageous? I looked over at Mrs. Ivory, who smiled and clapped excitedly with her eyes on the women. Or rather, girls.

And just like that, a light sound emitted through the dining room, something magical and majestic. A harp? And that's when the lights dimmed and one in particular dropped brightly on a woman in a long, golden gown.

She was beautiful; her hair was blonde, but unlike everyone else's, you could see her original dark brown roots growing out. Her thin, long fingers strummed against the harp strings, crafting a stunning melody. My heart began to race as music danced through the darkened room. *I hate music.* Clenching my eyes shut, I realized this house was so appealing to me because of the silence. There wasn't noise covering up—

"That's Misha." Conrad dipped toward me. "She'll be making it out soon," he added.

Looking at him and seeing his outline, I tilted my head. "Making it out?" I questioned. What a strange way to word it. But Conrad didn't say anything more; instead, his eyes stayed on Misha.

"What was her job here?" My voice sounded needy, and the urgency was easily noticeable.

Conrad sighed and leaned back into his chair. "You're replacing her, Demi."

But why was their previous housekeeper dressed up and playing the harp?

Suddenly, it occurred to me… They weren't celebrating me joining their staff, they were celebrating Misha making it out.

But making it out from what?

CHAPTER
SIXTEEN

THE REST of dinner was much more natural, and Misha joined us at the table. I so desperately wanted to speak to her and ask her why she was leaving the job that was now mine. But as I looked down at my over-flowing plate full of fresh, sizzling, and organic food, my stomach protested, and I thought of something my mother used to always tell me. *"When you're in a hole, stop digging. Because if you don't, it'll be easier for someone to throw more dirt over you and impossible for you to get out."* Why would I dig myself deeper into a hole when I had a chance to finally climb out of it?

This was a bunch of rich people drama—matching staff, a housekeeper they loved enough to buy a gown for and celebrate, her probably saving up enough and moving on to the next stage of her life. Maybe they enjoyed helping desperate, young women and then letting them go like a caged bird finally freed.

Nodding, I pinched my lips to the side as I studied the shiny silver forks. "This one." Conrad tapped one and smiled at me kindly.

"Thanks. I was about to brush my hair with one." I winced at my childish joke based on *The Little Mermaid* —the last movie I had watched... with her.

"I'm glad you're part of my world now." Conrad winked at me, and I swear it took every ounce of willpower for me to not hysterically cry or hug him.

"Conrad..." I began, but was tapped on my shoulder.

Flinging around, my eyes widened. She was even more beautiful up close. "Hello, I'm Misha." Her gaze held onto Conrad's for a moment and I could have sworn she look pained when he turned away. She sat in the empty seat next to me and put her hand out. She was very thin, but unlike the other girls, she wore a full face of makeup.

"Hey, I'm Demi." I took her hand but was stunned at how cold it was.

"You're... so different from what they prefer," she said in a saddened whisper.

"Yeah, I guess they needed their minority quota," I added with a small chuckle.

Apparently, Misha didn't find humor in my statement as she just looked at me blankly. "After you finish obtaining your nutrition, Bradley will bring you to my room. They'll let me discuss details of your new position that may be helpful for you, dear Demi." She clasped my hands between hers and blew out a small breath of air. "I have a good feeling about you. I really hope it'll be these beautiful soft fingers on the harp next." She lifted my hands and intertwined my fingers with hers.

You know those moments someone is doing something extremely disturbingly eerie, but you're in shock and you can't get out of the situation?

Yes, this was exactly that moment.

"I hope they'll let you keep this beautiful raven hair." She released my hands and tucked the straggling curl that had fallen out of my poor attempt at a bun. "But she's going to love wearing it…" Her eyes looked distant as she drew her fingers down my cheek.

"Misha, stop it," Conrad cut across me and pushed her hand off my face while I sat there like a statue, unable to move.

This girl was clearly mentally unstable. Maybe that's why I was replacing her? Maybe she had lost her mind entirely.

· · ·

"You must protect her, Con." She smiled sadly before standing and smoothing out her long gown. "Goodbye my handsome, Con. I'm sorry that I wasn't good enough. I'll see you in a bit, darling Demi." She wiggled her fingers at us and glided to the other end of the lengthy table. Looking back down at my barely touched meal, I lifted the biggest spoon and began shoveling it into my mouth. I wasn't going to be that girl who said she lost her appetite over an unsettling conversation—those were the people who had the luxury of knowing when their next meal would be.

The scent of sandalwood and cedar floated off Conrad as he leaned in and whispered, "Hey, don't worry about what Misha said. She's… a little off."

"Sometimes I think the people who are accused of being a little off are the ones who are the most truthful. Perhaps it is the ugly truth that makes them seem off?" I chewed some creamy potatoes while feeling Conrad's eyes still on me. I hated how the job, with everything I needed, had a house full of unsettling opulent people. I started to think about how long I'd need to work to save up and find a new job and a new home.

Hmm, with no bank account—and maybe three dollars and some change to my name—I'd need this job for at least the next… I don't know, infinite years.

Middle class families could barely afford their groceries, so how would a girl like me afford to survive?

I needed to stick to what I was here for. *I'm here to clean...* But the thing that had the pit in my stomach growing was thinking about what kind of messes I was actually here to clean up.

CHAPTER SEVENTEEN

EVENTUALLY, after staying mostly quiet for the rest of dinner—and eating every last drop of food off of my plate—Bradley came to 'retrieve' me.

"Good night, Demi," Conrad said sheepishly, looking at me with hopefulness. I felt a bit guilty for being crass with him. He was, after all, one of the only normal people in this house that I had met.

"Good night, Conrad. Thank you for your kindness. See you later." I smiled.

His face completely shifted and broke into a huge grin that had me smiling even bigger. "See you later, Princess Ariel." He winked at me before Bradley cleared his throat.

"Shall we, Miss Rao?" He bent his arm, and I assumed he wanted me to take it.

"I'm not holding your hand, creep." I shook my

head and stood as Bradley's jaw tightened from amusement he was trying to suppress.

"You must say goodnight to Dr. and Mrs. Ivory before you meet with Misha by the peony garden." Bradley nodded where the couple was sitting.

I held my breath for a moment, acknowledging the fact that my job hadn't even begun and I already dreaded interacting with Dr. Ivory. How was Mrs. Ivory married to such a... well, a man with an ego that would probably make his head burst any second?

"Smile," Bradley hissed. "You look like you're paying your respects at a funeral." He nudged me as we stopped in front of them.

"Shall I curtsy while I'm at it?" I rolled my eyes at him.

"Darling Demi, how was your dinner? Did you eat enough?" Mrs. Ivory asked me with genuine concern.

Her voice was so soft and smooth, the way a mother's voice should be—the way I had always wished my mother would have been. But for my mother, I had a price tag on my head. That's all I was for her, a means to an end.

"I did. Thank you so much, Dr. and Mrs. Ivory, for this lovely dinner and the job. I look forward to beginning tomorrow." I clasped my hands together. I really meant what I was saying; I couldn't believe that I had a real job.

"You're welcome, dear," Dr. Ivory said, throwing me the biggest surprise of the evening.

"Get a good nights' rest, and let Bradley know if you need anything. Off you both go. I'm sure Misha is eager to help you get ready for your new role." Mrs. Ivory wafted us away.

I followed Bradley out of the stunning dining room, taking the exquisite, rich, and colorful space in one last time before going back into the blindingly white house. The doors opened for us, and when I looked at the women holding the door, the uneasiness came right back. I took in their short blonde hair, white sheath dresses, hollowed cheekbones, and how their eyes stayed on the floor as we exited.

Looking over my shoulder as we walked ahead, one of the women who had to be no more than twenty rolled her eyes upward without moving her head and mouthed something at me.

Scrunching my face, I shook my head. I couldn't make out what she was trying to tell me.

So, she did it again and this time, there was no missing it.

Her thin, pale lips breathed out, "Run."

My heart dropped, my hands grew cold, and I flung back around, catching up to Bradley.

"Bradley, I'm safe here... right?" I asked with sheer desperation and froze in my spot.

"Don't stop walking, Demi," he mumbled as he continued to walk hastily, cutting into sharp turns at the end of each hallway.

Picking up my pace, I followed until we got to a wall of nothing but glass. Outside it was pitch-black, but I could see specks of shimmering stars in the sky. I couldn't even see a door, but one tap later, and a part of the seamless glass opened.

Bradley turned toward me and sighed. "You're safe as long as you don't go looking for the answer to that question. Misha is waiting for you. She has a flight to catch tonight to go back home, so don't waste time. You need to get to bed on time as well. Tomorrow is a busy day and an early start. They've been eager to have someone new clean The Ossis area of the estate."

"The Ossis area?"

"That's what you were hired for, Demi—to clean the most private area of The Ivory House. That's what Misha's job was. Didn't you read the contract properly? Didn't Conrad explain that?" Bradley furrowed his brows and rambled so quickly that my heart began pattering.

"No?" I felt foolish for sitting there like some high school girl with a crush when I was supposed to be paying attention to details of my new employment. How reckless could I have been?

"Demi, we don't have time right now. Just go meet

Misha. Walk outside, make a left, and you'll see the peony garden. If you don't see it, you'll definitely smell it. Misha will be waiting for you on the swing… She loves the swing." He pointed into the darkness as if I knew what he was talking about.

"I'll come back to pick you up and take you to your room in approximately twenty-one minutes." Bradley patted my shoulder as I walked through the door and into the slight chill of the night air. I couldn't see the moon; I couldn't see anything beyond the stars. Rubbing my arms, I turned back over my shoulder to ask Bradley if he'd walk me to the garden, but he was already gone, leaving nothing but a dark, empty hallway behind me.

"Hell," I groaned and begrudgingly dragged my feet in the strange platform shoes. I began sniffing the air like I was a dog. I couldn't see any flowers. I didn't even know what a peony smelled like. But as soon as I grew more irritated, I did smell something.

Something beautiful, sweet and comforting. A small gate no higher than my waist was engraved, 'The Peony Garden.' Unlatching the small lock, I strolled through and inhaled the incredible aroma. Small fairy lights were strung up all over and provided enough light to see the stunning blush-pink and white flowers. It was like an absolute dream. A kind of place you'd want to get married in.

Cutting through, I could see a picturesque, intricately carved swing, and I heard a light creaking echo through the fragrant air.

"Misha?" I called out. I could see her silhouette on the bench swing and looking into the distance.

"Hi..." I took a seat beside her, almost falling since she didn't stop swinging. Her head was pressed against the bar of the swing, and she didn't even look at me.

"Misha, thank you for meeting with me..." I started again and planted my feet on the ground as hers dragged. Stopping the swing, her body suddenly folded in half.

"Misha!" I screamed and quickly pulled her back up. I looked at her in the darkness and I noticed all the blood dripping down her neck, soaking into her silk gown. "Oh my god!" I shook her shoulders as my entire body tensed and I couldn't breathe. The scent of peonies choked me as I repeated her name over and over.

Grabbing her hand, a knife clattered to the ground and I lifted it up.

"No, no... Why, Misha? Help! We need help!" I shrieked as I pressed my fingers against her wrist, praying I'd feel a pulse. Nothing. She was lifeless. I grabbed her body, holding it against mine, and began to cry as her blood splattered across my flesh.

Stomach acid teased my esophagus as the scene felt all too familiar. It felt haunting. Reminiscent of times I'd tried endlessly to suppress in an altered state of my conscious.

"Demi?" My body shook violently as I laid Misha onto the swing and turned.

Dr. and Mrs. Ivory stood there in a matching all-white scrub set and looked at the knife I had clutched in my hands.

"Oh, darling Demi, what have you done?" Mrs. Ivory slowly walked over to me as I aggressively shook my head.

"What? No, I didn't... Please, you don't understand." I couldn't breathe, I couldn't move. My vision grew fuzzy and suddenly, it was all too much. My body and mind were in overdrive.

Mrs. Ivory lifted a small needle and tapped it. "It'll be okay, darling Demi. We will protect you. We will protect you because now, it's your turn to be the favorite girl."

"I didn't..." I coughed and choked on my saliva as panic had a hold around my neck.

And with a trifling sinister smile, she pressed the needle into my arm, and the all-white world around me turned black.

CHAPTER
EIGHTEEN

"HELLO, MISS RAO." A woman's voice woke me from a deep sleep as I gradually opened my eyes. I fully expected to awaken and be on some weathered park bench where a police officer was asking me to leave.

But instead, I was in the room from last night. *My new room.* A woman with bright blonde hair and thick wrinkles across her forehead and eyes was looking down at me.

"Who are you?" My voice sounded hoarse, my eyes sticky, and my mind completely disorientated.

"Miss Rao, it's a pleasure to meet you. I'm Carla Cross. I was the one you emailed your inquiry for this position at the Ivory House."

"Carla... Cross." I nodded slowly, remembering her name. "I don't know what happened last night..." But that was a lie; I did remember as I looked around my small new bedroom. I remembered Misha's body gushing blood; I remembered her striking face, lifeless, as her thin body folded over. I remembered lifting a sharp knife as Dr. and Mrs. Ivory walked out and assumed I had done the heinous crime.

But I didn't. I'd never... right?

My heart began to race as my chest tightened. My mind desperately tried rationalizing with itself, not knowing fact from fiction.

"Miss Rao, you were found covered in Misha Stover's blood after her throat was slit, and your fingerprints were all over the knife that matched the cut. Here are the images from the cameras that point at the gardens." Carla neatly lined up the black and white photos across my lap as my mouth parted in shock. This was huge misunderstanding.

I didn't murder her, I didn't...

I had found her.

"No, I swear to you, I didn't do it." I lifted an image as tears began to pour out of my eyes. It looked terrible. There I was, holding the knife with Misha's body in my arms, faced away.

It didn't matter what I said. According to these photos, I was guilty.

They were going to call the police. Then the police would find out about my past. They'd find out that these pictures weren't lying because this wasn't the first time I held a knife in my hand with a young girl bleeding out in front of me.

The difference was yes, I had killed her, but not Misha. No, I didn't. I'd never hurt someone. I was forced to the first time. I was...

"Demi." Dr. Ivory came in, followed by a woman pushing a small silver cart, who was wearing a short dress and an old-fashioned nurse's hat. The cart didn't make a sound—the wheels didn't even screech against the floor. My breathing hitched as panic settled in. *What is this place?*

"Dr. Ivory! You have to help me! I didn't do this..." I began, waving the images around.

"Demi, how can you deny what these images are clearly depicting?" He glanced back at the nurse who stabbed a needle into the small vile. *Tap, tap, tap.* Her nail clicked against the needle as contents of it sputtered out.

"No, I swear to you. I found Misha out there, and she was... swinging and bleeding, and then I think I fainted?" The words coming out of my mouth sounded incoherent and so loud, my ears were ringing.

But he wasn't looking at me; instead, he nodded at the nurse behind me, who moved slowly and held the needle as if it were an award.

"Demi, you murdered Misha. We have the images

here and video footage from our security staff." My lips parted as I stared at the man in front of me. Platinum blonde, meticulously brushed hair, the sharpest and brightest green eyes imaginable, and not a wrinkle in sight.

"Dr. Ivory, I think I just need to leave. Can you call Raina? She lives down the road…" I started as the nurse grew closer and stopped right by my arm.

I felt exhausted and my body ached. It had to be well past midnight. The entire day had come and gone, but it felt like it was ten days built into one. Attempting to pull myself upright in the plush bed, I couldn't, as if my limbs were paralyzed.

"Demi, the thing is, once you're a part of our… family, we protect you. Luckily, you signed the contract and now are ours." Dr. Ivory wiggled his index finger at the nurse, who immediately flashed me a smile before bending and grabbing my arm.

"Oh no, I'm not sick, I'm fine!" I looked between both the nurse and Dr. Ivory.

"You need rest, darling Demi. Tomorrow is your first work day and, my dear, you made quite the… bloody mess out in the peony garden. You'll need to clean that up as your first task." Dr. Ivory patted the top of my head before leaning down and kissing my forehead. "Sweet dreams, Demi." He turned and left.

What? He wanted me to clean up Misha's blood? They thought I killed her?

No... I didn't. Looking at the nurse as she slid the needle into my flesh, it occurred to me...

What if I did kill her?

The problem with trauma is that when you experience something that disturbs your mental equilibrium, you don't know if you can even trust yourself. You don't know if your mind is honest and if it's capable in remembering things accurately. Considering, I had... I had held a knife in my hand and taken an innocent life before—one I loved with all my heart. What if I blacked out? What if I blanked?

Is the Ivory family now protecting me? Is this what it's like to have a family?

Grinning at the nurse, I let go of the tangled breath in my lungs. I closed my eyes and went to sleep.

CHAPTER
NINETEEN

WAKING UP IN A WARM, safe, and comfortable bed is something I don't think I'll ever get used to in this lifetime. Every single 'bed' I've slept in has been in either a closet, a bench, on the floor, under a bridge, or a lucky night or two in a shitty motel where the walls are paper-thin and a prostitute is moaning next door or gunshots are echoing in the sky while bed bugs nip at my flesh.

"Good morning, darling Demi." A soft voice had me turn my head in the direction of the window where sunlight was pouring in.

Mrs. Ivory was sitting in the chair by my bed, filing her nails. The light screeching of the file pad going back and forth in harmony against her well-manicured nails filled the room. Had she been watching me sleep?

I cleared my voice that was hoarse with sleep and dryness. "Hi."

"I hope you're feeling better because today is your first day of work," she chirped and stood quickly.

My neck was stiff, my stomach was rumbling, and the last thing I wanted to do was have to work today, but that's why I was here. I wasn't here because some rich people found a poor girl they wanted to help rehabilitate and set free like some sort of wounded butterfly. No, I was here because I needed a roof over my head and money to save in hopes that, eventually, I'd have a sliver of a future.

"Yes, ma'am." I nodded and licked my lips.

"Don't do that," Mrs. Ivory hissed at me, and the sudden shift in her voice startled me.

"I'm sorry?" *Don't do what?*

"He'd be repulsed if you do that. Use the lip balm in your room, for goodness sake, Demi." She wiggled her finger at me with her eyes fastened onto my lips. Standing slowly, she moved toward me and leaned over. Squinting, she brushed her fingers across my lips as I froze and held my breath.

"Ouch!" I cried out as she peeled off the loose, dead skin from my lips.

"Repulsive." Mrs. Ivory clicked her tongue and shook her head before she turned away and immediately left the room.

As soon as the door shut behind her, I touched my lips and lifted my finger.

"Fuck." The sight of blood on my finger reminded me of the previous night. Part of me questioned if everything that happened with Misha was a figment of my imagination? Wouldn't Mrs. Ivory have mentioned it? A girl died. They wouldn't just brush it off. Right?

"Miss Rao, day one on the job and already creating a mess?" Bradley appeared, and I knew these noiseless shoes and doors were going to give me an early heart attack.

"Bradley, I… I swear, I didn't touch her. She was…" The realization of the magnitude of what happened last night twisted my stomach as acid rose into my throat.

"She was a beautiful light. Why, Demi?" Bradley glanced around the room and at the corners of the ceiling.

"I didn't kill her," I jeered. "If I killed her and they really believed that, then why haven't they called the police? Why is everyone acting so fucking nonchalant?"

"Demi." Bradley sighed and paused. "Demi, you killed Misha. The end. This isn't some extended novel where you get to dig into the beginning, middle, and end. This isn't a story you need to figure out. This is a simple one-line sentence you will accept as your truth.

If you want to live here, work here... you will accept anything they tell you as your truth. Even if they tell you a lie, you will make it your truth. It's the only way you will..." Bradley brushed his hand across his tired scowl.

"It's the only way I will, what?" I sat up and ran my hands through my unruly hair.

"Survive."

The one word shook my entire being. My heart raced while my palms grew moist. "I don't want this job anymore. I think this has been... a mistake on my end." My feet hit the cold floor and I walked around Bradley.

The slapping of my feet against the floor seemed even louder with the impeding silence that radiated all around me.

As soon as my hand met the cold metal doorknob, another grabbed my shoulder and jerked me backward.

"Are you reckless? You can't just leave the Ivory House. You signed the contract. You have to work here for the next four years. Did you not read the damn contract, Demi?" His face flushed as his fingers gripped into my skin harder.

"Foolish Conrad is too busy flirting, and now...

you're the one who will pay the price." Bradley quivered with anger. His eyes seemed glossier, his jaw was clenched, and out of nowhere, he snapped out of the trance-like state and let go of me. "I mean, you signed a contract with your new employer, Miss Rao. Please be respectful of it and the family. This is a house many would kill to stay in."

Blinking, I felt like I was in some kind of twisted dream. Misha was murdered in the peony garden last night—the girl who held the same job as me up until last night. What was in that contract that I had not seen?

Was the only way out of this job… *death?*

CHAPTER
TWENTY

I HAD no idea what was happening. I didn't know how to process what had happened in the last twenty-four hours. But here I was, sitting in a chair, having some woman named Becca gel my hair back into the tightest bun as if I were a ballerina about to take the stage.

I was staring at Becca through the reflection of the mirror as she focused on my hair. She couldn't be much older than me. Her blonde hair was in the same kind of bun, and she was wearing an all-white outfit. Her skin was covered in a thick layer of makeup and her green eyes were darker than most of the staff and family in the house.

"Hey Becca, how long have you been working here?" I asked. Uneasiness was still churning in my stomach considering I had just seen a woman hemor-rhaging out on a swing in the middle of a garden and my new employer was insisting I had done it.

"Two years," she answered without moving her eyes or hands from my hair.

"Do you like it?"

She froze and looked back at me through the mirror. "I used to live in a group home. A different kind of hell. The Ivory family took me in, and I have everything I could ever need."

"Are you a maid, too?" I asked quietly.

"No. I'm a keeper and beauty expert." Becca straightened her shoulders and pursed her thick lips that were painted in a strange nude color.

"What's that?"

"Demi, the less questions you ask... the less answers you'll need and the better off you'll be." She took a small brush and neatly combed the tiny hairs across my hairline.

"Done!" She beamed and placed her hair tools neatly across the vanity in front of us.

"Look, for girls like us..." Becca murmured and glanced around. "This place is a safe haven for girls like us, the ones who come from nothing but a background of intense trauma. You're not here to dissect the family and their hobbies or tendencies. Clean, eat, exercise, and enjoy living in Charlotte's largest estate with the most prestigious family."

Becca busied herself while I mulled over her answer. "Your outfit is hanging in the powder room, and your cleaning supplies are right outside the door. Follow the hall all the way down and make the first two lefts; you'll end up in the peony garden."

"Okay, thanks, Becca." I nodded and tried to absorb her words. She was saying the simple truth. This life was going to be a hell of a lot better than being slaughtered or raped in the middle of the night at some bonfire with a group of misfits that I belonged to.

Becca left me alone in the small room, and I quickly grabbed the hanger off the bathroom door. Unzipping the bag, I tugged out the short white dress, and to my surprise, found a white lace thong and a strapless white lace bra.

"What in the world? Why do I need to wear lingerie under my work clothes?" I laid it out on the bed and brushed my hand across the fabric.

Shaking my head, I peeled my nightgown off and put everything on. Standing in front of the mirror, I tugged on my white platform shoes and took a deep breath.

There I stood, wearing all white, with a sleeked

back bun and no makeup. I reached to the vanity drawer, where I found a neat line of tubes of lipstick and lip balm. Glancing over my shoulder, I figured it'd be okay to put some on considering Mrs. Ivory ripped the dead skin off my lips with her fingers.

Grabbing a tube of lipstick, I rolled it up and looked at the creamy nude color. Maybe I should stick to some basic Chapstick. I didn't know the rules about makeup, and I didn't need to get into any more trouble. My trembling fingers grabbed the lip balm, and I quickly rubbed it against my lips.

Smacking them together, I turned and left the room, and just as Becca had said, there was a small white cart with a trash bin, a bucket full of what smelled like bleach and soap, and a mop, along with other cleaning supplies.

"Okay, Demi, you can do this…" I whispered to myself and began to push it in the direction of the peony garden. I was terrified of what I'd see. Did they remove her body? Had they really left all the blood there for me to clean in broad daylight? The estate was gated and secluded, but still… this was insane.

Once I made it outside, I slowly pushed the cart across the cobblestone path and dragged my feet to the spot we were in last night.

Standing still, I looked all around me in shock. The

small swing was moving against the breeze, but it wasn't the wind that was moving it.

It was a woman who looked just like...

"Hey, Demi, you totally skipped our date last night." The girl slid off the swing and walked toward me. She was wearing the same long, gold gown, with the same makeup and hair. Everything was the same, minus a clear difference in her face. Her eyes were a little bigger, her nose slightly smaller.

"Misha, remember? We met last night." She stuck her hand out and waved me toward the swing.

Glancing around the swing, there wasn't an ounce of blood anywhere. Rubbing my head, my slicked-back hair started to hurt; it felt like my skin was crawling and my head was spinning.

"Are you sure? I swear... I swear the Misha I met last night was..." I looked around wildly as my panic rose.

"Are you alright, Demi?" She grabbed my hand and tugged me to the swing. Sitting down, my chest tightened. It was all meticulously clean. The fresh scent of peonies wafted throughout the air and not a single ounce of anything was out of place.

"Didn't I do such a great job last night? The harp is a must to learn, and I'm sure you'll learn it, too. I think they are going to pick you..."

I stared at the woman in front of me. Sure, she

looked like Misha, but she sure as hell wasn't her. Squinting, I could see a small scar run across her cheek that I knew without a doubt Misha did not have. I remember thinking how perfect and flawless her skin was. How her makeup looked like it had been done professionally.

"Okay, I'm about to catch my train soon but basically, you will be assigned to The Ossis wing. It's the most private wing of the estate. Dusting is key. Dr. Ivory is very, *very* meticulous about dust. You also will be in charge of the pulchritudo floor, which is really Mrs. Ivory's belongings and prized possessions. Pulchritudo means beauty and it will make sense when you get there. Make sure to use the boar brush only. She'll lose it if she finds out you've used anything but that. Hmm... what else?" She tapped her perfectly manicured, blush-pink nails against her chin.

"Oh, why, of course. The most important of all the rules is absolutely never, ever speak or make a single sound on the Ossis floor. Do not speak to them, engage, or shift your facial expression."

"Speak to... them? Who?" I could feel my forehead crinkle as I looked at Misha 2.0 sitting in front of me.

"Oh... the caged girls." She tilted her head at me in confusion. "I figured Bradley had already taken you

there since you're going to be their main caretaker."
She clicked her tongue and stood.

"I'm not a caretaker; I'm a housekeeper. I really
can't even take care of myself, so I highly doubt I could
take care of some dogs in cages."

The Misha imposter erupted into shrill laughter,
slapping her hands over her mouth immediately. "Oh
my, my, my... Demi." She continued snorting and
laughing into her hands as tears dripped from her eyes.

"Dogs... dogs in cages. The caged girls aren't..."
She began laughing again and shook her head.
"Okay, I must get you to the Ossis floor to begin
cleaning, but it was a pleasure meeting you, Demi.
Time to go!"

Misha stood and gripped my head between her hands,
pressing a kiss onto the top of my head. "I love your
black hair..." she said sorrowfully before tugging me
up and pointing to my cart. "Let's go!" She rushed off
rapidly, and I clutched the cart and followed
behind her.

I would act as normal as possible; I'd clean today
and then tonight, I'd pack my bags and escape. I
wasn't going to stay here. Who cares about some
ridiculous contract? They don't own me; I'm not their
property. Who does Dr. Ivory think he is?

Nodding, I turned the cart around a corner as Misha glided down the narrow, dimly lit hallway.

"Yea, fuck the patriarchy." I smiled to myself, thinking about how I was about to give that man the middle finger and sneak out with my dignity intact. These psychos were trying to convince me I was a murderer. They wanted to force me to eat a certain way, dress a certain way…

Nope, I'd find another job. Maybe some shady motel would hire me and could pay me under the table. I didn't have a bank account—I couldn't risk my name being on legal documents—but I'd find something.

This was all too much.

"Here we are." The woman who claimed to be Misha paused and took out a golden card. "This is your badge to get in and out of the Ossis wing. Mop all the floors and dust the wall in Dr. Ivory's office. You'll know which one. Bradley will pick you up in approximately an hour to take you to the next part." She slid it over to me and moved out of the way to allow for me to use it.

Tapping the strip against the small keypad-style lock, I waited a moment and then magically, the door began to quietly open on its own.

Walking slowly, I pushed my cart through the door. There were shut doors on both sides, and I had no idea where I was supposed to begin. There wasn't even a door handle. Standing in front of the first door, I raised my hand just about to knock, but instead it opened immediately on its own.

Stumbling back a bit, I waited until it was completely opened before peering in. It was a stunning office. "Hello?" I called out, my voice echoing in the empty space.

Loosening my shoulders, I glanced up at the ceiling and noticed a small device that moved.

A camera. *They're watching me...*

Grabbing the mop, I dipped it into the bucket and quickly began to mop the already-spotless floors.

Making my way farther into the room, I stopped in front of the massive wall behind his desk. The textured wall in shades of cream and white was stunning, and I'd never seen anything like it. When I asked Bradley about it, he brushed me off. That must be the wall that the woman claiming to be Misha had told me to make sure to dust. There were three desktop monitors on the waterfall-style, smooth marble desk. An oversized cognac brown leather chair sat behind it, with two bookshelves on opposing sides of the textured wall. The strangest thing in the space that stood out like a sore thumb was the popcorn machine in the corner beside a large window that was covered by curtains.

Putting the mop back into the bucket, I walked

around to the bookshelves, fully expecting them to contain the same style of medical textbooks the other ones had from yesterday.

But instead, my lips parted as I stared at them. Peeling one out, my eyes widened. They weren't medical textbooks, they weren't thriller novels… they were romance novels. The kind that have a handsome man on the front cover. Flipping it open, there were so many lines highlighted.

I looked around once more. Was this Mrs. Ivory's office? No, it couldn't be. Dr. Ivory's medical degrees and awards were displayed on one of the walls.

Pulling the chair out, I sank into it and placed the book on the desk. *"With my hands tied up, he ran his tongue down my neck, shoving it into my mouth as he parted my legs and pushed inside me, roughly."*

Closing the book, I felt uncomfortable. Dr. Ivory read smut? Why did he highlight passages?

"What the hell are you doing?" My heart jumped as Bradley stormed in.

"My God, you are an idiot." It was like a flash how fast he was moving around, before he yanked me out of the chair and grabbed the book from my hands.

"What is wrong with you?" he hissed at me, splatters of his spit touching my skin.

"Wrong with *me*? You lied to me! You implied I killed that girl. But boom, some random Misha replacement arrives and acts like nothing happened. What is this? Some sick game? I'm done; I'm leaving tonight." Resentment, fear, and anxiety were building inside me as my hands trembled.

Bradley pushed the book back into its place before grabbing my arm and bringing me to the far-right corner of Dr. Ivory's office.

He looked up at the ceiling and turned his back. "Demi, what do you not get? You cannot leave when you want to... the only way out of this estate is in a hearse."

My stomach dropped. "That's the dumbest thing I've ever heard. I don't even have anything to pack. I'll just walk through the front doors and close it on the way out. I'm not their property." I knocked my shoulder into Bradley's and immediately went to open the door.

But there wasn't a door handle. "How do I get out?" Frustration was clear in my voice as I flung back around.

Bradley stood with his arms crossed, watching me race around the office and eventually tugged open the curtains.

Except, I fell backward because the curtains weren't concealing a window that looked outside. The curtains covered a glass window that looked out into an insanely bright, all-white room that blinded me.

But it wasn't the room that terrified me; it was the fact that a woman was in it. She was laying in the center on a small cot.

"What the...?" I walked backward, staring at her and flicking to the popcorn machine that was sitting in the corner beside the glass.

"I'm calling the police... This is crazy, Bradley. This is *illegal*." I was shaking, my entire body went cold as I forced myself to blink and try to find a phone.

"Bradley, what is going on? Why are you working here? What is this?" I was running around like an animal in the middle of a busy interstate. I had no clue what direction I should be going in, no clue if there was even a point of running, because suddenly, I realized the outcome would be dangerous, no matter which way I went. Slamming my hands against the walls, tears stung my eyes.

"Demi. Please just stop," he whispered. But he wasn't angry, he seemed desolate.

For me.

Dropping to the floor, I pressed my face between my legs, trying to gulp in long breaths of air.

"The caged girls... aren't dogs. They are... girls?

Humans..." I drifted as my world seemed to close in around me.

"Yes."

That one word ripped me to shreds. They say lying is immoral, but lying is actually a protective mechanism that helps guard us from something like this.

A truth we can never come back from.

CHAPTER TWENTY-ONE

"YOU NEED to dust the wall. Afterwards, I have to take you to the cages to clean them." Bradley dipped down and, using both arms, lifted me upright.

"Listen to me, Demi. There is no way out, except one. One way out in a sense that you'll never be harmed." He held both of my shoulders as his face turned red.

"Okay, tell me the one way out?" I whispered as tears ran down my cheeks.

"If they give you the title."

"What title?"

"The favorite girl."

The favorite girl? What was that? So many questions swirled in my mind as I looked through the glass window in front of me. The woman on the bed had not even moved. I crept toward it and put my hands on the glass. I had to help her… I had to save her.

"Why is she in there?"

"Demi, she's in there by choice. The caged girls sound worse than it is. These are all women who signed up for an experimental study. They are all psychiatric patients of Dr. Ivory's friend, Dr. Decker Sterling, who were unable to do well with treatment. Now, they are here to be rehabilitated through The Ivory Experiment."

I didn't believe him. I didn't want to. I couldn't.

"They really signed up to be called a caged girl and live in a glass cage?" I grinded my teeth together as I shook my head. Realization of the way the popcorn machine was right by the window made my blood grow cold. "Wait… Does he watch her while eating popcorn?"

"Yes."

"I'm done. I don't care if they signed up. I don't give a fuck; I'm out of here." I smashed my hands against the door, screaming at it to open.

My heart pounded against my chest so hard, I swore it would burst through my flesh at any moment. The door wouldn't open… there wasn't a door handle, there wasn't a key, there was no way out.

I'm trapped.

"Bradley, please, I cannot breathe. I can't breathe." I clutched my palms around my neck, choking on every ounce of air around me.

Cold hands turned me around as I pressed my back against the door, hyperventilating. My vision was hazy as my anxiety gagged me.

"I'm going to count to three, and then you're going to take a deep breath and pull yourself together… Because if you don't, Demi, then they won't let you have the option of taking even one more breath," Bradley said through clenched teeth.

I began to cry, not in a sad, heartbreaking way, but in a defeated, exhausted way. The kind of cry that only comes out of your body when you know all your options have been depleted.

I tried to inhale through my nose but instead, I opened my mouth and swallowed air as I sobbed against Bradley.

"This is not okay… this is not okay," I cried out.

"Listen, you're going to be alright, Demi. It'll all be alright. You just have to play by their rules. You have to become the favorite girl and when you do… you'll get to leave."

"They killed Misha. That girl wasn't her. Wasn't Misha the favorite girl?" I sniffled, not caring that I had soaked his expensive suit with my snot and tears.

"She wasn't the favorite girl. They've been waiting for you. Now, you just have to pretend to be a part of this family. Do as they say and don't fall to pieces."

"Waiting for me? What about you? Why are you here? How long have you been here?"

"I've been here for thirteen years. I'm a felon who fell into the same trap you did. A simple, yet glamorous, promise of a safe place to live and a steady job. They know I'm loyal enough and won't leave. They... they have something on me—something they know I'll never leave behind."

"Shit. This is... horrible, and I don't even know how I'm supposed to do this, Bradley. I'm scared. Really, really scared." My body shook as I forced myself off a man I had just met.

"Fear is a simple reaction, but strength is a decision. Make the decision that can save your life." Bradley shook me as if he were hopeful I would break out of this state of panic.

"Bradley..." My chest tightened as I tried to calm down.

"Tell me something you've always dreamt of." I knew he was trying to divert my attention.

"When I was little... I wanted Nikes. So, I took a pair of raggedly sneakers with holes and with a Sharpie, I drew the signature check mark on them." I shrugged.

A long pause of silence fell between us. "That's really sad." Bradley's forehead creased as he looked at me with pity. "By the way, I found this in the trash. I think it was with your things." He tugged out the crumpled Biltmore Estate brochure and my lips parted.

Taking it from him, I shook my head. "I don't need it anymore. I guess I'm in the closest thing I'll ever get to being there." I tossed it into the trash bag.

He cleared his throat. "You should always have some kind of dream, Demi."

"No, girls like me… we don't dream. Dreams are meant for people who can make them come true. Nightmares, on the other hand… those are guaranteed."

Blinking rapidly, he shook his head. "Shut the curtains, wipe down his desk and the shelves, and dust his wall."

"What is that wall made of…? I've never seen something like it. It's so bumpy and—"

"You don't need to know. But most of all, *you don't want to know*, Demi." Bradley pointed his finger in my face. "Just clean it," he gritted through clenched teeth and shoved the duster from the cart in my face.

At this point, my fear was evolving into anger. Anger that I was born with bad luck, anger that I never had a chance to live, anger that every single person in my life, besides one person, hurt me.

Lifting the duster in my hand, I rammed it against Bradley's perfectly coiffed hair. His lips parted in shock as his eyes widened. "What the hell was that?"

"Get out of my way, Bradley. I have to *dust*." I shoved him with all my might and walked around him.

Looking ahead through the glass window, the woman on the bed was still laying there. I was going to get her out. I was going to save her and myself. I had escaped before; I had survived.

And I can do it again.

I started to dust the strange wall and all the ridges of it. Growing closer to it, I froze as I notice small grooves and creases. Running my finger against it, I stopped breathing.

Was it wood? Was it...

"It's human bones, Miss Rao. Yours will be up there if you don't stop playing Nancy Drew," Bradley said quietly.

Exhaling, I cringed as tears rolled down my face. My fingers trembled against the plastic handle of the duster and I could feel the acid rise in my throat. Puffing my cheeks, I turned and ran to the cart, grabbing the small garbage bag and dry heaved until vomit spewed from my mouth.

"No," I cried through my gagging. Sinking to the cold floor, I began to cry harder.

"You're dismissed, Bradley." A familiar voice that didn't make my skin crawl caused me to lift my head.

Oh, great. Conrad Ivory was standing there in a light cream suit, like he walked out of a damn modeling campaign, while I sat crumpled on his dad's office floor, reeking of vomit with the backdrop of a bone wall and a woman held hostage.

The worst part of all, this handsome man in front of me had to be just as psychotic as them. I didn't want Bradley to leave; I didn't want him to leave me alone with anyone from this family. He glanced over his shoulder at me with his hands tucked behind his back.

Pinching his lips to the side, he shook his head slightly before the glass door slid open and he left.

Scooting, I pushed away as much as I could while wiping my mouth with the back of my hand.

"Don't get near me. You are all deranged. You're all going to get caught. How can you be a part of this...? What is this?" I trembled as Conrad squatted down and looked at me intently.

"Demi, you are so lucky it was me watching the cameras and not them. You need to get off this floor, grab a damn mop, and do what the job entails. Clean and live. Simple. I need you to trust me." Conrad's voice was smooth and soft, not aggressive or rushed like Bradley's.

My heart rate began to slow as I tilted my head with realization. "Your eyes aren't green." I squinted at him in disbelief.

His hand shot up to his face as he looked away. "Shit," he mumbled.

"You have light brown eyes. Why do you wear green-colored contacts?" My breathing kept hitching. I felt like I was having an allergic reaction and began clawing at my skin. Tears blurred my vision as I receded up to the glass window and pressed my hands against the floor. My back constrained against the glass as I stared at Conrad in bewilderment.

Conrad's eyes widened as he looked through the glass window behind me. "Demi... whatever you do, don't turn around."

There's this theory that if someone tells you to not eat an apple, you'll want to eat an apple, even if you wouldn't have wanted it until they mentioned it.

And like the apple, as soon as he said don't turn around, my body flinched and I did.

The screams that left my mouth echoed so loudly, my own ears were ringing.

The woman who was laying on the bed wasn't laying anymore. No, she was standing there, with both palms pressed against the thin glass separating us, and she was smiling at me.

CHAPTER
TWENTY-TWO

I KEPT SHRIEKING until my voice grew hoarse. I couldn't stop staring at her while tripping over my legs and stumbling into Conrad, who immediately slapped his clammy hand over my mouth to muffle my cries.

I started to bite at his palm, but that made him slap the other hand over my mouth, too.

"Listen to me, you have exactly five minutes before my mother or father checks the cameras, and when they see this shitshow, they will, without a doubt, put you in a cage and you'll be one of those girls. So, Demi, I'm begging you to stop. Stop screaming. Pull yourself together. Now!" he whispered loudly into my ear with his hot breath blowing against my skin.

"Now, are you going to calm down?"

"Mm-hmm…" I nodded aggressively.

"Okay." He released his hands from my mouth, and

I looked at the woman in front of me. She was wearing a short white dress; her hair was shaved off, and light stubble was growing in patches. Her eyes were bloodshot and the bags deepened around her eyes.

"Hello," she mouthed with her cracked lips and bemused eyes. The curve of her lips tipped upward in a demented smile. She began tracing the glass around my face without letting her grin drop.

"Don't engage with her. She's getting moved soon." Conrad tugged me away and quickly shut the curtains.

"Why is she in there, Conrad?" My voice shook as I closed my eyes with my hand across my pounding heart as if I could steady it.

"She's in there by choice."

"If she has psychiatric issues, then why is she not seeing a psychiatrist? Why would she need your dad?"

"My dad is helping them, Demi. He's doing a free experimental study—it's actually FDA approved. He's saving the lives no one else could." Conrad tilted my head up, forcing me to open my eyes and look at him.

"Do you actually believe that?" I squinted at him as his fingers traced my jawline.

"Yes, I do."

"You're living in denial, because denial allows us to be blind to the truth we don't want to see since our minds don't think we're ready to handle them." I moved his hand off my face.

"You may be right, Demi, but denial also keeps me alive here, and it's in your best interest to submerge yourself in it, too. Please, Demi."

Forcing myself to nod in agreement, I walked to the cart and looked around the meticulously clean room. "I think I'm done here. What do I need to clean next?" I whimpered.

I could see Conrad release a breath of relief as he waved the small gold card across the glass door.

"Today was more of a trial day, and I think you deserve a short day, all things considering. Besides, Raina is here to see you. Apparently, she brought a bag of your belongings you left at her house and wanted to check on you. I didn't know she knew you."

"Do you know Raina well?" I was eager to see her. She'd help me; she'd figure out a way to get me out. I'd find a way to get her to see that this wasn't some sweet family who lived close by to her. This family was unhinged. I wasn't about to be a part of the next true crime podcast: 'Brown, unidentifiable girl abducted by wealthy Caucasian family and sliced like deli meat.'

"Yeah. Kind of." Conrad shrugged, then glanced at my outfit. "I'm going to take you back to your room so you can change and then go see her."

"Okay." Pushing the cart through the narrow hall-way, Conrad abruptly stopped in front of me.

"Let me." He grabbed the handle and began to push the cart for me.

Why did he have to be the son of psychopaths?

The halls all blended together, and if I didn't have Conrad to guide me, I would never have known which way I was going. This wasn't a house; this was a monstrous estate that was monochromatic and sterile. There was no end and no beginning. It was the perfect trap. And I was the perfect victim.

The temperature shifted as soon as we left the Ossis wing— warmer in the rest of the house and not biting cold like it was down there.

A shiver ran up my spine as we got to the hallway with what I knew was my bedroom.

Key word: was.

I never even slept in it. I blacked out on my first night here, and now the day was already winding down. "Just wave your card over the door, and it'll open. Sometimes your card won't work and you'll have to be collected. I'll wait for you out here." Conrad left the cart in the middle of the hallway and had one leg pressed against the wall, watching me as I tugged out the small gold card and waved it over the door.

As soon as it opened, I slid in and waited for it to automatically shut. Spinning it around the room, I felt sadness knowing I had assumed this was some ticket out of my own personal hell and series of bad luck. Instead, my life was spiraling downhill like an avalanche.

Opening the small closet, I found a few new outfits had been neatly hung. Two were identical to the dress I was already wearing, along with a white blouse and slacks.

"Wow, so much variety." I rolled my eyes and tugged out the slacks and blouse. Peeling off the sheath dress, I threw it on the bed and quickly dressed. Running into the bathroom, I pulled the itchy, tight bun out and let my wild curls hang over my shoulders.

I couldn't wait to get out of this place; I didn't even need to pack anything. The best thing about not having anything to my name was that I never got attached to any place. I never had a real home... I didn't even know what that felt like.

The greatest part of never having anything is never losing it, either.

As soon as I walked through the door, Conrad pushed off from the wall and let his eyes do a very obvious once over.

"I like your hair down." He gave me a lopsided grin, but I didn't laugh, I didn't smile. I was ready to get out of here. What I had seen in the past two days had my mind spinning. A girl in a 'cage?' A murder I know without a doubt happened in the peony garden. And magically, no one was saying a thing about it. No one cared. This was their normal.

I followed Conrad through the hallways and counted seconds until we reached the main room I had initially met Dr. and Mrs. Ivory in.

"Raina!" I breathed out as her presence immediately comforted me. She looked up at me over her teacup and smiled. My face sunk as soon as I saw a small bag next to her. She had brought my things.

"Demi! Wow, one day at the Ivory Estate and you look like a changed woman!" She jumped up and gripped my elbows, tugging me into her. I took a deep breath and realized her scent was so very familiar.

Peonies.

"Hey Rain," Conrad said behind us. I turned over my shoulder and looked at him. He acted like they barely knew one another, yet he had a nickname for her.

"Hey Con." She winked at him. *Oh no, did they date?* Raina was married with a toddler. She was older than both of us by a good amount of years.

"Demi, I used to babysit Conrad." She tapped me.

I don't know why I felt so much relief considering I would never see any of these people again within a few hours. "Oh, okay. So, I was wondering if I could have a word with you? *Privately*?" I shot Conrad another look.

His jaw clenched as Raina grabbed my hand and led me out through the front doors.

As soon as the sunlight hit my face and we walked down the concrete steps, I wanted to take off in a full sprint. But I had nothing. Literally nothing. They'd catch me within minutes and drag me back in, knowing I had seen too much.

"Raina, I don't want to work here. I think that they are doing something very dangerous and truthfully, very illegal. I was wondering if you could take me to your house so I could maybe apply to some other jobs. Don't worry, I'll find a spot to sleep tonight. I just need to get out of here."

"What? Demi, why? This is such an amazing opportunity! I've known the family for years. You're being irrational, sweetie." She let out a small laugh but grew closer to me and lowered her voice. "What kind of things do you think they are doing that's illegal and dangerous?"

"Raina, I saw this girl… this woman. She was in an all-white room, and she was clearly heavily medicated and… Raina, she was caged. I mean, they literally referred to her as a caged girl. And then, last night, this girl named Misha—who, apparently, was leaving the house for good—wanted to talk with me. But when I went to meet with her, her neck was sliced." I motioned to my own neck while stumbling through my words as if I couldn't get them out fast enough.

Raina blinked repeatedly with her lips tightly pressed together.

"The entire house is all white, and you have to wear these padded shoes and all white outfits. Everyone has blonde hair and green eyes, except… Did you know Conrad has brown eyes but wears colored contacts?" I couldn't even believe the words that were leaving my mouth.

"Demi, Demi…" She brushed the hair from my face and looked at me with concern. "Sweetie, you need to take a few deep breaths and calm down. You know, I think that you have had a really rough life and, all of a sudden, you're in this massive estate with a prestigious family and your mind is starting to go into overdrive."

She didn't believe me. Of course, she didn't. I was the vagrant girl she found on the street in ripped clothes, smelling like a sewer. She probably assumed I was some disease-infested, drug addict stereotype.

"Raina, I'm not high. I'm not drunk. I'm not disturbed. This house…" I looked behind us at the sprawling estate with ivy running across the pristine white stucco. "This house has secrets. Deadly secrets. And I don't think that girl in the room is the only one being held against her will. I think there's more."

"Demi, you are probably exhausted from all this overstimulation. Dr. Ivory is the best orthopedic surgeon in the southeast, and Mrs. Ivory is a socialite and philanthropist. People like them do not do dangerous things, because they have everything to lose. If you leave this house, you'll be sleeping on a bench in the middle of Freedom Park, and winter will be here before you know it. Jax isn't going to let you stay with us because of Kai. At the end of the day, you're a stranger. I'm not trying to be malicious; I'm telling you the reality and magnitude of your decision."

Raina held my face between her palms and smiled. "How about this, I'll come by every so often and check on you? And you can come visit us whenever you want. We're only about a mile down the road."

Brushing my hair behind my ears, I thought about what she was saying. Homeless shelters were overflowing, and I didn't have close to enough money for another night in a motel—which would take me easily a month of swindling to get it. I couldn't use my legal name or social security to get a job even at McDonald's. I didn't have options, and if I left, I'd be killed or assaulted before my twentieth birthday.

Looking back at the house behind me, I nodded slowly. "What are they doing to that girl?" I whispered.

"Dr. Ivory helps women who have been otherwise dismissed by physicians."

"But he's not a psychiatrist... he's a bone doctor?" I questioned.

"Honey, doctors go through the same training in medical school and even part of residency. I'm a dermatologist, but I still remember and know enough to deliver a baby if I had to. The Ivory family is running a free experimental study to help reset individuals who probably would have been dead if they didn't get taken in.

"I promise, Demi, everything is legal. You just need to go inside, clean their house, do as they say, and enjoy a safe place to sleep, warm food to eat, and a roof over your head. Look, the pay is great. Save up for a year and then you can go get a place and a different job," she reasoned with me.

"A girl had her throat slit in the garden..."

"Demi, you probably hallucinated. You didn't sleep well; your brain is in overdrive. Going from life on the street to a mansion is a huge shock for your cognition." Turning me around, she gave me a soft shove. "Go back in. I'll check on you in a few days."

Was she right? Was my mind playing tricks on me?

CHAPTER
TWENTY-THREE

"HI SWEETHEART." Mrs. Ivory's face lit up as soon as I walked back in. A light aroma of chocolate chip cookies radiated through the foyer. "I baked some of my special cookies for you. I know it's been a bit of a challenge settling in. Come on." She looped her arm with mine and led me to the kitchen.

"Did you know I came from nothing, Demi?" Mrs. Ivory crooned as she plated the fresh cookies from a baking sheet.

"I'm sorry?" I was taken aback by such a straight-forward, yet unintentional, thought.

"You heard me, dear. Just like you, I came from nothing. That's why Ian and I hire women whose life has not been so kind. Ian may seem a bit crass to you, but in reality, he saved me. I was his favorite girl." She smiled absentmindedly.

His favorite girl? Wasn't Bradley rambling about that earlier?

"What do you mean, you were his favorite girl?" I took a cookie off the plate, but Mrs. Ivory swatted my hand. "Ouch!"

"Demi, they are hot. Wait a moment, dear," she said with a slight smile. The oven behind her began to beep, and she swiftly turned. Tripping over one of the island stools, she took a tumble and fell to the ground. Leaping out of my chair, I hurried to her, but my shoes skid across the tile. Mrs. Ivory was on the floor, bald, except for small amounts of dark stubble across her scalp. Shrieking, she crawled on all fours until she reached the blonde wig that had fallen.

"Mrs. Ivory!" Mortified for her, I bent to help her as she hurriedly pulled the wig back on.

Her skin was flushed red, her hair stuck out in ten different directions, and her breathing was erratic. She used my arms to steady herself. "Well, that was humiliating," she murmured under her breath with one hand across her heart.

"Are you alright, Mrs. Ivory?" Suddenly, I couldn't help but wonder if she was sick. Was she losing her hair due to an underlying medical condition or treatment?

"I'm not ill, if that's what you're wondering. It's bloody alopecia—chronic hair loss. I'm not dying,

Demi; so, you can stop looking at me like I am," she snapped, clearly agitated.

"It's time for you to go back to your room to bathe and sleep. I expect a full day of work from you tomorrow. Dr. Ivory will not be pleased if he sees that the Ossis wing isn't properly cleaned by tomorrow evening. Bradley will take you into the rooms as well. Go on now." She waved her hand at me.

My stomach rumbled, and I assumed asking for a cookie wouldn't be the most appropriate thing to do. I wondered about dinner, but Mrs. Ivory left the kitchen before I could even ask.

"Shit," I whispered, realizing I didn't even know my way back to my room.

"Let's go." Bradley's voice echoed behind me, and I couldn't believe the amount of relief I felt with his presence.

"You have to stop, Demi." He grabbed my arm and guided me out into the hallway. He was walking so quickly I was having to break into a light jog to keep up with him.

"Bradley, let go of my arm." My teeth grinded against each other as I slapped his hand off me. Pushing me against the wall, he planted his hands on opposite sides of my body, growing so close I could feel his warm breath against my face.

"Demi, Dr. Ivory wants to get rid of you. But the thing is, he doesn't mean to fire you." His eyes widened and the vein in the side of his head was protruding out.

"If you run, they'll find you and they'll kill you. You have to prove to them that you are trustworthy. Demi, this is not a joke," Bradley hissed and swiftly pulled away while glancing at the ceiling.

I knew it. I knew this wasn't in my head. These people were vile.

"Bradley—"

"Demi, just clean and keep your mouth shut. You're on his radar, and it's not a good thing to be on it."

Nodding, I swallowed the lingering saliva to coat the dryness of my throat. I was terrified. I didn't want to die, but I was trapped here. I was nineteen and had never even lived my life.

Like an unsuspecting animal, I fell into the trap of a predator. The first time not by choice, but the second time, I walked right into it.

Pushing off the wall, I followed behind Bradley, trying to keep my tears back but they kept falling down my face. It was exhausting when your entire life was a series of unfortunate events.

Once in front of my new room, I looked up at Bradley. The first time I saw him I thought he looked

like some kind of character from a sci-fi movie—
perfectly coiffed blonde hair that was meticulously
held in place with way too much gel, a serious scowl,
and mossy green eyes that felt hostile like some kind of
reptile. But now, as he grew closer to me and brushed
his thumb against my cheek to wipe away the lingering
tear, I wasn't so sure.

"Don't cry, Demi. It'll be okay. We'll get out. But
you have to trust me." He pinched his lips to the side
and gave my shoulder a quick squeeze.

"I'm hungry," I nervously whispered as my heart
raced. I couldn't believe I was feeling some kind of
emotional connection to Bradley.

"Your dinner is in your room. Eat, bathe, and sleep.
Tomorrow is your real, last first chance to survive."
The door opened behind me, and I walked backward
into it. The door shut slowly while Bradley and I stared
at one another.

Blowing out a breath of air, I thought about everything Bradley just said and everything Raina had told
me. Everyone was telling me something different. But
the one thing I knew with absolute certainty was I had
to pretend to be content here. Bradley wanted to
escape. He'd been here for a while, meaning if he
thought he could simply walk through the front door
unharmed, he would have.

"Just clean and keep your mouth shut, Demi," I told myself as I looked at the wrapped plate sitting on my small vanity. Peeling the wrapping back, I couldn't help but smile. Grilled chicken, roasted asparagus, a sweet potato with a dollop of butter, and on the side, a bottle of water and piece of dark chocolate.

If I left this place, I'd die anyway—likely starving to death. Grabbing my plate, I sat on the edge of my bed and began to eat. When you've been on the verge of starving to death, you know that you can never let food sit. You eat it because you simply cannot believe you actually have it. Or before someone takes it from you.

After inhaling my dinner, I took a hot shower, brushed my teeth, used fancy creams and lotions all over my body, and slid the small white gown on. Looking at myself in the mirror, I didn't have that glaze of dirtiness anymore, and I didn't reek. I didn't have this strange taste in my mouth that made me nauseated.

Yes, I was terrified... but in some sick way, I was also thankful. The Ivory family wanted me here; they needed me. Dr. Ivory clearly had some kind of OCD with cleanliness. Now that their last housekeeper had either left or died, that meant they wouldn't hurt me. They needed me. I just had to trust Bradley had some kind of plan brewing because tomorrow, I had to wake up and see things I knew would change everything.

Tomorrow I had to be a happy little housekeeper and pretend to be completely content being trapped in a dangerous house with dangerous people.

CHAPTER TWENTY-FOUR

I TOSSED and turned all night, contemplating all the ways I'd escape. I could sneak out of my room, unlock the front door, or climb out of a window. I could pretend to meet Raina and leave. But Bradley's words coursed through my mind, and I wasn't too sure I was willing to risk my life.

I got dressed in my uniform, slid on the ridiculously padded shoes, tied my hair up, and left my room. I started to walk toward the end of the hall until I recalled the turn and luckily, Bradley appeared pushing an all-white cart.

"Good morning, Demi." Bradley paused and waved at the cart.

"Morning." I grabbed the cart handle from him and began to push it behind him.

"Today you'll be cleaning the Ossis floor rooms.

There are very strict rules, Demi. You must not speak or make any noise, and you must not make eye contact with anyone you may encounter. Before we go in, you'll need to stop in the dressing room."

"The dressing room? And eye contact with who?"

"Lower your voice, now!" Bradley shushed me with his finger, and I noticed he wore long sleeves and white gloves.

Walking quickly, we eventually ended back up on the Ossis wing, and Bradley swiped his gold card in front of the door.

"Are you helping me clean?"

"No. I have to make sure you don't screw up." He gave me a pointed look. "Now go into the dressing room; Becca's in there with your breakfast. She'll help you, and then come right out so we can get started."

"Hi Demi." Becca bowed slightly, then pointed to the salon style chair. Sinking into it, I looked at my reflection and Becca quickly draped a cloak over me.

My eyes widened as she reached for the scissors, and I jerked back and quickly put my hands on my hair. "Oh, no, I don't need a haircut." I laughed awkwardly.

"Demi, you must. Your hair is too thick and there is no way it'll fit in the wig."

"Wig?" I turned and looked at Becca.

"Oh honey, you can't go to the Ossis floor with all this unruly, black hair." She clicked her tongue and immediately grabbed a handful of my hair.

"I said no." I slapped her hand off me.

"Don't be difficult, Demi," she said with a chill in her voice that had my heart racing. "You either put this on or you let me cut and dye it. But there is no way they'll let you in there with black hair." She lifted a short blonde wig, and I couldn't help but break into laughter.

"You're kidding me, right?" Disbelief was clear in my tone.

"No," Becca replied dryly.

"Well, I'm going to wear the stupid wig, because there is no way I'm going to go blonde. It wouldn't work for me." I rolled my lips together tightly.

"Fine. I'll try to fit it in there, but if it falls or moves at all and the caged girls see you, then that's between you and Dr. Ivory." She tugged at my hair, balling it up and brushing it aggressively.

"This is going to take ten pounds of gel," she muttered as she began plastering the goop in my scalp and didn't even try to brush it lightly. Once in a tight bun, she paused. "Well, I'm a magician." Fastening the blonde wig on top of my head, she tilted her head and studied me carefully. "You kind of look alright as a blonde."

Running my fingers through the soft hair, I didn't disagree. Surprisingly, it didn't clash completely with my olive skin. "Yea, I guess."

"Now, put on your gloves and this white cardigan. You're ready to go." She shoved the items at me and looked at the time. "You have three minutes before you're late."

Peeling the gloves and cardigan on, I stood and walked toward the door. I felt ridiculous in this outfit and wig. What were the cages?

Bradley's eyes widened as soon as I walked through the door. His Adam's apple bobbed slightly as he let his eyes linger on my new hair.

"I know... it's awful." I dropped my eyes to the floor.

"No, it's not. It's just... not you," he mumbled and started to walk before he stopped and turned to me. "This is cage number one. Remember, Demi, don't talk, don't engage, don't look at her. Just clean the space and leave. Do not make a single sound."

"Okay." I nodded as he waved his card in front of the door.

"Go ahead." I pushed my cart that had these strangely large wheels that were layered in some kind of foam-like material so no sound came from it.

As soon as I walked in, I slammed my eyes shut.

It was blinding.

Bright, white, and frigid. The floors, the walls, everything in the room was a stark white.

My breathing was so fast that I swore I was about to have a full-blown panic attack. The room was one thing, but the woman chained to the bed in the corner had me on the verge of shattering. I felt a hand slap over my mouth and an arm wrap around my waist, pulling me right back out of the room. When the door shut slowly, I opened my eyes and looked up. "You would have ruined it!" Dr. Ivory looked at me with fury searing through his eyes.

"There's a… a girl chained to the bed." My body shook as I looked for Bradley, but he wasn't there. Where was he? I needed to leave. I needed to run, now.

"You foolish girl. I don't know why they had to have you. I really don't. But you better shut your mouth and clean that room or else you'll be chained to the bed. This is my experiment; my medical experiment. I'm helping these girls, and you are going to wreck everything I have worked so hard for." Dr. Ivory dropped his hand to my neck and tightened his grip. "Do you want to be in the cage, Demi?"

"No, please, no," I whimpered as I instinctively reached my hands to his and tried to pry it off, but his hold only grew stronger.

"Then go in the room and clean it. I don't want to see a speck of dust, and if I do, I'll put you in a cage. Understand?"

"Yes," I whimpered as he loosened his grasp.

"Go," he whispered with his eyes squinted. A simple gesture and word that made me shut down completely and do as I was told—a survival mechanism, and one I was completely used to doing.

CHAPTER
TWENTY-FIVE

I WALKED in and stopped as soon as the door shut behind me. A small camera in the corner of the room was how Dr. Ivory had seen me. The girl in the bed had a thick blindfold on and large headphones over her ears.

What is this…?

I took the mop out of the bucket and began to slowly swipe it across the floor. My eyes were aching from the brightness of it all, and how the walls and floors blended together was disorienting.

I felt numb. What kind of medical experiment was he allegedly running? I mopped until every single spot of the white tile floor shined, then grabbed the small wipe and started to clean every surface, terrified Dr. Ivory would see a speck of dust and strangle me.

The girl didn't move; she probably didn't even

know I was in here. I wanted to peel the blindfold off her eyes as badly as I wanted to tear the headphones off her ears. The wig on my head started to itch, and I felt like the stale air was suffocating me completely.

How was I supposed to clean her bed? The sheets looked fine, but I didn't know if I was supposed to get closer and clean around her.

The door began to open slowly, and I quickly moved away.

Bradley walked in, carrying a tray of food—simple white rice and a small cup of plain yogurt. After Bradley set it down, he pointed to the door and nodded, placing his finger on his lips, signaling me to stay quiet. Pulling the headphones and blindfold off the woman, he handed her the tray. She looked at him, but he didn't make eye contact. Then she lifted her eyes and looked at me. Hopefulness filled her otherwise hollow eyes, and parting her lips, I swore she was about to shout for me to help her, but she didn't.

Instead, she smiled at me.

Just like the girl we saw through the glass in Dr. Ivory's office.

If they were being tortured, why would they smile? Why wouldn't they bang, bash, scream, and cry for help whenever they saw a new girl in the same space as them?

Were these women really outcasts the Ivory family chose to rehabilitate?

My mind spun while I waited in the hallway. Nothing made sense.

Bradley came out and the door silently shut behind him. "Good job, Demi. Let's finish the rest of the hall, and then we will be done. See, it's not so bad." He shrugged and started to walk to the next room.

"This is it? This is what I have to clean? The Ossis wing and then the formal wing?" I questioned in a low voice.

"Yes." Bradley pushed his own cart that had identical meal trays lining the top. One bowl of plain white rice and one cup of plain yogurt.

"Who cleans the rest of the house?"

"Maids who don't live here. Maids who never go into any other parts of the estate," he answered and paused in front of the next door.

"Why did they choose me?" I froze before the next door, already dreading what laid behind it.

"Because you have nothing." Bradley's words stung, but it wasn't because he said it so matter-of-factly, but more so because it was the truth.

"Let's go. Don't look at her, don't speak."

The door opened and I immediately looked down. My eyes were already burning and sensitive from the shocking visual adjustment in and out of the first room.

I pushed my cart in and this time, the girl in the bed wasn't wearing the blindfold, only the headphones. She was staring off at the wall, without blinking a single time.

I didn't feel like I was even in the room; I felt like this was some kind of prank, and there had to be a reason this was happening. But I did as I was told because suddenly, I realized if the Ivory family was dangerous enough to do this, then what would they do to me if I didn't obey?

I carefully mopped until the white floor glistened and then grabbed the dusting cloth. Bradley quietly walked around the small cot and tugged a white bucket from the floor. I hadn't seen it in the other room, or maybe I had missed it?

Oh no. I was probably supposed to clean it.

He closed his eyes and scrunched his nose as he carried it to my cart. My eyes widened from the pungent odor that emitted from it as soon as he grew closer. Pointing to the bottom of my cart, he slid out a concealed tray-like compartment and dumped the contents of the bucket into it.

I gagged at the urine and feces in the concealed compartment. Bradley's face grew pale as soon as the noises rose from my mouth came out. Shaking his head quickly, I knew I had to be quiet, but I couldn't stop. But then I caught a glimpse over his shoulder, and the girl on the cot had sat up on her knees. Tilting her head, she watched me choking on my own saliva.

Her lips parted as my heart pounded against my chest.

Say something. Please, I thought to myself.

"Run." The word wasn't audible; she mouthed it as soon as Bradley had turned away to push our carts out. *"Save him."*

Him? Who?

An arm grabbed me from behind, tugging me out before the door slid shut.

"What was that?" Bradley hissed, pushing me against the opposing wall.

"Bradley, tell me what the hell this is or I'm going to scream," I panted with anger and dug my nails into his skin, prying his hands off me.

"Finish the rest of the rooms and then we will talk," Bradley huffed with distressed eyes.

"No."

"Demi, they'll put you in one of these. They are watching. So, slap a fucking smile on your face and go."

My eyes shot up to the ceiling, looking in every direction. I felt paranoid. I couldn't see someone watching me, but I could feel them observing me. My skin was crawling as my anxiety coursed through my body.

I tried to compose myself, and I gripped the cart, pushing it down the hall with Bradley behind me. We went into the rest of the rooms, and one by one, I saw a new girl. No hair, thin, and void of any emotion. All of the girls had green eyes with the whites streaked with red.

I was going to call the police tonight. There was no way I was going to let these lunatics do whatever it was they were doing. I could save these girls. Bradley mentioned I'd be getting a cell phone soon, but until then, I'd have to use the landline. I saw one in the kitchen and the drawing room. Relief began to spread over me. A few more hours and then the police would be swarming this estate, and I'd pack a bag of things and run as far as I could from this madness. I'm sure Raina would help me out with a night or two until I figured out my next move.

CHAPTER
TWENTY-SIX

ONCE I WAS BACK in my room, I quickly peeled off the itchy wig, then tore off the stiff gloves and dress. I climbed into the shower, intent to scrub away the horrors I had witnessed. Sometimes when you see something deplorable, you begin to question if you can even trust yourself. But I wasn't going to doubt myself, not this time. The Ivory family had something going on here; something so dangerous and deadly, I was scared to walk the halls alone, but I had to. There weren't any phones in this small hallway that apparently housed the live-in staff. Beyond Bradley and a chef, I hadn't seen anyone else in this hallway. And of the staff members I had seen elsewhere, they all had one thing in common—no one spoke, and everyone kept their eyes down.

Tying my hair in a ponytail, it sopped into my shirt

as I slid the platform slippers on. At least they'd help silence my footsteps. I waved my small gold card in front of the door. None of the doors had locks, they were all automatic, and usually opened as soon as I got to one or Bradley waved his card.

Clicking my tongue, I tapped my shoe against the floor. "Come on..." I shook my head as the door remained closed. Pressing my hands against the smooth, white surface, it wouldn't budge. I started to feel claustrophobic. Knowing you're trapped some-where, with no way out, may be the worst form of trepidation. I couldn't scream, I couldn't shout. Backing away from the door, I blinked away the tears that stung my eyes.

What was worse? Being trapped inside a small room or being trapped, knowing that just outside this door you could be slaughtered like a pig if you angered the people on the outside?

I sat on the edge of my bed, gripping the thin quilt that sat atop the twin mattress.

I had to sleep. I had to wait until tomorrow morning when Bradley came. Maybe he'd have my phone? Maybe I could find a way to use one while they thought I was cleaning? There was nothing I could do now. I looked at the delicate teacup full of steaming tea. Grinding my teeth, I knew it would help me calm down. Lifting it up, I pressed the peony-infused concoction against my lips and sipped it. Minutes later, I was yawning and climbing into bed as fatigue ravaged through my body. My eyes shut without any effort, and I reminded myself it was for just one more night.

Drifting off into a deep sleep, I let go of the fear and anxiety, and let myself sleep in this bed-bug free bed one last night. Because tomorrow night, I'd be on a park bench, shivering in the cold with nothing to my name and no one to even think twice about my existence.

Even in a deep sleep, I felt a presence in my room. *I'm being watched,* my subconscious screamed. But this time it wasn't a camera, it was a person. I slowly opened my eyes, but my room was completely dark and I couldn't even see the ceiling.

"Hello, darling Demi." I jolted upright, gasping for air. Turning my head left and right to the point of my neck cracking, I searched for the body behind the voice.

I could see an outline as I jumped out of my bed and began to scream at the top of my lungs. I was shoved onto my bed with strong force and another hand slapped against my mouth.

"The more you fight, the more I'll crush you," he said through clenched teeth and specks of his saliva hitting my face.

I gagged against his moist palm. The panic rang in my ears to the point where I couldn't identify who it was. My eyes were hazy from sleep, with anxiety and darkness abating me.

"Calm down, my exotic little bird," he crooned closer to my ear. "I wish you had gotten the IUD. Our in-house OBGYN had a bit of an accident, and our replacement is due any day now. Granted, I could do it myself…" He let out a dry laugh, and I instantly knew it was Ian Ivory.

His arm had mine pinned down so tightly, I felt like a small prey in the dark forest, completely thrown off by a vicious predator. Pressing against me, I could feel his crotch harden.

"No. Please, no," I cried against his palm.

"Oh no, I can't touch this beautiful body until I know if you're pure or not." He sighed with disappointment.

"Did you know that the hour of three in the middle of the night is considered the most demonic of all hours, Demi?" I clenched my eyes shut as the tears streamed down my face and into his palm.

His fingers slowly raked over my cheeks, his breath cold against my lips. "The Devil's Landing is between three and four a.m. So that's the time when I wake each night and visit my caged girls. They are pure, so very pure. You've seen them, haven't you?"

Dr. Ivory rasped. I refused to open my eyes, telling myself to calm down so he'd unpin me. Coaching myself to act completely impassive and unbothered while my new employer pressed onto me. "Visiting them allows the Devil to not be superior than me." He sighed.

Slowly he removed his hand from my body, and I laid still, thinking I'd lunge forward and fight him, but that was senseless. I was one hundred and twenty pounds, and he was a muscular man towering over me. One blow could kill me. He had the darkness on his side, he knew the space and he had been watching me for who knows how long.

"I just visited them, my lovely birds. Daphne prefers I call them the caged girls but really, they are my precious birds." A small light flicked on and which was even worse. He was walking around my room, spinning in slow strides, moving his arms up and down like a puppeteer.

"You did a splendid job cleaning the cages. Although, I did find this…" The light turned on brighter and caused me to slam my eyes shut again.

"Demi, I don't like any messes. None. This is why you need to be using the roller on your entire outfit before you come out." I squinted at the thin black strand of hair dangling between his thumb and index finger.

"I wore the wig…" I stammered nervously as I deflected his stare.

"Well, the wigs work better when all that mess is gone." He pointed angrily to my long, thick, unruly black hair.

"No, please…" I shook my head, looking into his pale green eyes. I slowly sat up in the bed and tugged the blanket over my body, clutching it tightly.

"Well, darling, it'll absolutely go. Don't worry, I only prefer certain areas of girls bald. Perhaps we can cut it and bleach it; after all, the black doesn't go with our aesthetic." A sinister smile curled his lips as his eyes dropped down my body.

"I would like to leave." I let out quickly as he backed away to the door.

"No one leaves the Ivory Estate unless they are released. Just like birds. Chirp, chirp!" He mocked. But his tone was hostile as his hands clenched into tight fists until his knuckles turned pale. Chills scattered across my arms as I looked at the man in front of me. If you saw him walking outside, you'd stop and think how truly handsome he was. How he seemed well-established and definitely wealthy. You'd never assume he was a monster. But that's the thing about monsters; they don't lurk in the shadows like stories convince us… no, they prowl right in the open.

CHAPTER TWENTY-SEVEN

I LAID in the bed the rest of the night, completely still and devoid of any emotion. I was scared that if I closed my eyes, the monster would come back. So, I waited until the small alarm that was already set hummed out an eerie tune, and I climbed out of bed. I was going to tell Conrad what his dad had done and then he'd help me. Showering quickly, I pulled out the white sheath dress, stockings, and gloves, but rebelliously left my hair to air dry into a curly mane.

"Fuck you, Dr. Ivory," I mumbled as I stood in front of my door, waiting for it to open.

A minute later, it did. Bradley's eyes widened as he looked at me. "We have to stop by Becca's room so she can help you..." he trailed with his arms behind his back.

"I'm not tying it up; I'm leaving this hell today. I

need to see Conrad. Ian Ivory assaulted me last night."
I wanted to break down into tears of humiliation
because that's what women were conditioned to do—
feel humiliated based on a man's actions. But instead, I
bit back my quivering lip and tried to sound as confi-
dent as I could.

Bradley looked at me with complete desolation and
sympathy building in his eyes, moving closer to me he
slowly exhaled and put his hands on my elbows.

"Are you okay?" His voice wasn't the same; he
sounded genuinely concerned. I hated when people
asked me if I was okay. It only made it worse and just
like a switch, I began to cry.

"Bradley, please take me to Conrad. He's their
son... he'll help me out of here. I can't do this. I'll call
the police and then he'll help us all. Bradley, Dr. Ivory
called those girls his pure birds... he implied that he
was going to check if I was a virgin." I gripped my
hands into his forearms.

Looking down, he turned away and pushed my
cart to me. "It was nice to know you, Demi Rao."
Bradley began to walk down the hall with his cart full
of covered meals. I quickly followed behind him,
knowing my card didn't work anywhere and I'd be
trapped in the middle of a hall.

"Bradley, slow down!" I called out as he took a step
through the main door.

"They're going to kill you today," he said without turning around. "I wish you'd understand that you don't leave the Ivory Estate unless they *let* you. And to do so, you must shut your mouth, work, and make them love you. When they do, they might choose you."

"Choose me?" My voice shook.

"As the favorite girl." He shook his head. "It's the only way out. How many times do I need to tell you?" He looked back at my cart. "If not, they'll either kill you or cage you, but if you're lucky, they'll kill you."

"Please just do the job, Demi. Please." He sounded defeated, exhausted, and tired of reasoning with me.

"Bradley, I'm so scared," I whimpered as he went to get my cart and bring it back to me.

"You should be petrified. And you should also be glad that you're still alive and can feel fear. Now, let's go. You have to get your hair fixed and have an appointment." Bradley ushered me out of the door.

"An appointment?" I followed behind him, but he didn't say anything else and I didn't push. Instead, I savored the trivial amount of ignorance I knew would be the only way I didn't have a full-blown panic attack.

We were in a part of the house I hadn't been to before. The same fluorescent lights beamed and brightened the all-white walls and floor.

"He's waiting for you. Afterward, we will go back to Becca and then I'll take you to the floor you have to clean today." Bradley gestured to the second door on the left.

"Can you come with me?" I trembled as I sluggishly moved in front of the door, waiting for it to open.

"No, I can't. But I'll wait here."

The door slid open, and I went inside. I was starting to realize there was no way out. I was imprisoned here.

A man in all-white scrubs stood in the corner, washing his hands while an operating table sat in the middle of the room with a giant light above. Medical tools were neatly lined on a tray and cabinets were full of identical bottles and syringes.

"Oh no. I don't…" I began to breath heavily and walked backward. The man slowly turned and stared at me as I bumped into the already closed door.

"Please, Miss Rao, take a seat. It's time for your bi-annual physical assessment as agreed upon in the contract. I'm Dr. Cowell." He sat on the circular chair and moved to the table, pointing to it. I looked over my shoulder and knew I couldn't get out until I did whatever this doctor needed to do.

Moving to the cold, steel table that was papered, I held my hands together in hopes they'd stop shaking.

"Any previous health concerns?" He flipped through a stack of papers. I looked at him, stunned. I had never been to a doctor's office; I never even had a physical.

"I don't know," I answered honestly.

"Well, in that case, we will run a full panel of blood work, I'll do an exam, and then we can insert your IUD."

"I don't need an IUD." I felt my face grow warm as I anxiously swung my legs until Dr. Cowell grabbed and stilled them.

"We tell you what you need, and this is what you need. Lay down, now."

"Why do they want me to get an IUD?" I rolled my lips together as my heart thumped against my chest.

"So, you don't conceive. Now lay down, Miss Rao. I have other patients."

Conceive? I laid down as Dr. Cowell forcefully adjusted my legs into the stirrups. Peeling my stockings off, along with my panties, had to be one of the most humiliating feelings in the world. "Relax your muscles," he demanded as my legs trembled. "Relax!" This time he yelled it, which only made me clench every muscle in my body all that more.

Taking a few deep breaths, I closed my eyes as a cold speculum was inserted and my teeth chattered.

"You're pure." He clicked his tongue and after that, I felt my mind shut off. I didn't want to relieve those days; I didn't want to weaken myself more with memories that haunted me of my sister protecting me so I wouldn't be assaulted.

"You are a pure woman. I'm pleasantly surprised."

I didn't hear what he said next because all I could think of was my beautiful sister. And just like that, I didn't feel anything anymore. *Being numb is the safest place to be.*

CHAPTER
TWENTY-EIGHT

AS PROMISED, when the door opened, Bradley was waiting there. My lower abdomen was cramping, but more than the physical pain, I was emotionally drained.

"I'm sorry," Bradley whispered.

"Why are you sorry?" I asked as I pushed the cart toward the end of the hall.

"I'm sorry that you think I'm not helping you, because I am, Demi. I'm just telling you the truth, and sometimes, it's the truth that hurts the most. But, the truth is also what will save your life here." He licked his lips and brushed his hand across his face.

"Okay." I nodded. He was absolutely right. This was a fight I couldn't do alone. Bradley was the one person I'd have to lean on and trust in order to escape.

But I didn't want to just get out; I wanted to save those girls...

The way I couldn't save my older sister.

The memories flooded my mind. I wasn't raised in Gatlinburg. I wasn't born here. I could still picture it all. Us, boarding the plane from our small village in India with the strange men with light skin and hair I'd never seen before. My sister clutching a worn teddy bear, lacing her fingers into mine as our parents counted through stacks of money. They didn't even look at us; they didn't kiss us goodbye or shed tears of sadness.

Instead, they smiled. The paper in their hands brought them more happiness than their own daughters.

"Demi? Becca's waiting for you."

"Yeah." I walked in to the small salon-like space.

"I'm so excited to cut this off. You're going to fit in so much better and besides, then you won't have to wear a wig. The wigs get really hot and itchy." Becca clapped her hands excitedly.

"I love my hair." I sank into the chair and looked at the mirror, twirling the thick, frizzy strands between my fingers.

"Well, you'll love this look even more. And they will, too. Fitting in is the best!" She grabbed a brush and began to comb out all of my hair, then snatched up the scissors and cut it swiftly. The slicing of the blades hitting my hair just before it fell to the ground had me clench my eyes shut. I didn't want to fit in.

Four hours later, Becca had me turned the other way and spun me around. "Ta-da!" she exclaimed with jazz hands.

"Holy shit." My mouth dropped open as I stared at the girl in the reflection. I didn't even look like myself. My waist-length hair was cut short, and it was now bleach blonde. My hair clashed against my otherwise tanned skin, standing out like I was some kind of side character in a Marvel movie.

"Your lips are chapped horribly. See this line in the middle? Yuck." She pointed out the line that was embedded in my bottom lip as she tinted my lips in a creamy, nude lipstick.

But it wasn't from being chapped; it was from being sliced opened when I was seventeen and tried to run away for the fourth time.

"Now you'll have higher chances of sealing the deal as the favorite girl. Poor Misha…" Becca shook her head with a frown.

I spun around on the chair and looked at her. "She was murdered, Becca. In the peony garden," I spewed out, finding some strange kind of relief that Becca knew something had indeed happened to Misha.

"Mm-hmm… she was. But at least she's free. There hasn't been a favorite girl in years."

"I don't understand what being the favorite girl even means? Why aren't you trying to be that?"

"Me?" Becca tossed her head back, breaking into laughter. "I don't want to leave my home—" She covered her mouth as she quickly tried to silence herself.

"Home?" I questioned, completely stunned by her reaction.

"Demi, I was married to a man who beat me daily. He almost killed me multiple times, and I can guarantee you, had Daphne and Ian not taken me in and given me an entirely new identity, he would have found me and done it. This is *home*." Becca waved her arms around.

"But the… the caged girls," I whispered.

Becca's face lost its color as she slowly walked away from me, turning to her vanity and cleaning her scissors with an alcohol wipe. "The caged girls were drug addicts." She glanced at me through the mirror. "Drug addicts who were a burden on society. The Ivory family saved their *lives*. You just don't get it… They are saving the weakest women and helping to guide us toward a brand-new life. You should be grateful, Demi." She pointed the scissors directly at me with pursed lips.

"Drug addicts?" I whispered, completely confused. Was that what Dr. Ivory's experimental study was? But the all-white rooms, no sound, no visual changes, and all-white food...? How was that healthy? Those women were trapped in a colorless, soundless boxes. This wasn't rehabilitation... this was complete sensory deprivation.

"The favorite girl is the one who wants to go back into the bloodcurdling world and fly free. Dr. and Mrs. Ivory don't like it, but they have enormous hearts and only want what's best for their girls. The thing is... I've been hearing some whispers that they are trying to find a favorite girl who will eventually be the next *Mrs. Ivory*." Becca smiled happily.

"Why would Daphne... Mrs. Ivory be okay with that? Is she planning on divorcing Dr. Ivory?" I stood and shook the straggling hair from my body.

"No silly! They want the favorite girl to marry Conrad and eventually take over the estate and carry on their study. Dr. Ivory is starting to feel as if he can't carry it all out in the upcoming years. Besides, the wedding would be stunning! Can you imagine being the next Mrs. Ivory?" Becca clutched her chest and swooned over the thought of marrying Conrad.

"So, the favorite girl will be asked to marry Conrad and take over... all of this?" I asked curiously.

"Yes! Now you need to go and clean the pulchritudo floor. Mrs. Ivory has an event tonight; she'll want her room in the best shape."

Nodding while every ounce of this insane information circled my mind, the door opened and Bradley was there. Ironically, I felt like a caged girl, too. Weren't we all? Locked in with no way to escape? Our wings damaged and paralyzed with no option.

"Wow." Bradley sucked in a breath as soon as he saw me, and immediately realized his reaction was out of character.

"It's horrific, I know." I looked away and gripped my cart.

"Nothing about you is horrific, Demi," Bradley said so quietly, I swore I had made it up in my head. I paused and looked at him. I wanted to smile. But as soon as I thought how kind the words Bradley said were, I thought about the magnitude of the dangerous situation I was in. Should I believe Becca? Were those women all former-drug addicts who would have definitely been dead by now, and this is just some outlandish medical experiment to help them with withdrawal?

I barely had an education, so I didn't have a clue about medicine. But Dr. Ivory was disgusting. He was on top of me in the middle of the night, threatening me. He was calling those women his 'birds.' Rubbing my face, I knew I had to do something. I had to help these girls; I had to save them and myself. There were better resources out there for these women.

I just needed to sneak away and call the police.

We wove through hallways, and it seemed like a mirror reflection of each 'wing.' Every hallway identical, even the decorations were duplicates. There was no color, and the walls and floors stitched together.

"I'm going to the Ossis floor to give… them food." Bradley looked at his cart. "I'll come pick you back up after. It'll take you time to clean Mrs. Ivory's room. She's very particular that you brush everything."

"Brush everything?" I raised my eyebrows and swallowed the saliva in my mouth that was coating my otherwise dry mouth.

"I'll see you in a little bit." Bradley shrugged and turned away.

"Bradley!" I called out behind him.

He flung around and put his index finger against his lips. "Shh!" he shushed me with fear in his eyes.

"What are they getting to eat today?"

"Plain rice and yogurt." Bradley's lips tightened into a straight line as he stared into my eyes. I could tell he wanted so desperately to say something else, but he didn't. He walked away and the door silently slid shut behind him.

The knots in my stomach grew tighter but then suddenly, the door slid open and I did what I knew best.

Survive.

Holding my breath, I walked through with my cart. Thankfully, the room wasn't stark white. Exhaling as I paused in the center of the room with parted lips, my breathing grew quicker as my heart started to pound harder.

When Bradley said my job today was to 'brush everything,' I wasn't sure what he meant. But as I stood there in Mrs. Ivory's 'special' room, I saw the endless wigs, neatly lined on shelves with spotlights over them.

My lips trembled and my body grew cold as I walked to the wall.

"No... Oh no, no...." I stammered as I blinked repeatedly. Tiny, golden placards were drilled into the shelves that held them.

Rows and rows of wigs; all blonde, with different styles and lengths. Squinting, I ran my finger against the engraving.

Jackie Indigo (Brunette, virgin)

Gabby Mian (Brunette, dyed)

Kealey Remington (Blonde, dyed)

Elise Moretti (Brunette, dyed)

Silvia Sully (Brunette, virgin)

Jessica Miller (Red, virgin)
Kori Wimberly (Blonde, virgin)
Erin Harlow (Brunette, dyed)
Paige Cooper (Dark-brunette, virgin)
Cristina Navy (Red, dyed)
Caroline Sage (Blonde, dyed)
Amanda Calloway (Brunette, dyed)
Kelly Shah (Blonde, dyed)
Allyson Montgomery (Brunette, virgin)

Rows and rows of names and hair colors? My chest tightened as I looked at each wig that was now platinum blonde. Closing my eyes, I tried to count the rooms I cleaned. Five? Or was it nine? It was too hard to remember when the shock was cutting through every ounce of my body as I robotically cleaned around a human who was in a room with a shaved head and everything was a blinding white, including their meals.

"Demi, have you even started brushing them yet?" I spun around to find Bradley shaking his head at me.

"Bradley... those... the caged girls... This is their hair?" I didn't know whether I was asking a question or saying my thoughts out loud just so I'd be able to believe them.

"They are Mrs. Ivory's precious wigs. You need to

brush them. She's been extremely agitated since they couldn't find someone to do this job in quite some time," Bradley replied stoically.

"Where did these wigs come from? What are these names? Who—"

"Demi, here. Boar brush only. Do it." Bradley shoved a fancy-looking brush into my hands and physically turned me toward the wigs.

I looked at the bristles and trembled as I reached for one of the wigs and head-shaped mannequin stand.

It was Gabby's. Who was she? Was she here? Was she trapped in one of those terrifying rooms? Those cages?

I began to brush the hair, cringing as the brush struggled to get through the knots. I couldn't hold back the fear pounding through my chest as I thought about how these wigs came to be.

"Bradley, how…" I started.

"Don't ask what you don't want to know, Demi. Just don't." He left the room, and I swore, as soon as the door slid closed, I could hear the girls who once had this hair on top of their heads… *scream.*

The room felt colder, darker, and more sterile when I was in it alone. My racing thoughts grew loud and echoed amongst the cries of the women who existed under this roof and were being forced to live like puppy mill animals.

But I stood there and brushed each and every wig, hoping that doing so would fill the time because I could no longer breathe here. I realized now that the air in this house wasn't pure or clean; it was plagued with death, just like a morgue.

CHAPTER
TWENTY-NINE

THE DAY WENT FASTER as I actually did my tasks. I didn't ask any more questions, I just worked. I worked until I got a lunch break, and then worked until dinner. But I counted down seconds until the house grew quiet because I knew that before I went back to my room, I'd sneak to the phone that sat in the kitchen and call for help.

We ate dinner with the staff, and no one really spoke, but everyone wore the same type of outfit. The women wore short, white dresses with stockings, hair pinned up, light makeup, and clean nails. The men were all dressed in white pants and white, tucked-in, button-downs. And we all wore the same platform shoes that made zero noise against the floor.

Everyone besides me looked content, smiling and stealing glances at one another while shoveling hot, delicious food into their mouths. It was true, the food was unlimited—I made sure to have seconds. I'd miss it. I'd be back at the dumpsters behind restaurants before I knew it, but at least I'd be alive... If I didn't starve to death, or freeze to death, or be attacked by another predator lurking in the shadows. Suddenly, I froze as I looked at the staff around me.

That's why these people didn't care what the Ivory family did behind closed doors. They knew that they were here to work, eat, sleep, and be safe. Safety had varying meanings, but that's why people stayed. Stayed in toxic relationships and situations because even if short-lived, safety is comforting, consuming, and more than anything, gave us a sense of false hope.

After we all cleared our dinner plates, everyone began to head to their rooms through the back hallway, which I had finally memorized.

"Ready?" Bradley came up beside me.

"I'm going to have some dessert. You can head back; I know my way now." I offered a forced smile to Bradley as he looked at me curiously.

"I'll just wait." He shrugged and leaned against the staff kitchen island.

"Bradley, please stop babysitting me. I'm fine. My card is working now, and I'm getting a hang of the hallways and everything. I'll be in my room in ten minutes. You can check on me if you absolutely have to." I rolled my eyes and took a thick slice of chocolate cake, my absolute favorite.

"Fine." Bradley hesitated but eventually left. As soon as he did, I took a huge bite of cake and raced to the phone. I didn't have much time. Someone would be in here to clean up the dishes and kitchen soon.

I punched 9-1-1 into the landline. One ring later, an operator answered.

"Hi, I need help, I'm being held in the Ivory Estate as a prisoner and they've got other girls here, too. Help us!" I rambled as fast as I could, then slammed the phone down and speed-walked back to my room. The halls all looked the same, and suddenly, with panic coursing through me, I didn't know where I was going. "Shit, shit, shit." I panicked as I stopped and turned in a circle.

My breathing grew faster, my palms moist as I sank to the floor and clutched my knees to my chest.

"Demi?"

I looked up and saw Bradley, but he wasn't in his uniform.

"Come on." He reached down and helped me off the ground, then led me back to my room.

"You look so different." I looked at his gray joggers, black V-neck, and messy hair as he stood outside my door. "You look… normal."

. . .

"Demi, I *am* normal. We're just in an abnormal environment." He looked sad as the door shut between us.

I put my hands up against the door, wishing we could have talked more. He knew this wasn't normal; he knew this was completely deranged. So, he wasn't some brainwashed fool. But then, why was he here? He seemed well-educated and well-spoken. It didn't seem like Bradley came from the streets like me or many of the other staff here.

I went into the bathroom to shower. This might be my last one for a long, long time.

Suddenly, I felt sadness. Sadness that this is how it was ending for me. How a promising job turned into something from a horror movie. I was grieving the chance to finally turn my life around.

My damn luck. I savored the heat from the shower as I lathered my hair with the luxury shampoo, and I wrapped myself in the plush towel before getting into the buttery-soft lounge wear.

My shorter hair was still foreign to me, but it felt nice and light. Swiping the fog from the mirror, it wasn't just my reflection staring back at me…

It was also Mrs. Ivory's. The warmth of the shower no long wrapped around me, instead, the cold presence of Daphne Ivory did.

"Darling girl, whatever have you done?"

I didn't want to turn around. I didn't want to face her.

"Officer Tate is here... and he'd like a word with you. Apparently, they received quite a panicked call from you. I thought we were keeping you happy." Mrs. Ivory looked genuinely unhappy.

"I... I don't know what you're talking about." Turning slowly, I faced her. Her eyes were slightly tinged with red.

"You know I love my girls... *all* of them. Every single one of you is a precious bird to me." She grabbed my face between her palms. "I won't let him take you from me. I won't." She tucked my hair behind my ear. "You're special to me, Demi. We've just met you, yet it feels like we've known you all along." She smiled at me. "Now, the authorities would like to speak with you, my special hummingbird." She put her hand in mine, and walked me out of my room.

My nerves were shot as I glanced over my shoulder. "Mrs. Ivory, you don't have to stay here. You can come with me," I whispered up at her. She felt warm and everything she ever said seemed genuine. Her husband was clearly a monster, and she was probably trapped here, just like the rest of the people in this estate.

"You're so silly. Why would I leave our home, Demi? And you're not going to leave, either," she said with excitement as we turned to the formal living area.

A police officer in a pale gray uniform was sitting across from Dr. Ivory, who gave me a look that had my entire body ice over.

"Miss Rao?" The officer stood and reached his hand out. "I'm Officer Tate." He tapped his hat with the other hand.

Nervously, I looked around the room. Conrad was sitting beside his dad, and he leaned down, widening his eyes at me and slowly shaking his head. What did that mean?

"We received a call of distress from you, ma'am."

Dr. Ivory let out a dry laugh as Officer Tate chewed on a wet toothpick obnoxiously. Tapping my thumbs together, I looked at my feet. This was it. I had to speak for myself but also for the caged girls.

"There're at least five girls in the Ossis wing in these white… rooms. And one is in Dr. Ivory's office… you can see her through the glass. They are all being held prisoner." My words shook as I spoke. It was completely silent, and I felt the heavy gazes locked on me.

"Miss Rao, that's an awfully intense accusation, and we don't want to waste taxpayer money, now do we?" the officer sang out in his southern drawl.

"I swear! Please!" I pleaded.

"Okay, well, why don't we take a look around with you?" Officer Tate looped his fingers into his belt loops and nodded at Dr. Ivory, who smiled at him in a way that had my stomach curl.

"We can all head over together." Dr. Ivory glanced between Mrs. Ivory and Conrad. Following behind them, I dragged my feet slightly. This was it. Those girls would be freed. I'd leave with this officer, and maybe stop by Raina's house for a night. I'd start over and find a new place.

Once we got to the Ossis wing, Dr. Ivory swiped the card and waved for Officer Tate and me to go through first.

I didn't want that creep behind me, but with a police officer beside me, I felt safe enough. I glanced at Conrad, who had a look of worry on his face. Maybe this would be a way to set him and Mrs. Ivory free, too.

"This is the first room I cleaned." I pointed to the door and it opened slowly. I looked inside the room and looked at the officer. "See!" There she was, the first girl I saw, chained to her bed, wearing a short white gown with her head shaved, eyes closed, and thick headphones over her ears. "There! She's chained up!" I slapped my hand over my mouth and shook in relief. Part of me thought in some crazy way they'd have removed all the girls... the evidence.

Officer Tate walked into the room and looked all

around before turning back again. His forehead creased as he looked directly into my eyes. "Miss Rao, let's go take a seat." He rolled his lips together, brushing the scruff scattered against his jaw.

"Wait? You have to unchain her!" I tried to push past him and run inside the room, but he gripped my shoulders and pushed me out of the room before the door slid shut.

"Let go! You have to help her! And there's more; this whole hallway is full of girls just like her!"

Officer Tate's nails dug into my upper arm as he dragged me to the formal living area. "Miss Rao, do you have a history of mental illness?" The officer peered at me as he pushed me onto the sofa.

"Mental… illness?" I stammered with my brows lowered. I was appalled by the accusation. "You saw her. She was right there." I waved my hands wildly, completely flabbergasted.

"Conrad! Conrad, he won't lie." I stood and raced over to Conrad, who had his head dropped low.

"Demi, those are empty patient recovery rooms my dad uses for his outpatient clinic. It's been a long time since we've even had a patient," he said without a hitch.

"No… there was a girl. Let me back in and I'll shake her. I'll take the headphones off." I began shrieking and panicking all at the same time. This couldn't be happening.

"Dr. Ivory, would you like me to take her somewhere?" Officer Tate began restraining me as I tried to lunge forward.

"No, you know we take care of them," he said with a grin.

"I know you do, sir. You see, Miss Rao, the Ivory family gives jobs and homes to women like you, who would be dead on the street if it weren't for their kindness. Our city is a safer, cleaner, and better place thanks to the Ivory family. It's time you show appreciation to those who are saviors of our otherwise progressive city," Officer Tate hissed in my ear as his nails dug into my arms.

There was no point attempting to fight this enormous man. My mind was spiraling, and I was exhausted with myself. I crumpled over, loosening my body as if I were a ragdoll. Once I did, he let me go and I sank into the sofa. Was I delirious? Was I losing my mind? Was the Ivory family truly rehabilitating these women? No one was crying or running, but one of the girls did mouth 'Run' to me.

Didn't she?

"Miss Rao, if there is nothing else, then I need to leave now. My wife is at home waiting for me."

"Oh, how is Isabella?" Mrs. Ivory chirped and her eyes lit up.

"She's everything I could have ever wanted. It's as if I dreamt her up myself." Officer Tate winked at Mrs. Ivory and turned to leave.

My mind was spiraling and my stomach was churning from everything.

"Demi, sweetie, let's get you to bed." Mrs. Ivory reached down and lifted my hand into hers.

"Actually, Conrad will take her. Won't you, son?" Dr. Ivory boasted. I felt numb. It felt as if I were watching a movie, but here I was, living it.

"Yes, father," Conrad replied softly before moving toward me, dropping his opened palm in front of me.

"Come on, Demi." He nodded as I placed my hand into his. Following him out of the formal living room, I felt my peripheral vision grow fuzzy. I had to sleep; I couldn't do this any longer with a mind that was completely scrambled.

Once we got back to my room, I expected Conrad to wait outside just like Bradley did until the door shut completely to ensure I hadn't left again.

But he came inside, and the door shut behind him.

"Demi…" He grew closer to me, opening his hands he planted them under my elbows. "You have to stop. My father, he won't… he won't be as forgiving. My mother has taken a liking to you, and so have I, so we are doing everything to keep you…" he trailed, quickly averting his eyes.

"Alive?" I winced as I filled in the word for him, knowing without a doubt in my mind it was the truth.

"Demi, please, promise me that you'll just stay strong and know that one day… we're going to be okay. We're going to have our fresh start. It's always been the plan. You and me." Conrad brushed a strand of hair out of my face. "I can't believe you exist. The hair is perfect. They really kept their promise to me," he breathed out in admiration.

I froze. Everything he had just said had me completely confused. What promise? But before I could even ask, he leaned in and tilted my chin upward just before locking his lips with mine.

Closing my eyes, every emotion in my body shifted.
My first kiss…

I took a moment before opening my eyes once his lips left mine. And as soon as I did, my cheeks heated as Conrad smiled down at me. "Be good for me, *Demilion*. Our time is coming." He winked and turned to leave as I stood there speechless.

But it wasn't speechless because I was some love-struck girl. No, I was speechless because I wanted to know. I wanted to know why he had just used the nick-name only one person had ever called me.

My dead sister.

CHAPTER
THIRTY

DEMI – *Two years ago*

"Just close your eyes and count to three, then you'll fall asleep," she whispered in my ear.

"I can't. I'm so scared, Layla," I cried into my palms, terrified they'd hear us. Slivers of light seeped through the cracks of the closet we were forced to stay in for twenty-two hours a day.

I had learned to ignore the scent of urine, the pile of feces in the corner, and the sweat-covered clothes. I had learned to ignore the screaming women and the men roaring with laughter.

Sleep was something I didn't know how to do without Layla—my sister essentially comforting me as if I were a petrified toddler.

"Go to sleep, go to sleep, my sweet Demilion," she cooed. I couldn't help but smile as she brushed her fingers through my knotted hair and massaged my scalp.

We'd been here for years now, but time didn't mean anything. There were no birthdays, there were no holidays to help mark the passing of another year. We lived in the shadows. We were already dead. Our parents sold us to traffickers that couldn't believe their luck acquiring two young, beautiful girls. 'Exotic' was what they called us.

One of the men, Trent, who ran one of the largest trafficking rings in Nashville, raped my sister multiple times a day. He'd tie her up and then have me watch as he'd brutally beat and rape her. He called her 'his wife.' She'd look me in the eyes sometimes and tears would stream down her reddened and bruised cheeks as she'd whisper with a small, forced smile, "It's okay, Demilion."

Demilion, the nickname she gave me. She said it's because I was her greatest wish come true—a built-in best friend, a sister. She told me she made wishes on dandelions every single day, hoping for a baby sister, and then, just like that, I eventually came along.

Our parents were the perfect example of humans who should never have reproduced. They were poverty-stricken and told us we were going to chase the American dream. Layla and I were so excited to fly for the first time when my parents put us on the airplane. We couldn't believe our lucky stars. Once there, they pretended we were meeting with a babysitter, an older woman wearing pearls, waiting for us at a park bench. Smiling, she pulled out two mints and handed it to us. She told us she was going to take us somewhere fun and new; she told us that we were going to love our new lives. My parents didn't even think twice. They took the cash from her, watched the strange men come for us and left immediately. "Ma!" I called out after them, but they didn't even look over their shoulder.

Layla was my everything. She was only three years older, but she was a mother, a father, a sister, a protector. She was everything. Our captors had a television running and old movies played on it. We'd watch through the crack. I remember watching *Titanic* and thinking Rose was brilliant for not risking her life for Jack. I admired her for not making room for him and letting him die.

One day, Layla found a way out for me. She said she'd distract Trent by being defiant, and when he grew angry and abusive, I needed to run. She said that the rest of the men were going to be making a transaction—that's what they called it when they sold another girl or had her go out and perform sexual acts for money.

"I don't want to leave you," I whimpered.

"You have to, Demilion. Run and never look back. Charlotte is six hours away... I've heard it's a safe place. They've got resources for girls like us. Go there." She nodded with so much hope in her eyes, I swore it hurt even more. "I'll meet you there. The Queen City, for two queens, right?" She smiled and brushed the hair from my face.

I had never felt more terrified in my life. I didn't want to leave Layla here in this hell. No one had ever touched me; they said I was protected and was to never ever be touched. But Layla wasn't so lucky. I had no idea why they spared me. Sometimes when darkness overtook my mind, I wondered, was it because I wasn't as beautiful as her? Was it because I was younger?

Hours had passed, and Layla had me wrapped in her arms while we sat there in the closet. We could hear the music from neighboring apartments blasting. Guitars strumming, piano keys echoing, musicians practicing their art form. I hated it so much. I loathed how the music always felt like a backdrop to the horrors that were happening right inside this small apartment, and no one heard since the music obstructed it all out.

"Wife!" Trent's loud voice boomed through the wood panels of the closet that had become a safe haven to my sister and me. My eyes filled with tears as I clutched Layla's arm tighter around me.

"Don't let me go," I whispered hurriedly.

"I'll never let you go, Demilion, from here." She rolled her lips and tapped her heart, and I knew she was holding back her tears. "I'll see you in the Queen City." She nodded as the door slammed open, and Trent's hairy arm reached down and yanked her from me.

"I love you, Layla!" I screamed out. For some reason, it was as if I knew that would be the last time I'd get to say it.

"I love you, Demilion," she said as she was dragged away. Her eyes crinkled and a single tear rolled down her beautiful face.

Drawing my knees to my chest, I sobbed. I didn't know how long to wait before I should sneak out. We'd never run away before, because we knew better. It was made very clear that if we ran and were caught, they'd slaughter us like pigs on a farm. They swore they'd gut us and make each other watch as we died simultaneously.

What felt like an eternity later, I heard screaming. *Layla.* This was my cue. I lunged up, pushed the door open, and raced out of the room. Sprinting down the hall, my feet jerked on the worn carpet as I gasped.

Trent was gone, the door was wide open, but my

sister... my beautiful sister was laying on the dirty, stained carpet, surrounded by an ever-growing puddle of her own blood. Her face was almost unrecognizable.

Dropping to my knees, I began to cry so hard, my body felt like it'd break any moment. But just as I began to sing a soft lullaby—the one she always sang to me—Layla's eyes shot open. I stumbled back into my hands as the whites of her eyes were tinged with blood.

As she moved her face slightly, I cried out seeing her bottom teeth punctured through her lip.

"Layla!" I slapped my hands over my mouth.

"Demi... lion," she rasped with blood dripping down her chin.

I reached in, clenching my eyes shut and tried to help pull her lip from her teeth, but she shook her head.

"So much pain," she breathed out as her eyes rolled backward. She lifted her finger slowly, and I followed to what she was pointing at.

A bloodied knife sitting in the carpet right by us.

"Can't do this anymore... please." She closed her eyes as I processed what she was asking from me. "Knife." I could barely understand her with her mouth completely smashed.

. . .

"No… no, Layla. Let's go. We're going to get you out of here." I looked around for a phone. I stood and ran around the compact apartment like there would actually be a phone just waiting for me.

But then I saw a badge. Tilting my head, I walked to it and lifted it up. Trent was a police officer… "Oh my God," I wailed.

We're trapped.

"Demilion." I flung around and picked up the knife, then brought it back to my sister.

"What do you want with this, Layla?" I sank back down and put her head in my lap, massaging her scalp with my fingers, knowing she was in agonizing pain.

"Kill me."

"No, no… no." I sobbed as my eyes grew blurry, and I looked at my sister's weakened body. "Just come on, stand up." I tried to pull her thin frame against mine, but she made a noise that sounded like an animal trapped in a hunter's net.

I saw her leg and realized it was completely twisted in the opposite direction.

"Layla." I dropped us both back to the floor, completely defeated and drained. My sister's body was shattered, physically and emotionally. She was dying. They'd never call for help; they'd let her endure every ounce of pain.

"This is the only chance you'll have. Please… Demi,

run. But don't let me…" She paused as tears rolled down her face, then she opened her eyes slowly and looked at me. "I'm… already dead." She looked at my hand, trembling against the knife. "You have to live for us both."

"I love you so much. Forever." She began to cough, but her bottom lip was still caught in her teeth, and it tugged so hard, she choked on her own blood.

I couldn't stop crying as I lifted the knife. "I love you so much, Layla. Always." I slammed my eyes shut as the knife slid into my sister's body.

I plunged the blade over and over again, until I heard the crackling of her cries stop. Until I knew she was no longer suffering like roadkill.

And in that moment, I died, too.

CHAPTER THIRTY-ONE

I GOT into bed and stared at the ceiling. No one in this world knew that Layla called me Demilion. I had no friends, and I had no family, so Conrad calling me that made no sense. Between every scenario and every single thought rampaging through my mind, I couldn't sleep, though I knew I needed to. I didn't know what to do. Part of me didn't know if I could even believe myself. Why would the police allow a family to do something illegal? Charlotte was a huge, well-established city. Did I suffer from so much of my own trauma that I couldn't handle this?

Eventually the questions I couldn't answer ceased, and I fell into a deep sleep.

A slight buzz from the small alarm clock echoed and woke me. For the first time in a very long time, I felt well-rested. I didn't feel hungover or deliriously fatigued. I felt... better?

Peeling the soft blanket off my body, I had to find answers. I know without a doubt that Conrad and his parents knew far more about me than they let on. I needed to talk to the girls... the caged girls. I had to find out if they were here by their own free will to actually be helped for a drug addiction or if they were being tortured. I was leaning toward the second option, but I needed to know for sure. The more I thought about the caged girls, the more questions began to form. Why did they only eat all-white food? Why did they shave their heads? Why did everything have to be completely silent? What about the room full of wigs? No, this was wrong. I had to find a way out and not just for me, but for them, too.

I showered, shaved, brushed my short, blonde hair that I was still not used to, and slid into the white ensemble. Staring back at my reflection, I licked my thumb and brushed my thick brows into place. The door of my bedroom slid open, and Bradley was waiting right outside. Seeing his face had become oddly comforting to me now.

"Bradley." I sighed as I walked toward him.

"Demi..." He glanced up at the ceiling before moving two steps over and tugging me to the side. Throwing his arms around me, my eyes widened as he quickly hugged me and my body stiffened in shock.

"I'm glad you're alive. Can you stop being fucking reckless?" he said softly into my ear, his warm breath sending chills down my entire body.

Pulling away, I looked at him and smiled. "I thought you didn't like me."

"I don't." He rolled his eyes and pushed my cart toward me. But this time it wasn't cleaning supplies; it was his usual cart full of steel-covered meals.

"Wait? I'm not cleaning?"

"They want you to serve the food first, then we will pick up your cart so you can clean Dr. Ivory's office before our next tasks."

"And what are you going to do?"

"Help you."

"Fine." I pretended I had a say or a choice in what my role here was, but I didn't. I rolled the cart behind Bradley as we made our way to the Ossis wing.

"What does Ossis even mean?" I questioned.

"Bones."

My breathing hitched as Bradley continued to walk without stopping for a moment. I knew Dr. Ivory was an orthopedic surgeon, but why would he call a space in his house 'the bone wing' if it was a floor of women they claimed to be helping.

There are questions you want to know the answers

to, and others where you know that if you find the answer, you'll be worse off. This was a question I knew I had to push aside. I didn't have the mental strength to handle something more. This was already too much.

The first door slid open, and my heart immediately began to pound rapidly. The girl was laying on the small cot with headphones on.

"Is she listening to music?" I asked Bradley, but he immediately slammed his hand over my mouth and shook his head, implying I needed to stay quiet. I saw a small table that I was supposed to put the food on. Reaching into my cart, I uncovered the meal and saw the small cup of plain milk, white rice, and yogurt—all white.

Trudging slowly to the bedside table, I held my breath as I gently placed the food down. The girl was lying down with her eyes closed and her hands intertwined.

The silence in the icy room felt all the more frightening. I turned slowly but accidentally bumped into the table and knocked over the fork, which crashed onto the tile with a loud *clang*.

Gasping, Bradley's mouth dropped as I turned to pick it up, but just as I turned, I fell backward as the girl flung upright with her eyes wide and a smile spread across her face.

"Noise." She giggled excitedly as my shaking fingers trembled against the fork.

Before I could speak or even think, Bradley grabbed my arm and yanked me out of the room. The door slid shut and he pressed me against the wall.

"What the hell was that, Demi?" he seethed.

My entire body was covered in goosebumps as I trembled with the image of her pale face, hollow cheekbones, and dried lips curving into a delirious smile.

"What do you mean? You tell me what the hell that was? Why did she act like noise was so shocking? How does a colorless, soundless room have anything to do with withdrawal and coping with a drug addiction?"

"Demi, stop. You're spiraling again." Suddenly Bradley looked at his phone.

"I have to go back inside the room... damage control," he huffed as he read a lengthy message. "Go into the next room, but don't drop anything and don't make a sound. I'm serious, Demi. They're watching you."

Nodding slowly, I made my way down the hall and waited in front of the door, but it didn't open automatically.

"Use your badge," Bradley hissed with irritation. I

looked down at the badge and glided it over, and it worked.

Slowly pushing the cart inside, I couldn't believe how frigid each room was. These girls were in short white gowns and mostly bald. They were thin and had a small blanket on each of their beds. There was no way the coldness in the room wasn't torture for them.

Carefully lifting the plate, I shook while I placed it on the table, making sure to back away slowly. But just as I moved from the meal, I stopped.

The girl sat up and stared at me. The bags under her eyes were deep and the bright green stood out strangely against her almost translucent skin.

"Hello," she rasped so softly, that if it weren't for the way her lips moved, I would have assumed I was hallucinating.

"Hey..." I whispered. Looking up at the ceiling, I saw the camera directly facing the young woman. Turning halfway, I pretended to busy myself with the cart.

"Are you okay?" My words shook as I tried to keep my lips still and keep my voice as low as humanly possible.

"Yes."

I looked at her with astonishment. "Really?" I breathed out as I flicked my eyes to the camera.

"Yes. It's safe." She grinned. But it wasn't a smile

that was filled with joy; it was a forced, rehearsed smile. Her dry, cracked lips shriveled back into a frown, showing me, it was a mere façade.

"Okay…" I looked into her eyes. Squinting, I could tell they were green-colored contacts. I left the room and went next door, repeating my actions. But this time, I was met with the woman who had mouthed the words, 'Run.' I looked at her as she was sitting up, blankly staring at the opposing wall. And unlike the other women I had encountered, her hair was starting to grow back and I could see specks of soft brown.

Placing her food down, she didn't even flinch. She didn't have headphones on, so I knew she heard the slight noise that emitted from the plate grazing the table.

"Hello…" I whispered under my breath.

She didn't look at me. Walking closer, I leaned in and tapped her shoulder.

She didn't move.

She just sat there as if she were a statue and continued to stare at nothing.

The door slid open, and Bradley appeared. Jerking me away from the young woman, I could hear his breathing change. I quickly grabbed my cart and moved closer to the door, but then I froze as I watched Bradley linger behind.

What is he doing?

He bent over and dropped to his knees, sitting eye-level with the young woman. *Oh my goodness, is he about to do something intimate with her?* My stomach tossed as I blinked rapidly, knowing I'd intervene if he dared to touch her inappropriately.

But then he whispered, "I love you, sis. I'm so sorry. I tried everything. There's no way out of hell." His words shattered me, and the air from my lungs dissipated with the realization that Bradley was working here because of her.

His sister was one of the caged girls.

CHAPTER
THIRTY-TWO

I STOOD THERE, trembling with what I had just witnessed. Bradley leaned in and planted a delicate kiss against the young woman's cheek. He turned back toward me, though his gaze remained on the ground.

"Bradley..." My voice crackled as I flicked my eyes between both of them. No response. He pushed past me and walked into the hallway. I followed him and the door slid shut behind us.

"Bradley, please talk to me. That girl is your sister?" I couldn't believe what was happening.

"Bradley!" I raised my voice as he pressed his forehead against the wall and planted both hands by his face.

"Yeah," he said desolately.

"Bradley, we have to get her out. What the hell? Is she here because she was an addict? What did you mean you tried everything but can't help her? What is going to happen to her now?" I asked rapidly as my heart rate spiked and my entire body went into the state of panic.

Sighing, he turned to face me. "She's someone's favorite girl."

Jerking back, I titled my head and eyed him. "What does that even mean? I thought I was supposed to become the favorite girl?" I felt stupid for even asking such a ridiculous question when I didn't even know what the title meant.

"Demi, you've always been the favorite girl. *Their* favorite girl. But my sister is someone else's."

Running my hands through my hair, my breathing became erratic. "I don't understand…"

"Demi, my sister has been chosen. She'll be leaving here in a week. Come on… we have a wedding to plan." He waved me toward the exit as if he didn't just say the most outrageous statement.

"What do you mean, I've always been the favorite girl? And who's wedding do we have to plan?" I had to break into a light jog just to catch up to him.

"Demi, just stop. Please. I cannot handle any questions when my entire life is crashing down in front of me, and I have no way to piece anything back together." He rubbed his hands across his face as we exited.

"Let's get your sister out of here—"

"Fuck, Demi! You just don't get it. There is no way out of here. This is hell, and we're all going to burn. The sooner you accept it, the better off you'll be and the less you'll scorch. But if you play your cards right, you won't even burn... you'll get to live happily ever after." He paused and suddenly, his facial expression shifted to annoyance. "Oh, I forgot to ask... how was your first kiss?" He rolled his eyes.

What? How did he know Conrad had kissed me? How did he know that was my very first kiss?

Embarrassment pooled inside of me as we continued to walk in silence.

I didn't recognize the path we were taking, and I looked at the framed images as we walked down the narrow hallways. Each one was black-and-white, with couples on their wedding day. Slowing my pace, I studied them carefully. The men were all significantly older, while the women were frail and young...

I wish they were in color. I couldn't tell what their hair or eyes looked like. I couldn't tell for sure, but I could swear the women looked just like the caged girls. The caged girls with hair and wedding gowns on.

"Demi, come on," Bradley said blankly. Opening the two doors, we walked in together, but we weren't alone. Surrounding an oversized round table, Dr. and Mrs. Ivory sat there with an older man I had never seen before, Becca, and Conrad. Three identical binders were laid neatly in front of the man.

"It's nice of you both to finally join us," Dr. Ivory said with annoyance as Bradley nodded toward one of the empty chairs for me to sit.

Sinking down, I looked around the table, catching Conrad's eyes. He winked at me, causing my cheeks to immediately grow warm, and beside me, Bradley grunted with irritation.

"Now that everyone is here, we are so very pleased to introduce our next client, Dr. Mason Davenport. As many of you know, his brother, Dr. Liam Davenport was once a client of ours as well. His selection, Oakley, was one of our best products—the perfect and most compliant blonde you could find. Dr. Davenport is here to select the make, model, and year of his purchase," Dr. Ivory boasted proudly.

Wait... the Ivory family sold cars? No wonder they were abnormally wealthy. I leaned closer to the table, wanting to see the details of the folders. I didn't even have a driver's license, so car buying seemed so foreign to me. "Demi, as a valuable member of our family, we'd love for you to flip through one of the folders as well. Perhaps you can help Dr. Davenport here decide on some of the finer details. Plus, you're the closest to our merchandise these days." Dr. Ivory smiled at me in a way that made me realize the purchase wasn't a car.

With shaking hands, I tugged the folder open and immediately choked on the air around me. I wanted to throw up. I wanted to scream. I wanted to cry.

But just as soon as I was going to react, I felt a hand grip my thigh. Glancing down, I saw Bradley's hand squeeze my leg under the table, and when I made eye contact with him, he gave me a pleading look that clearly said, 'Conceal every emotion in your body or you'll be dead.'

"Definitely want a 2005 model. The younger ones are the best…" Dr. Davenport licked his bottom lips and grinned at me.

"Well, we only have one 2005 model and she's in pristine condition." Mrs. Ivory clapped happily. "Demi, open the folder to page five," she added.

My fingers felt numb as I turned the page and begged myself to not start hysterically crying. Page five had an image of one of the girls—Bradley's sister.

My heart broke as I glanced at him. His eyes were fastened on the image of his sister standing on a platform wearing nothing but a beige bra and matching panties.

Shoving the folder toward Dr. Davenport, I slid my hand into Bradley's shaking hand under the table.

Gripping it tightly, he squeezed my hand back.

"She's definitely a favorite girl," Dr. Ivory quipped. "Her bones are flawless. No signs of deterioration. Completely submissive after intensive white-therapy, and as you can see here," he pointed to another page in a separate binder, "she's a confirmed virgin."

Dr. Davenport let out a sound of excitement that left me disgusted, and Bradley dropped his head lower.

"Now, this is my wife's expertise. You can select from the various hair styles shown on page thirty. We'll secure it onto your item, and we have a one hundred percent guarantee that their hair will grow back in, which we will style to your liking, free of charge. She'll be brand-new, just for you."

"I can't believe after five years on your waitlist... it's finally my turn. I've been waiting for her. I can't wait to..." He and Ian Ivory exchanged a nauseating look with a wicked laugh.

"Well, you do remember the wedding night must take place in the holy room. This is our way of coping with letting one of our beautiful birds fly free." Ian cleared his throat.

"Of course. I've heard nothing but incredible things about your wedding ceremonies and... memorable wedding nights." Dr. Davenport continued to flip through the pages.

Squinting, I could see one of the pages. Images of green eyes were lined up from light to dark.

"I think she'd look better with the forest-green shade, don't you think?" Dr. Davenport looked at Mrs. Ivory, who was scribbling notes down excitedly in a pink leather journal.

"Absolutely! She's got the perfect porcelain face and that shade will truly pop." The rest of the conversation began to blur, and all I could hear were the hairstyles Becca happily explained, preferences on wedding gowns, and music choices.

"Now, my favorite part." Dr. Ivory lifted a cream-colored binder that stood out against the white ones.

"Bridal lingerie." He licked his index finger and began flipping through the pages. "Here. Mmm... this is my absolute favorite." He shuddered and turned the binder toward Dr. Davenport.

"Oh, now that is simply delectable. Yes, I want my product in that."

"Now, now, Mason. Don't forget once she's designed for you, she's no longer your product but rather your beautiful blushing bride."

"What do you think, Bradley?" Dr. Ivory asked. "Bradley?" This time, anger laced his tone.

"Yes, sir?" Bradley looked at him with defeated eyes.

"Do you think product number five will look good

in this for the wedding night?" He sneered, and I swore it took every ounce of willpower not to jump across the table and gauge his fucking green eyes out. "Look at it, Bradley. Look at the outfit and tell us exactly your thoughts." Dr. Ivory knew what he was doing. He was torturing that innocent young woman's brother.

The binder slid over toward us, and I looked at the image.

A black lace outfit, combined with a dog collar-looking choker and leash was on the page, and the page beside it contained a white lace outfit with the same dog collar and leash. Suddenly it all started to piece together. The 'white-therapy' had to be some distorted way to make these women submissive? But how?

This wasn't some kind of rehabilitation; this was molding women to be subservient wives for these disturbed men.

"Bradley, answer me!" Dr. Ivory roared and I flung back into my seat.

"It's a great selection, sir." Bradley sounded like he was obstructing on his own voice.

"You'll have a front row seat to the holy room cele-bration," Dr. Ivory added before laughing and slapping Dr. Davenport's back.

I looked over at Conrad, who was sitting there like

a statue, completely unphased by what was happening. How could he allow this to happen? He didn't live here full-time, but this was his home he flocked to for holidays and summer breaks from medical school. Granted, he'd been here for as long as I had. Was he really in school?

"Okay, everyone, we have a wedding to prepare for. Tomorrow will be here before we know it."

"Tomorrow?" I spat out loudly.

Everyone turned toward me, including Conrad.

"Dr. Davenport leaves for California in two days, and he needs his wife to be with him." Mrs. Ivory's jaw ticked as she looked at me.

"Okay." I nodded and avoided her gaze. That meant Bradley's sister would be leaving here. What was his plan? Would he try to escape? Would he try to save her?

But then I recalled what he had said to her. He said he tried everything.

There was no way out of here. We all had a one-way ticket to hell, and I was starting to realize that the ones who would eventually leave were just going into a different side of it.

CHAPTER
THIRTY-THREE

BRADLEY and I walked back to our wing in silence. I had a multitude of things I wanted to say to him—millions of questions to ask him, comforting statements to say to him—but I took one look at him and knew that the best thing I could do was be silent and let him process the horrors he was faced with just moments ago.

We got back to my room and the door slid open. Bradley kept his eyes on the floor as I walked inside. "Bradley, will you come inside for a minute?" I asked quietly.

He didn't answer but took two steps forward as the door slid shut behind him.

His eyes lifted, and I could see the tinges of red from what had to be him doing everything in his power to not breakdown.

"What's her name?" I asked and put my palms out in between us.

Placing his hands into mine, he replied. "Daisy."

"Daisy... that's so pretty." I offered a small smile as he sighed and held my hands. "How can we save her?"

His Adam's apple bobbed. "Demi, I've been here for years, ever since Daisy was sold." He closed his eyes. "They hired me knowing I'd never leave because they told me if I tried anything, they'd slaughter her in front of my eyes. So, I stayed; I watched her suffer, I watched them torture her. But I also watched her breathe and knew she had a heartbeat."

"Who sold her?"

"My mom sold her to a man named Trent Smith. We're originally from Tennessee, and he's the largest trafficker in the state."

Trent... Smith?

"How... how is that possible?"

Bradley's forehead creased as his eyes drooped slightly. "Demi... none of this was a coincidence. Trent Smith works for Ian Ivory. Just like a butcher has an animal-supplier; Ian Ivory has a supplier for trafficked women."

Backing away from Bradley, I began to pant with my chest constricting. "No..." I shook my head with tears running down my cheeks. "I saw the ad, the listing. I applied for this job. Raina..." I paused, thinking about how Raina just so happened to be driving exactly where I was.

"Raina dropped that paper off to your motel room in hopes that'd make the process easier for you. Raina was paid to follow you and pick you up. Raina is basically the Ivory's adoptive daughter, and her husband Jax once worked here."

"How'd they escape? How did they manage to not tell anyone about what's happening here?"

"Demi, you just don't get it." Bradley rubbed his forehead as if it were aching. "It's not white-therapy; it's white-torture. We all went through it. You're the first they haven't done it to in years. For two years, we all lived in those sound-proof rooms, eating nothing but plain white food. No sounds, no color, no stimulation. It stripped us of emotion. It made us completely submissive and devoted to this family."

"But you don't seem submissive. You seem like you're just pretending so you could be here for Daisy?"

"I can't imagine leaving this place. I'm messed up, Demi. I wanted to help Daisy escape, but thought I'd probably stay here and work for the family. Because if they caught me, they'd put me back into a cage. No one speaks to you, you hear no noise, no sounds, you see no color or anything. They shave your head and put you in all-white. You stare at four white walls all day and eat white food so your senses are depleted."

Fear churned inside of me as my legs trembled and I forced myself to sit down. "Why do they do this?"

"Because they need staff. Loyal staff who will help them with their business. They sell these women as mail-order brides essentially, and their wait list is filled with the world's richest men. Each woman is guaranteed to be completely obedient, subservient, and designed to be exactly what that man wants. Each woman sells for one to three million dollars."

I couldn't believe my ears. This had to be some sick nightmare. I pinched my skin and flinched when my nails dug into my flesh hard enough for me to know this was reality.

"Trent… knows I'm here?" I began looking around the room wildly, terrified that the man who made me kill my sister was here waiting to kill me, too.

"Demi… you were sold to him. The reason they never hurt you was because you were always intended to come here. You were always intended to be a part of this family."

"I don't understand?" I placed my hand over my heart, praying it'd slow down.

"Trent has folders, too—binders full of the women he's bought from parents, kidnappers, and more. Conrad hand-selected you from a folder."

"Conrad?" I gasped.

"You've always been the favorite girl, just like Mrs.

Ivory once was. You were chosen to marry Conrad Ivory—just like Dr. Ivory's father bought Mrs. Ivory for him—and eventually, the two of you will continue this family legacy."

I sat on the edge of the bed, unsure of everything. "What?"

"You're going to be the next Mrs. Ivory."

"Conrad picked me out of a binder?" I repeated the statement to myself.

"Yeah. He liked that you weren't pale, while his father hated you for your skin color. He prefers..."

"Only white people?" I filled in, looking up at Bradley.

"Green eyes, blonde hair, and white skin is the Ivory family specialty. Dr. Ivory believes that it continues the legacy. If the girls have brown hair, they dye it. If they don't have green eyes, well..." Bradley pinched at his eye and tugged the small contact out, "then they change that, too."

"Conrad wanted you. He thought you were breathtaking, which... you are, Demi." Bradley stared at me and moved closer, sitting next to me on the bed.

"But he wanted a tanned-skin woman with blonde hair. He also didn't want you to have green eyes, so they don't make you wear the contacts... yet. But as soon as you become his wife and eventually take over this... business, they'll make you wear them." Bradley tucked the short hair behind my ear. "For what it's worth, I liked your black hair," he said sadly.

"I'm not going to marry Conrad." I furrowed my brows and looked into Bradley's eyes. One eye was a light brown, while the other had a green contact in.

"You have to, Demi. If you don't, they'll cage and torture you. They'll torture you so badly that you'll wish you were dead or had just married him."

"If they are so big about submissive wives, then why aren't they caging me? Why aren't they forcing me to withstand white-torture?"

"Because Conrad told them he'd never take over the business if they did that to you. He said you were already submissive enough. You do everything you're told; you haven't run away. Sure, you called the police, but that doesn't mean anything. The police—"

"Bradley! What are you doing in here?" Conrad's voice cut through the heavy conversation, stunning us both. Bradley jumped up and fastened his hands behind his back.

"Mr. Ivory," he bowed his head. They couldn't be more than a couple of years apart in age, yet Bradley was acting like Conrad was his boss.

But then again, wasn't he?

"Get out." Conrad's teeth gritted together as Bradley quickly moved out of my room. I looked at him once more before the door slid shut.

He tilted his head and looked at me with sheer sorrow.

"Did he touch you, Demi?" Conrad took Bradley's spot on the bed next to me. Instantly, I scooted back as I looked at the handsome man in front of me.

"Did you order me from a magazine to be your wife?"

Conrad looked like someone had slapped him across the face. "Demi… Bradley had no right, and he will be dealt with."

"No. You won't do anything to him!" I shouted and stood.

"Listen to me, Demi. I don't want my soon-to-be wife being a fucking whore. Did he touch you? Did he touch what's *mine*?" Conrad's eyes dropped below my waist as he shot up and grabbed my arm. I tried to wriggle out of his grip, disgusted that this man was even breathing the same air as me.

"He didn't do anything, and I'm not yours, you psycho." I tried to shove him off me, to no avail, and I bumped into the small vanity. Conrad gripped my wrists tightly between his hands and flung me onto the bed.

"If I don't see blood, I'll know you're a disgusting slut and ruined. If I don't see blood, you'll never become my wife; instead, I'll make sure you rot in the cages until you die, and then I'll give my father your bones for decoration."

I began pushing my feet against the bed, trying to sit up, but Conrad moved even faster, hovering over me. He unzipped his pants and looked at me with evil in his fake-green eyes.

"Don't do this, Conrad," I whimpered as he pressed his legs against mine, pinning me down.

"You know what… you're right. It shouldn't be this way. I'll have you prove yourself to me in front of your dear friend Bradley, in the holy room on the night of our nuptials. I think we will be pressing pause on Dr. Davenport's wedding; instead, tomorrow… you and I are going to be wed." Moving off me, Conrad adjusted himself and smiled.

"I can't wait for you to be my bride, Demi. And just to make sure you understand how this will go… well, if you don't smile on your way down the aisle to me and marry me tomorrow, I'll make sure Bradley and Daisy are tortured and murdered in front of you. I'll make sure that your next meal is the meat from their bones." Blowing an air kiss, he abruptly left the room, leaving me to crash my face into the pillow and sob hysterically. Nausea rose inside my body as I gagged and cried loudly.

Trent Smith was the man my parents sold Layla and

me to for money they desperately needed for the survival to dig their way out of poverty. They didn't care about their two daughters, who were nothing more than burdens to them. They didn't care about the abuse or repercussions. I closed my eyes and saw Layla's crushed face. I could hear her wheezing, holding on to every last breath as her teeth cut through her bottom lip. I cried as I pictured myself violently stabbing her to make sure she was dead and freed from the pain Trent and our parents had succumbed her to. Her limbs were tangled and broken... her body wasn't hers. Sometimes setting someone else free means imprisoning yourself, and that's exactly what I had to do.

And now, I was going to marry Conrad Ivory. And I'd do whatever he wanted me to in order to protect Bradley and Daisy. Even if it meant I was going to be a caged girl in a different way.

CHAPTER THIRTY-FOUR

THE NEXT MORNING, I defiantly slammed the alarm clock countless times, but it wouldn't stop. The agitating buzzing kept sounding as if it were taunting me that this was not my apartment where I could do as I pleased. This wasn't some job I could feign an illness and call in sick. No, if I didn't obey and abide by their rules, then this was a death sentence.

I was hoping Conrad was simply agitated, jealous even, that Bradley was in my room alone with me. There's no way he'd marry me today. I almost laughed at the idea of it all until a moment later, the bedroom door slid open.

"Demi! What are you doing in bed still?" Becca stormed into my room, wearing a stunning short white dress with white tights and the same cushioned platform shoes. Her blonde hair was in ringlet curls, and her big, green eyes popped against the makeup she had layered on.

Why's she so dressed up? Swallowing the lump in my throat, I pushed upward in bed. "I'm not feeling well. I don't know how I'm supposed to work today." I forced myself to cough into my clenched fist and sniffled.

"Oh well, good news for you... you don't have to work! Honestly, I don't think you'll have the same job anymore now that you're going to be the next Mrs. Ivory!" Becca wiggled her fingers excitedly.

My breathing hitched as I realized the magnitude of it all. Conrad wasn't joking around; he was going to force me to marry him. *Today.*

"I think there has been some major misunderstanding. I need to talk to Mrs. Ivory." I tossed the blankets from my body and quickly ran into the bathroom as my stomach flipped. Gripping the bathroom sink, I dry heaved as my body broke into a cold sweat.

No, no, no... I cannot marry him. I will not marry him. You can't be forced into marriage.

"Darling Demi..." His voice sent chills up my spine as my name left his lips, and when I looked up into the mirror, I saw his reflection behind mine. Freezing, I didn't want to turn around.

"Come with me, dearest little bird," he cooed with his hands stretched out toward me. Turning around as slowly as I could, I looked into Dr. Ivory's eyes.

"Please?" He nodded at his palms. My body was covered in chills as I swallowed and he squinted at me.

Placing my hands into his, I flinched as he closed his bony, cold fingers around mine. Guiding me to the bed, I swore my heart stopped in fear as flashbacks of this man hovering over my body in the middle of the night battered my mind.

"I've convinced Conrad to give you more time before your nuptials."

Lifting my eyes to Dr. Ivory, I couldn't believe this was the person helping me—and I knew better than to trust him. "Really?"

"Yes. You still have to get acclimated to our family, and it must be terrifying to think you're going to marry someone you haven't even gone on a date with yet. So today, my sweet girl, you and Conrad will be spending the day together in the gardens, having a picnic and planting your own peony bush. Planting a peony bush in our gardens is a tradition for each to-be-wed couple in the Ivory family. We've done it for generations." Dr. Ivory sat at the edge of my bed and tugged me onto his lap.

"I'll sit beside you?" I didn't know why the statement came out as a question, but it was the most awkward feeling sitting on a man's lap when he was clearly sexually aroused while discussing my marriage to his son.

"No, you'll sit right here where you belong... on me," he breathed into my ear from behind. He raked his fingers across my spine as if he were counting each vertebrae.

"I'd like to share why peonies are so very treasured in this family. Did you know there was once this gorgeous nymph named Paeonia? She was mesmerizing and consumed Apollo, the son of Zeus. Aphrodite, the goddess of beauty, grew jealous of Paeonia and turned her into a peony flower." Dr. Ivory paused as I tried to interpret the meaning behind the Greek mythology story he was telling me.

"I always thought that the story was flawed. I can guarantee you, Demi, it wasn't Aphrodite who turned Paeonia into a flower. It must have been Zeus. He wanted the woman who was meant for his son, and if he couldn't have her, then no one should. But you see, sweet little bird, I'm not a monster. I want my son to have you, taste you, feel you... enjoy every single part of you."

It felt as if all the blood in my body had drained. I was sitting on Dr. Ivory's lap, facing away from him with my back against his chest. Pulling me in closer, he bit at my earlobe before licking it.

"No!" I tried to jump off, but he tightened his grip around my waist and tossed me onto the bed, pinning me down with my wrists above my head.

"Conrad will taste you first, because I'm an amazing, selfless father, but I can promise you... if you don't willingly let me have my turn, I'll turn you into a beautiful flower myself and put you in my garden where I can admire you all to myself." He licked my entire neck before shoving his tongue into my mouth, kissing me as I cried out in protest.

"Mmm... delicious," he groaned as he pushed off me. I scrambled up my bed to the pillows and hugged my knees to my chest.

"I can't handle your beauty, Demi. You know, I always assumed I enjoyed a certain type of woman. But it's true, my Conrad has excellent taste. I love the way your sultry brown eyes look at me. I love how I know you want me just as badly as I want you. I love how I know you're untouched, and you're a tight little virgin, dying to be pleasured." Peeling his scrub bottoms off, I cried softly as fear, panic, and terror muddled inside of me.

"No. Please, no," I whimpered. Looking around my room, there was no escape. I couldn't even open the door myself.

He pulled his briefs off and I slammed my eyes shut, whispering to myself that I was going to be okay. But I didn't believe an ounce of what I was saying; I wasn't going to be okay when this man forced himself on me.

"Demi, open your eyes. If you don't open them... Bradley will die," he warned.

Flinging my eyes open, I knew better than to gamble with this devil. His hand was around his hardened penis, and he smiled with satisfaction as he began to stroke himself. "Demi, yes... Oh fuck, you're so tight, gorgeous," he moaned out, staring into my eyes while he pumped faster.

Stomach acid rose in my mouth as I cried harder and began to shut my eyes again. "Close them and he dies," he grunted as he licked his palm and continued pleasuring himself. Prying my eyes open, I swallowed the burning acid in my mouth as it scalded my throat.

Ian Ivory turned around and opened my dresser drawer. Peeling a pair of my panties out, he walked closer to me, and said, "Hold them with two hands."

"Please, no." My voice trembled as I begged for him to stop. I prayed the tears flowing from my eyes would blur my vision completely.

"If you care for Bradley, you'll do as you're told, Demi. Do not play with fire because you will only get burned." Ian forcefully opened my hands as I made a face of disgust at the feel of his clammy fingers against my skin.

Holding my panties in my palms, he began stroking himself again until he closed his eyes and yelled my name in pleasure. His semen soaked my panties that were in my shaking hands as I sobbed harder.

Once he was done, he looked at me and grabbed the underwear. "Now, open your mouth," he hissed.

I couldn't stop sobbing, and as soon as my lips parted, he shoved the dampened panties into my mouth. The saltiness of his semen caused me to immediately gag as he pushed them farther in.

I began choking, unable to breathe with my nasal passages completely clogged and my mouth stuffed with the dirtied underwear. Bile rose in my mouth, and I turned away toward the floor and spat the panties and a mouthful of vomit out.

Ian laughed wickedly behind me. "Clean that mess up, Demi. Don't make my home filthy." I didn't hear him leave, I didn't hear the door open or close, but after a few grueling minutes, I wiped at my mouth and looked over.

He was gone.

I forced myself out of the bed and ran into the bathroom. Grabbing the mouthwash, I filled the cup and swallowed half of it. I wanted to clean my mouth, my throat, and every single part of me he had touched. Brushing my teeth rigorously, I climbed into the shower and waited for the water to steam before sinking down and crying while I scrubbed my body.

But no amount of stinging mint mouthwash or soap

could make me feel clean after that. My skin was raw as I shoved my finger down my throat forcing myself to vomit.

"Demi?" Becca called out and opened the shower curtain.

Slapping my arms around my breasts and drawing my knees up, I screamed, "Becca! Get the hell out!"

"Demi... calm down. I can't leave without you. I have to get you ready for your date. Conrad is waiting." She had changed out of the formal dress back into her usual white suit.

"Please hurry. They don't like to be kept waiting." This time, she didn't say it with her usual quirkiness or joy. This time she was hoping I'd do as she asked so there wouldn't be further repercussions.

"I can't do this." I cried and pushed myself up. Quickly rinsing my body off, I grabbed a towel and wrapped it around myself.

"Please, Demi. They'll hurt me if you don't."

Tears trickled down my face as my eyes burned the same way my throat did. I had no choice. Everything I did would impact someone else. I was numb. Completely numb.

Sinking down into the small stool, Becca opened her large makeup tote and hurriedly began working on my face. I didn't feel the feathering of her brushes against my skin, I didn't feel the irritation against my eyes as she lined them with eye makeup. I didn't feel her blow dry and brush my blonde hair. I didn't feel anything anymore.

Perhaps, I never had.

Perhaps, I never was meant to feel in this lifetime.

Spinning me around, she handed me a tube of lipstick. "It's best when you apply it yourself." She tilted her head with a semi-smile.

Rolling the tube up, I stared at the nude lip color and lathered it over my lips. I didn't want to look at myself. I didn't care to.

"This white sundress will be perfect for today." Becca pointed at the outfit she must have laid out while I showered.

I changed into it, then followed Becca out. The doors opened and sunlight immediately hit my skin, but it didn't feel warm and reassuring. It was just light reflecting against my skin.

"There's your prince charming." Becca clapped happily as she looked in the direction of Conrad, who was seated at a beautifully decorated table for two in the middle of the garden. But I didn't notice anything about him; instead, I noticed Bradley, who stood by his cart with food and drinks lining it.

They were making him serve us.

My heart ached as I walked toward the table and Conrad jumped up to pull the chair out for me.

"You are a vision, Demi," he said as if he had not just threatened me the night before. "I was distraught that my father pushed our wedding back another month, but I suppose we have a lot of things to do in order to have the most beautiful wedding."

"Bradley pour my bride her wine," Conrad barked at him.

"Did you know this wine is freshly crafted with ingredients from our family vineyard in Napa, and our peonies are also blended into it?" Conrad lifted the glass to his lips as Bradley hesitated before pouring the blush-pink liquid into my glass.

"Drink it," Conrad demanded as my eyes locked onto Bradley's.

Taking a sip, I let the smooth liquid numb my mouth. I didn't care if it was poisoned… I actually hoped it was.

Chugging the entire glass, Conrad smiled proudly. "Delicious, right?"

I nodded. It was the first time I'd ever had alcohol, so I pretended the bitter taste didn't burn my throat. Or that I knew in a few minutes I'd probably be buzzed. Hell, I hoped it'd make me forget this entire day.

Bradley stood with his arms behind his back as we ate our meal, and Conrad talked about his dreams and ambitions. He rambled about his hobbies and his friends back at school he was excited to connect with when he was back at school.

"Am I going to be moving with you?" I asked curiously.

"Mother and Father want you to stay here if we conceive on our wedding night. They'd be able to provide you and our baby with the best care as I finish my medical training, sweetheart. We have exactly two months to conceive. I don't doubt that I'll be able to impregnate you on our wedding night or during our honeymoon. I'll visit you every weekend and then, we will eventually take over the family business together."

"Why do you need to become a doctor if you have this business?" I chose to pretend I didn't hear a word about pregnancy and babies. I chose to pretend that he didn't say those words to me. I knew my mind wouldn't be able to handle the thought of carrying a child from this family and being bound to them forever.

"Because there will always be weak girls who need to be... well, put down. But, my love, we don't waste our merchandise. The weak ones are perfect for well, fertilizing our soil or home décor. These peonies bloom from soil that is..." Conrad's tone had shifted completely. "Pour my bride another glass, Bradley."

. . .

"I don't think she should—" Bradley began.

"I hope a bastard like you doesn't actually think he has any say in what my soon-to-be wife does? Pour the glass or I'll smash your face with it," Conrad shouted violently.

"I don't want one." I looked at Conrad as Bradley poured a small amount into the glass.

"You will drink it, then you'll come with me so I can show you something…" he snarled. Grabbing my hand in his, we walked toward the peony garden—the same garden I knew, without a doubt, I saw a young woman's dead body bleed out in.

When we got to the garden, the swing was there, repainted in a fresh coat of white paint. I could see Misha's body bleeding out with her body crumbled on the swing. But when I looked at the swing today, it wasn't Misha's face I saw… it was my sister's. Stumbling back, Conrad constricted his grip on my hand.

"What is it my love?" He rubbed his thumb against the back of my hand as I stayed silent. "Bradley! Bring the plant!" he shouted again.

Bradley appeared, holding a small plant with tiny, closed buds and a bag of what I assumed were gardening tools.

"It's time for our Ivory family tradition."

What did he mean by putting the weak girls down?

What did he mean by using their merchandise to fertilize the soil?

Bradley laid a small blanket down by the gorgeous blush-pink peonies. The heavenly scent of sweet citrus floated around us, and it felt like such a paradox to the darkest place in the world.

"Here, dig a hole for us, will you?" Conrad handed me a small shovel. I so badly wanted to bash his face in with the shovel, but this was survival. What would I do? Kill Conrad in front of Bradley, then sprint out of a house that every single door stayed locked in? What kind of torture would Ian Ivory put me through if I did something to his precious and only son?

I sat on the blanket and began to dig, brushing at the soft dirt with my freehand. "These are the peonies you just drank the wine from, beautiful," Conrad said proudly as I continued to dig. He took the small plant out of the wrapping and suddenly, my shovel hit something.

Jamming the metal into the dirt again, I assumed it was a root, or maybe a clump of dirt that had grown cold and hard?

Brushing away the loose top layer, I let out the loudest, sharpest scream I'd ever heard leave my lungs.

"Oh my God!" I pushed away on my heels, flinging the shovel away and crawling on all fours like a terrified animal.

"What is it?" Conrad asked without emotion. Bradley lifted me from the ground and held me in his arms as my body convulsed and my voice grew hoarse from the shrieks I couldn't stop.

"Demi, it's okay... Just breathe," he whispered against my hair, brushing my back.

I couldn't breathe, my ears were ringing from the echoes of my own voice, and my heart was pounding so hard I thought it'd crush through my chest walls.

"I... It was... Brad... I..." I fumbled through my words that made no sense.

"Oh, babe... it's just this. This is what made the wine you just consumed so very sweet." Conrad stood and held up a finger. A crushed, stabbed finger.

My head felt fuzzy, and suddenly, everything went black.

CHAPTER
THIRTY-FIVE

I DIDN'T WANT to open my eyes. I wanted to force myself to believe that I was dead. That I didn't exist in this demented world. Should I flip over into the pillow and suffocate myself? Could a human even do that? I could slit my wrists with my razor... but this house was the equivalent to a padded room.

"Demi," a soft voice caressed into the depths of my darkest thoughts. The dark thoughts felt more comforting than my reality.

"Demi..." he repeated. Slowly opening my eyes, I saw his face.

Bradley.

"Hey." He sighed and sunk into the small sliver of space between me and the edge of the bed.

I didn't know why looking at Bradley made me want to cry. Maybe it was because I couldn't believe this man was forced to work for the family who was abusing his sister. Or the fact that he was able to stay composed and loved her enough that he willingly spends his life trapped in hell just to see her.

"You have to clean Dr. Ivory's office today. He's losing his mind with how dirty it's been and has wanted to find someone to replace you, but they can't find—"

"Someone as stupid as me?"

"Come on, Demi." Bradley stood and pointed to the outfit he must have laid out for me.

"Conrad… he had a finger…" I began and felt my mouth grow dry at the thought.

"They're proceeding with the wedding ceremony, and Daisy is getting married tonight. We have to clean Dr. Ivory's office, and then set up the viewing room." Bradley turned away as I forced myself out of bed.

"Bradley, look at me," I whispered.

"Change your clothes and meet me in the hall. It's going to be a long day." The door slid open and he left.

But just as the door began to close, I could hear Bradley sniffle, biting back his tears.

———

Standing in Ian Ivory's office felt equivalent to standing in a morgue. It was cold and the air circulating was that of death. I hadn't been in it in a while, yet it looked spotless.

"They have a team of cleaning staff. You're not even the maid, Demi; they just wanted to test you…"

"What?" I looked at Bradley, who hadn't said anything on our walk over to the Ossis wing.

He shrugged as he wiped down the desk. "Just a way to get you into their house without throwing you into the back of a van. And you fell for it," he said spitefully. But I knew he wasn't trying to be hurtful. Hurt people, hurt people, and that's all he was doing. He was displacing his heartache on me.

And I was going to let him.

"Why do we have to clean, then?"

"Because they love watching you…" His eyes shot to the camera in the corner of the room.

Grabbing a dusting cloth, I walked over behind Dr. Ivory's desk. It was the most elaborate and intricately designed wall I had ever seen. I began wiping the textured, white pieces slowly. Growing closer, I ran my fingers across the grooves. I knew it was a wall of bones. I think I had known all along but forced to not believe it.

"This is made from all the caged girls that didn't obey, right?" I looked over my shoulder at Bradley, who had removed the trash from the bin in the corner of the space.

"I don't know," Bradley continued to clean.

"Okay." This wasn't the time to pry and push him. Tonight, he had to watch as his sister was forced to marrying some old psychotic man, and there was nothing any of us could do about it.

We cleaned and left the room. Heading down a long, winding hallway, I kept wracking my brain to think of something, *anything* to say to Bradley. But just as I thought that I could convince Bradley of some genius plan to escape, Mrs. Ivory appeared.

She was wearing a fitted white dress, paired with white gloves to her elbows, and when I studied her hair, my blood froze.

It was one of the wigs I had brushed. One of the wigs made from the girls trapped here.

"Demi! My love! It's your first family wedding tonight. I cannot believe Ian had you cleaning. *Foolish man.* Come with me; Becca has your outfit and everything. Conrad is simply thrilled to be attending the ceremony with you. Bradley, this one is so special to you, too. Go on and freshen up. We have plenty of people working to make it wonderful." Mrs. Ivory swatted Bradley away while she gripped my wrist tightly.

"No, wait. Bradley!" I called out and tried to wiggle out of her grasp, but she jerked me so hard that I cried out in pain.

. . .

"Stop being a silly whore, Demi." Mrs. Ivory's eyes filled with anger as she dug her nails into my tender flesh. "You're going to be my daughter-in-law. You're going to be my Conrad's wife. You better hope we see blood on your wedding night, or we'll make sure you do bleed," she seethed as splatters of her spit hit my mouth.

I didn't even check to see if Bradley had left or was still there. I looked down at Mrs. Ivory's fingernails that were deep in my wrist. She slowly moved her hand off mine, leaving tiny, crescent-like grooves behind.

"Shall we, my darling Demi?" Glancing up at Mrs. Ivory, fear grew inside me as she smiled, pretending like she didn't just say the most terrifying thing.

Was she referring to seeing blood to prove I was a virgin? But most of all, what did she mean by *we'll see blood*? Being forced to marry Conrad was one thing, but having to lose my virginity in front of his entire family...? No, this had to be a sick joke...

"Demi!" Becca's voice broke me out of the whirlwind of fear and consuming thoughts. I didn't even realize I had made my way with Mrs. Ivory to her room.

"Make her look beautiful. It's her first family

wedding, Becca dear." Mrs. Ivory pushed me toward Becca and immediately left.

"Oh, you're going to have the best time. I wish I could attend," Becca chirped as she shoved me into her salon chair.

I was emotionless, yet again; my mind and body felt divided. I wanted to run. A simple act that was completely unattainable in my situation. Even if I could run, there was nowhere to hide. I thought I was hiding here, tucked away from a group of men who profited by selling and abusing women. I thought I was hiding away from the man who essentially forced me to kill my sister. I was forced to put her out of her agonizing pain the same way a vet does to an animal.

But I was never in hiding, and they had found me. Trent and the Ivory family were interconnected. From Nashville to Charlotte, they were all working together.

"How are you enjoying your new hairstyle? I think it's so gorgeous on you, girl!" Becca was moving around me in circles, poking and pulling at my hair and face.

"Becca, you know they're forcing one of those girls... the caged girls, to get married, right? This isn't a wedding you'd want to attend. This isn't a wedding at all..."

Becca began layering makeup on my face with a

sponge, humming to herself while completely ignoring me.

"Becca!" I swatted her hand away from my face, catching a glimpse of myself in the mirror. The stress and fear were plastered all over.

"You know what your problem is, Demi?" Becca put her hands on her hips and looked at me with pursed lips. "You don't realize that when you're in a hole, it's already dark. It's already hard to breathe. No one can see you or help you. So why would you scream if you're never going to be heard?"

I sucked in a breath of air as Becca's otherwise optimistic demeanor shifted to one that made me feel all the more nervous.

I was nervous because she was speaking the truth. For once, she wasn't lying to herself or to me.

And that's the thing... the truth will always be more terrifying than a lie. Because the truth can't be altered, but a lie can.

CHAPTER
THIRTY-SIX

CONRAD WAS WAITING outside the room for me when the door opened. He was wearing a designer tuxedo, and although I didn't want to admit it, he looked extremely handsome—like the kind of handsome that made you forget what he was capable of.

"Demi, wow…" he breathed as I looked at the floor. Becca had left my hair in the sleek, simple bun but put a hefty amount of makeup on my face. I was wearing a fitted, short white dress, covered in tiny pearls.

I missed color. I never realized how much color my life had before it was stripped away, and I was living a life of blinding white and pain.

"Demi, sweetheart, listen… I'm so sorry about the garden. I'm so sorry about… I didn't mean to scare you, my love." Conrad came closer and I took a few steps backward. My back hit the wall and he caged me in with his arms.

"I know this is hard for you to believe, but your life as my wife is going to change significantly, and you're going to be living a life of luxury. We're going to be a family." Conrad leaned in and kissed my neck. I immediately turned my head the other way, praying I wouldn't breathe in his air.

"Baby, we're going to be married soon, and I cannot wait to have you. All of you…" he whispered into my ear before biting my earlobe. I let out a small whimper, slamming my eyes shut while reliving his father doing the exact same thing to me.

A voice cleared behind Conrad, forcing him off me.

"Of course, it'd be irritating Bradley," Conrad said with exasperation.

"Dr. and Mrs. Ivory asked for me to retrieve you both." His eyes lingered on me an extra moment, doing a quick sweep. When I met his gaze, his eyes were full of defeat.

He looked even more handsome than Conrad, wearing a white tuxedo and his hair slightly messy across his forehead. It was losing the stark blonde shade it was when we first met, and I found myself wondering what his natural hair color was.

"I can't wait for you to be out of here." Conrad

looped his arm into mine and dragged me past Bradley.

Glancing over my shoulder, my chest tightened. *Bradley was leaving?*

Once we walked what felt like ten miles in the damn, sponge-like shoes, we entered a large space I'd never been to before. Tables lined the back of the room but at the front were two rows of pews. The room was decorated with creams, whites, and the only other color was a hint of blush-pink from the peony center-pieces. My stomach tumbled as I realized the peonies were being grown on what had to be a cemetery. The finger...? There had to be a body somewhere in the garden. Swallowing the stomach acid that began to inch its way into my esophagus and mouth, I focused on my breathing.

"Come, my love." Conrad tugged my hand to take a seat next to his parents. Dr. Ivory looked over at me and licked his lips while his eyes slowly studied my entire body. Hiding behind Conrad, I quickly sank down next to him, and Bradley took the seat beside me.

He had a front row seat to his sister's wedding. A wedding she didn't want; a wedding he couldn't stop.

The opposing two sets of pews began to fill with older men, who all smiled enthusiastically. I peered at them, noticing they all held binders and highlighters as they settled into their seats.

. . .

"Who are they?" I mumbled under my breath, directing the question to Bradley. But he didn't answer me. His eyes were fixed on the front of the space, where a small arch was covered in tiny fairy lights and tulle.

Conrad wrapped his arm around me and said into my ear, "They are our most elite buyers, sweetie."

Buyers? And just like that, soft music began to play, and one-by-one, bridesmaids wearing identical long white gowns began walking in with peony bouquets in their hands.

But they weren't just women; they were the caged girls. Their heads were completely shaved, their bodies frail, collarbones protruding and eyes desolate.

Mrs. Ivory gasped with pride as they lined up in front of the arch. The men in the pews were mumbling to one another, pointing at images in their binders. I squinted and leaned closer to Bradley, hoping to catch a glimpse.

It was the same binder the man Daisy would be marrying had.

Make, model, year. Hairstyles, eye colors, and every single other detail in order for these men to take these women and build their own bride. My hands shook as I watched them eye the girls hungrily.

The lights dimmed and the music shifted as an older man walked down the aisle. "Mason looks dapper, doesn't he?" Mrs. Ivory whispered with a smile. The man had to be in his sixties, and I knew with certainty that Daisy was no more than nineteen years old.

His wrinkled face beamed with joy as he nodded at Dr. Ivory and took his place under the arch.

A moment later, Dr. Ivory stood and walked to join him. He was wearing a strange white caftan over white slacks and a shawl over his shoulders with a religious symbol in gold.

He's going to officiate the wedding?

Mrs. Ivory leaned in and whispered, "Bradley, I don't know what's taking her so long. Go and retrieve her and walk her down the aisle. This must be the proudest moment of your life."

A wave of doom washed over me as I watched Bradley stand and leave. How could this be happening? Please, let Daisy have miraculously escaped. Please, please…

Time stood still as my eyes blurred and my palms grew moist. The anticipation of what was coming had a grip around my neck.

"Oh, my heavens…she's a vision!" Mrs. Ivory exclaimed. I turned in the pew and, in that moment, my heart shattered into a million pieces.

They say the only way to overcome pain is to feel it. But in this moment, I prayed that the pain I felt for Bradley and Daisy was enough for them to not endure it.

Daisy was wearing a fitted wedding gown. She wore a long blonde wig, that I knew Mason, her groom, had selected. Designing his perfect woman was part of the process, but she wasn't a woman. She was just a girl—an innocent life that would never get to truly live.

Bradley had his arm intertwined with his little sister's and walked so slow, it didn't even seem like they were moving. As soon as they reached the pews, Daisy's face changed. She looked over at us and smiled.

She smiled so big, I could have sworn she was actually happy. But I knew the truth. *Sometimes it's not the number of tears we shed that measure our pain… sometimes it's the number of smiles we forge.*

She looked back at her older brother and gave him a look of reassurance, but he saw right through it. As soon as they reached Mason and Dr. Ivory, Bradley clutched his sister's arm tighter.

"Who gives this woman to be married to this man?" Dr. Ivory boasted loudly. The girls, or bridesmaids, all shook slightly at his voice. And it occurred to me, this was the first time they were hearing noise. The first time they were seeing more than white walls. Each of them had smiles plastered onto their faces, but unlike Daisy, theirs weren't fake or forced. Theirs were genuine. In some sick way, this was freedom to them. This was a happy place and event.

"Who gives this woman to be married to this man?" Dr. Ivory repeated. Bradley looked down at his sister, his eyes tinged with red as one single tear rolled down his cheek, crushing my soul.

"Me. Her older brother." His voice cracked as he said the four simple words that had to have destroyed him.

Daisy gave him a quick hug before eagerly placing her hands into Mason's. If I didn't know the back story, I'd have assumed this was an actual love-based marriage. That this was one of those mega age-gap stories—maybe the girl had some daddy issues, or maybe he was filthy rich and she was a gold digger—but here, I knew. I knew this was the most disturbing, forced marriage in which Daisy was completely brain-washed to become submissive through torture and abuse.

Bradley turned and sat back down next to me, and the room grew even darker. The only light was now on Daisy and Mason as Dr. Ivory read some scriptures. Looking down at Bradley's hands, I saw them tremble.

It was the first time I saw him scared. *And it frightened me.*

Reaching over, I snuck my hand into his and squeezed. Another tear rolled down his face, and I wished so badly that I could wipe it away. But more than that, I wished I could wipe away the cause of the tears.

CHAPTER
THIRTY-SEVEN

THE WEDDING CEREMONY went by in a blur, and I didn't even hear a word. But then when Mason dipped Daisy down and smothered her in a sloppy kiss, a part of my heart shriveled up. I looked over at Bradley and his jaw clenched.

"Now, Daphne will be guiding you both lovebirds to the holy room, and the rest of us will shift to the viewing area to complete the marriage of Mr. Mason and Mrs. Daisy Davenport." Dr. Ivory nodded at his wife, who immediately stood and ushered the couple out of the area.

Bradley gripped my hand so tightly, I squirmed in pain.

"Come, sweetheart." Conrad stood and slid his hand into mine to guide me in the dark to a different room. Bradley stood and followed behind us.

. . .

Once in the other room, I wheezed audibly in shock. There was a glass wall and movie theater-style recliners. Daisy and Mason were in the adjoining room, and we could see them through the glass. This was the room you could see from Dr. Ivory's office. My heart began pounding against my chest as sweat grew in the crook of my neck.

There was now a large, king-sized bed covered in all white sheets, and in the middle of it laid a small white towel.

"What is this?" I wiggled out from Conrad's embrace and grabbed Mrs. Ivory's shoulder, forcing her to turn toward me. "What the fuck is this? How can you let this happen? You... you should feel for these girls!" I screeched. The other caged girls had all taken their seats, and behind them sat the group of men with their binders.

"How... how can you do this? How can you people be this sick? And forcing Bradley to watch this?" I cried out, waving my hands wildly.

But just as I turned to Conrad, he lifted his hand and slapped me so hard across my face, I fell to the ground, clutching my burning cheek. A moment later, his shiny black shoe slammed into my ribcage, knocking the wind out of my lungs. "Behave yourself, bitch," he growled angrily. I lifted my eyes and looked at the man I would be forced to marry.

"What the hell?" Conrad screamed as Bradley jerked him back and punched him in the face.

"Oh, my heavens!" Mrs. Ivory yelled as she attempted to tug Bradley off Conrad. Conrad's face was covered in blood, and Bradley didn't look like he intended on slowing down.

"Bradley!" I forced myself up and grabbed his arm, stumbling back with him.

Conrad stood with the help of his mother and spat out blood-tinged saliva. "Oh, you just wait... Mother, I have to speak with Mason for a moment. I have a wedding gift for him to use in the holy room," Conrad said spitefully, then left the room.

Bradley's face grew pale as he realized the magnitude of what he had done. Guilt panged me as he lifted my chin up. "Are you okay, Demi?" he choked out.

I began to cry. I didn't care that the room was full of people watching us as if we were on the trailer to a movie they were eager to watch.

"No, I'm not okay," I whispered.

"It's okay to not be okay," he murmured before Mrs. Ivory broke us apart.

"Bradley, you are so lucky Mason hired you as a part of the package. If not, I'd bury you alive in the peony garden myself for laying a hand on my beautiful Conrad," she threatened, then turned to me. "And you... I'm starting to think Ian was right. You may just need to be a caged girl after all. I believe Conrad may have chosen you as the favorite girl prematurely."

Thoughts of being a caged girl filled my mind and I panicked. "What? No..."

"Well then you better prove yourself to us."

The lights turned off completely, and I could see Dr. Ivory's outline appear. Bradley immediately backed away from me and sat down.

Where's Conrad?

I begrudgingly sat down as Dr. Ivory set up a camera in the center aisle. *He's going to record this entire thing?* Once he took his seat, the room fell completely silent. I dug my nails into the armrests. Bradley had his eyes secured to the ground, and I prayed that he would just fall asleep or maybe dissociate from this hell.

Suddenly, a small screeching noise had us all squinting through the darkness.

Was that...

Oh no.

A woman I'd never seen before appeared, wearing an old-school server outfit with red and white stripes and a hat to match. She was pushing a cart full of movie theater popcorn, boxed candy, and bottled soda.

No… this can't be happening.

"Here you are." She extended items to each person, which they excitedly took from her.

"Sir?" She tried to hand Bradley a tray.

"Bradley, take the tray. You don't want to make Daisy's last night here harder than Conrad's already making it," Dr. Ivory barked.

What does he mean, Conrad's making it?

Bradley handed me a tray of concessions, which made me think about my first-date fantasy I would have as a child. I used to dream about being a normal teenager, going on my first date at the movies. My date would buy me popcorn and a box of M&Ms, which were my absolute favorite. I had first tried them when Trent dropped a few on the carpet one day, and I reached under the closet we were forced to live in and gave one to Layla while eating the dirtied one for myself.

I always dreamt of that date, though I had never been on a date in my entire life—I never had the opportunity. The one where he'd wrap his arm around me, we'd steal flirtatious glances at one another, and then he'd lean in to kiss me. My very first kiss.

My stomach flipped thinking that Conrad was my first kiss, and how his father's lips had been on me. I suppose all along I was being saved for Conrad, so he stripped me from any chance of a real life. I cringed that this was my new life. A life I'd never escape from.

But then again, my parents were also to blame. They were the ones who sold us in the first place. They saw their two daughters as burdens, but they also saw us as a source of money.

They saw us as objects, just like these men and this sick family.

I took the tray and put it in my lap, and looked over at Bradley. "Bradley, just close your eyes and pretend we're at the real movies. I've never been. What's your favorite?" I whispered as low as I could while Mrs. Ivory was busy chatting with her husband.

Bradley looked over at me, and the pain he felt internally was displayed on his face.

"Titanic." He shrugged.

"Titanic?" I widened my eyes in shock by his response.

"Yea… we all know there was room on the raft for Jack, too." He forced a small grin, and I couldn't help but wince as tears streamed down my cheeks.

"Just so you know… Titanic was one of the only

movies I've ever seen. And there will always be room on the raft for Jack. When I find us a way out..." I swallowed the lump in my throat because I knew I was lying to him.

There wouldn't be room for Jack or Rose because there'd never be a way out. Not alive at least.

CHAPTER THIRTY-EIGHT

THE MOMENT BRADLEY and I tried to close our eyes and pretend the horror of what was about to happen in front of us wasn't real, dissipated quickly.

"Ladies and gentlemen, we'd like you to quiet down as we will begin our showing. As you know, a marriage is not valid until our couples consummate it in the holy room. Today we have a special addition to the showing, and our groom has agreed to it as well."

I could hear the shift in Bradley's breathing, and I knew he wanted to snap, he wanted to kill everyone in this room.

"Don't do anything..." I pleaded in a hushed tone. He shot me a look knowing if he did, they'd kill him.

Or worse, they'd kill her.

"Enjoy watching two become one, my dear friends and family. I'm thrilled that we have another graduate." Dr. Ivory beamed before taking his seat next to Mrs. Ivory.

I laced my hands together as Mason Davenport undressed and walked to the bed. Closing my eyes, I decided I wasn't going to watch.

"And as a friendly reminder, if you choose to close your eyes at any portion of this showing that is years in the making... well, you'll be punished accordingly," Dr. Ivory added as he scrolled through his phone.

Looking over, I saw his screen was full of tiny squares. He was watching us all. This room had to have cameras everywhere.

"Bradley, Daisy is already going to endure worse because of your indiscretions with Conrad, but if you choose to not watch... then Demi is next," Mrs. Ivory threatened.

He didn't move, he didn't make a sound. He just kept his eyes open, blankly staring forward. I could have sworn he hadn't blinked even once.

Daisy walked back into the room, and my palms felt clammy. She was wearing the black lace outfit with a dog collar on her neck. But what made me want to vomit was that Conrad was holding the leash. He jerked her so hard, her tongue flung out of her mouth as she gagged.

"Fuck this," Bradley rasped and stood.

I grabbed his leg and shook my head. "Don't.

They'll..." I didn't have to finish the sentence since he already knew they'd kill us both.

Sighing, he sat back down, and I saw Dr. Ivory type something rapidly on his phone.

"Phase out, think of the Titanic," I whispered.

But then I couldn't think of a movie, I couldn't think of anything. I saw Mason grab the dog leash and throw Daisy onto the bed. She carefully positioned herself on the towel, and my heart sunk.

Conrad stood in the corner of the room, watching them both. Mason took his briefs off and pressed her legs apart. My eyes were burning; I couldn't watch this. But I could also see the glare from Ian Ivory's phone in my peripheral, and I knew he was watching us.

Daisy's head was propped up against multiple pillows, and her eyes slammed shut as an expression of pain grew on her face. Bradley made a sound like his heart was shattering. Mason began moving faster, rougher, and I knew this had to be torture for Daisy. Speakers turned on and we could hear Mason's moans mix with Daisy's cries. She was actually crying out in pain. He grunted, holding both of her wrists above her head.

"My beautiful bride, you are so tight... Let me see

you bleed for me… Prove to me that I'm your first," he chanted as he clamped his teeth into her neck.

Seconds later, he yelled out in ecstasy, tossing his head back and erupting into laughter.

"Move, Mrs. Davenport." He tugged the towel from underneath her. Turning toward us, he lifted it up and showed us the blood-stained towel as if it were a trophy.

"Ian and Daphne, you make the greatest creations." He waved and moved away from the glass before grabbing his briefs and tugging them back on.

Daisy didn't say a word, but then again, who knew how long it had been since she had spoken or been spoken to.

Who knew if she could even speak at all?

I didn't dare look at Bradley; I was too much of a coward to do so. I stared down at the concessions, thinking of the irony.

There was a time in my life I'd have devoured every ounce of the food on this tray. But now, I didn't want to even touch the food in front of me. I was scared if I ate a piece of popcorn or an M&M, then I'd be reminded of this moment, tarnishing both items forever.

Having to kill my sister was something that ruined me, but this… seeing an innocent girl be raped in front of her older brother, wrecked me.

At least I was able to put my sibling out of her agony and pain.

Bradley had to watch her suffer and wither away, knowing she'd only endure more once she was forced to leave this place with her new husband.

I waited impatiently, wondering if we'd get to leave. I wanted to talk to Bradley, I wanted to give him a hug and tell him something that would make him forget what he just saw.

But this family knew no limits.

And now, Conrad was going to make sure it was his turn to make it known that no one could ever win against the Ivory family.

Leaning forward, the speakers continued to echo every movement and sound inside the room.

Conrad began unbuttoning his clothes, then he dramatically threw each piece of his tuxedo to the ground as he arrogantly made his way to the bed.

He couldn't possibly…

"Mason just married her." My heart was pounding. "Daphne. Ian!" It was the first time I had ever used their first names.

"Demi, hush your mouth." Ian shot me a glare, then turned to his wife. "I told you that she needed time in the cages!"

Daphne shot me a look of disdain as I sank into my

seat. I didn't care if Ian was watching, I grabbed Bradley's hand and held it as tightly as I could.

Conrad was naked and Daisy looked at him in complete fear.

Shaking her head, she opened her lips to speak but no words came out. It was as if she didn't know how to speak. She was like a dog who was trained that if she barked, she'd be shocked.

Conrad looked over his shoulder and paused. "Demi, baby... consider this a sneak preview for you. My loyalty is still with you, sweetheart. And Bradley, you might be holding my bride's hand in there, but I'm about to ruin Daisy." He sneered and moved forward on the bed.

Mason sat in the corner, dining on a meal I hadn't even known was brought in. Watching eagerly, he took a sip of his champagne.

I began to cough as stomach acid rose, and I couldn't take it. Grabbing the small popcorn container, I violently threw up inside it as Conrad pushed himself onto Daisy.

Her screams caused my ears to ring, and her pleading cries caused my insides to curl. The way her eyes widened as he slammed his body in and out of hers had the hairs on my neck stand and my body shook so hard as I threw up until nothing but bile burned on the way up.

"Please!" I choked and wiped the corners of my mouth as I looked to Ian and Daphne. They had slid headphones on and had grins painted across their faces.

"Bradley, let's go... Let's go..." I shook him, but he didn't move. His eyes were glazed, his face frozen.

Placing my finger on the inside of his wrist, I could barely feel his pulse.

"Bradley..." I cried.

"Put a muzzle on that bitch! We're trying to enjoy our show. We paid one hundred thousand dollars for this ticket," someone from the other side yelled at me.

"Demi, stop," Bradley whispered without moving.

Conrad ran his tongue across Daisy's face, then bit into her cheek. He pulled out and stroked himself until he ejaculated all over her.

Her cries would haunt me for the rest of my life. And suddenly, I realized...

I could no longer hear Layla's cries, just Daisy's. But there was no relief, because those tears and cries blurred together and hung over me the way a storm cloud does.

I'd forever drown in the rain of their pain.

CHAPTER THIRTY-NINE

CONRAD PUT his clothes back on, and Daisy laid in the bed, motionless. I was convinced she was dead. But then Daphne and Ian appeared through the glass with a new white gown for her and a shawl for Mason Davenport.

Daisy looked like a ragdoll—completely pale and lifeless—as Mrs. Ivory helped her into the dress. Whispering something into her ear, Daisy nodded at Mrs. Ivory and leaned in for a hug. She hugged Daphne Ivory as if the woman wasn't a part of the most traumatizing event of this girl's life. She held on to her and rested her face against Mrs. Ivory's shoulder.

"Demi, whatever you do, you have to promise me something," Bradley finally spoke and looked over at me.

"Anything, Bradley." I blew out a breath and batted away the tears that continued to build in my eyes.

"Never disobey them. You'll end up in the cages and then... you'll become this. You'll hug and thank the devil and his wife for the opportunity to be raped in front of an audience. You were chosen, handpicked. No matter what, you have to just... do whatever Conrad wants, and he'll treat you well. Okay, Dem?" His eyes glistened and the way he used a nickname for me, even in the worst moment of his life, made my heart constrict.

"Where are you going?"

"Mason hired me to be the new butler at his house. I'll get to be there for Daisy. I'll get to see her free."

"I wouldn't call this free, Bradley," I replied softly.

"Trust me, Demi. If you're in those cages... well, this is paradise compared to what that is like." Bradley closed his eyes for a moment before standing.

"I don't want you to leave. I won't be able to do this alone." My tone was unsteady as panic laced my words.

"I don't want to leave you, either. But after what I did to Conrad, well... let's just say I'd probably be dead if I hadn't signed a contract with the Davenports."

Bradley glanced back through the glass wall.

"Come on, they are going to start the reception soon. We'll be able to sneak away for a minute if we pretend we're going to get something from the kitchen. I have something for you. I'm leaving in the morning with Daisy... so this might be our last night, Demi."

I followed his line of vision, where we watched Mason and Daisy rest on their knees while Ian Ivory blessed them, sprinkling water on them as Mrs. Ivory and Conrad looked on proudly.

"I'm going to kill him," I muttered to Bradley as I stared at Conrad, who had a smug look on his face.

"Demi..." Bradley said with concern.

"I can't live like this forever. I can't be the next Mrs. Ivory." We began to walk through the dark room as the rest of the guests were bustling around and chatting over glasses of champagne. The caged girls were interacting with the men, but they weren't speaking; they were simply standing and having to allow these old, wealthy perverts admire them and caress their bodies.

They're choosing their brides.

"You are going to be the next Mrs. Ivory, and you're going to stay married to him forever. Because that's the safest thing for you to do." Bradley lifted his brow and paused in the middle of an empty hallway. "Promise me, Demi," he whispered, growing closer to me.

I knew he was right. I didn't want him to worry about me, so I nodded and crossed my fingers behind my back. "I pinky promise." I held my pinky up between us, and for the first time in a long time, Bradley's face broke into a small smile.

"Seriously?" he groaned but lifted his and intertwined it with mine. Letting go, we quickly walked down the hall and cut through the kitchen.

"Where are we going?" I picked up my pace to keep up with him.

"My room."

It never occurred to me that I had never been in Bradley's room. He'd always dropped me off at my room.

We walked to a completely different hallway, and Bradley scanned his card. Walking inside, I gasped. "Bradley, this is stunning. It's like an apartment. Wow." I spun around. It wasn't all-white; it was decorated in gray, blue, and black.

"Why did they give you such a gorgeous space? I mean, I live in an all-white shoebox compared to this."

"I've proven my loyalty to the family, Demi. They take care of their own." Bradley went to a closet and dug inside as a chill shot up my spine.

Bradley had to do anything and everything they asked of him in order to survive. Not only for himself, but they probably used Daisy as bait whenever he resisted their demands.

"I know you won't get to wear them until after the

wedding, and the only time they'll let you is when you go out—"

"Wait… I'll get to leave the house?"

"Demi, Conrad already has a honeymoon planned for you in St. Lucia. They'll let you wear color and bring anything you'd like. It's an Ivory family tradition. A honeymoon in St. Lucia, because they are convinced it…"

"It, what?"

"For generations, the Ivory newlyweds always go there and each time, the new wife comes back pregnant." Bradley averted his eyes from mine.

Taking a few steps back, I wrapped my arms around my abdomen. "No, Bradley…"

"They're going to remove your IUD this week. By the end of the month, you'll be married and the next day, he's going to take you to St. Lucia in hopes you'll conceive." Bradley stood in front of me. "So here are two gifts for you."

Handing over a beautifully wrapped blush box with an ivory-colored bow, I tried to process the absurdity of this entire situation. I set the gift on Bradley's table and began to open it. Layla had wrapped small hand-crafted items for me when we were children, but I'd never received an actual gift from anyone in my life.

As soon as I peeled the wrapping paper away, I broke into tears.

An orange box with a giant white Nike logo.

"Bradley…" I opened it and couldn't contain my emotion. This was too much. I was crying so hard that snot began to drip and intertwined with my sobs.

"Hey, hey… it's okay, Demi. It's just shoes. And, they actually make noise when you walk."

"No, Bradley… it's not just shoes." I placed the brand-new Air Jordans down. They were pink, black, and white, with a light pink Nike logo across.

"Thank you for being the reason I have even survived here. I don't know how I'm going to make it without you." I threw my arms around him and pulled him closer. His scent and the warmth of his body was soothing and comforting, and for the first time in this house, I felt safe.

"Bradley, I want you to do one more thing for me," I whispered against his ear as he held me in his strong arms.

"Anything, Dem." He sniffled against my hair.

I closed my eyes. "Take my virginity." It wasn't a sexually charged thought; it wasn't the right time or mental state. It was a shocking thing to say to any man, especially given what we had both endured in the evening alone.

Bradley's breathing shifted; he didn't say anything and for a moment, we both held on to each other. "I can't do that," he finally replied woefully.

My voice cracked as I parted my lips and felt embarrassed to have to plead for this. "Please, Bradley. Nothing in my life has been by choice. If I have to live this life, I don't want to know that monster was the one who took literally everything from me. Please don't let Conrad be the one to break the last piece of me. Please don't let an Ivory man be the one who gets every part of me."

"Dem, you don't understand. I can't do it because they have to see blood on the wedding night. They frame the damn towel, and the husband keeps it. Do you want to know what happens to the women who don't bleed?"

Bradley was still holding me, but I had tilted my head away from his chest to look into his eyes. I shook my head, too afraid to ask.

"They end up on Ian Ivory's office wall."

Sucking in a breath, I stumbled back as my lips parted in shock.

"That decorative wall behind his desk you've been dusting off are the bones of all the women who didn't bleed on their wedding night. The Ivory family loses so much money if that happens."

I think the entire time I pretended they weren't real bones. No, I lied to myself. But now, I couldn't breathe, my hands were shaking, and I wanted to throw up, even though there was nothing left to come up.

I had been cleaning, scrubbing, and dusting the damn wall. Dr. Ivory had made a trophy wall of... *bones from innocent women.*

"He's an orthopedic surgeon, well... was. He no longer performs actual surgeries that aren't for his amusement. He rips the bones out of their bodies and saves them. He crafts out of them."

"The peony garden..." I trailed.

Nodding, Bradley took a deep breath. "The peony garden is where they bury the bodies. They are convinced those women fertilize the soil and produce the most fragrant peonies. The perfume anyone wears in this house or the wine we are forced to drink all come mixed from the peonies that grow from the ground of death." He rubbed his hand over his face before filling the space between us again.

"Demi, this has been the way of the Ivory family for generations. I really hope you have a son first." He brushed my hair from my face before tracing my lips with his thumb.

"What happens if I had a daughter?" My voice shook as I looked into his eyes.

"Oh, Demi—"

"No, wait, don't tell me. I'm not going to get pregnant. I'll figure something out."

"Well, for three months, you won't have to." Bradley turned and grabbed a second wrapped present. It was a small, thin rectangular package. Slowly peeling the paper off, I slanted my eyes as I stared at the bright blue packet.

"What..." I pulled the paper out from it, revealing four rows of pills. "Oh..." I felt a wave of relief.

"I was only able to get a three-month supply. It should give you some time to deal with everything around you and being married to him before having to get pregnant. And I have a way for you to hide them."

Bradley picked my Nike shoes up and gripped the heel of one. Sliding it off, he revealed a divot he must have had cut in.

"Bradley..." My heart had never felt this kind of emotion for anyone.

"I'm going to cut myself on my inner thigh or even... inside myself for the holy room. I'll figure out a way to bleed for the wedding night. But Bradley, I need you to do this for me. I need you to take—"

But before I could finish my sentence, Bradley gripped my face between his palms and slammed his lips to mine. Kissing me in a sweet yet possessive way, my heart pounded as I held his arms.

Moving me toward his bed, he helped unzip my dress. "Are you sure, Demi?" he asked me as I shimmied out of my dress, suddenly feeling even more vulnerable in nothing but the lace lingerie that I was forced to wear.

"Yes. I've never been so sure about something in my life. And for the first time in my life, I'm getting to choose." Bradley nodded and unbuttoned his shirt before removing his pants. I could feel my cheeks warm as I looked at his muscular body. He had perfectly carved abs, his arms were strong and defined. I looked down as he came up to me and unhooked my bra.

My arms immediately shot up to cover my breasts. This wasn't how I pictured this moment to go. But given my other option of Conrad Ivory raping me in front of his parents and random people, this was a scene right out of a damn romance novel.

I awkwardly moved to his bed, sitting down and then adjusting myself so I'd be on his pillow. He crawled into bed with me, and I turned toward him.

"Bradley, will you take the contacts out?" I asked with slight awkwardness. His forehead creased as he curiously looked at me.

Sliding his finger into his eyes, he gently took his contacts out and revealed a beautiful shade of light brown.

"Is the blonde your real hair color?" I asked as he stared into my eyes.

"No, it's dark brown."

"Why do they make you do this? This blonde hair, green-eye obsession? Isn't Mrs. Ivory a brunette, too?"

"Yes, but they don't care. Ian is obsessive-compulsive with everything, and this is something that would kill him. He needs his home to be a specific way. He's obsessed with the idea of perfection. It is thought that green eyes are demonic. Evil, really. That the green-eyed demon is superior than the black-eyed demon. I mean witches, monsters, demons all possess green eyes historically. They are wicked."

I shook with chills. Ian Ivory wanted to live a wicked, demonic life. "I love your eyes." I immediately looked away.

"Demi, I love everything about you. I loved your curly black hair. I love the way you never listen and talk way too much. I love that... I love that even when you've seen nothing but horror, there's still hope inside those stunning brown eyes."

He moved closer and his warm, minty breath grazed my skin. "You're absolutely sure?" His fingers traced my abdomen, sending goosebumps everywhere.

I leaned in and kissed Bradley. His lips were so soft against mine, and everything around me blurred. I closed my eyes and didn't see the holy room, or Conrad attacking an innocent girl. For the first time in a long time, I just felt peace.

I didn't have the luxury of time. Bradley was

leaving in the morning, so this was it. He took my panties off, then his briefs. He kissed me back intimately before parting my legs.

"I'm going to put my finger inside you first," he said lowly, doing exactly what he had said.

I started to moan and make sounds I couldn't control as he rubbed my clitoris. *It feels so good.*

"Demi, we don't have much time before someone starts looking for us." Bradley began to kiss my neck. I knew he was feeling guilty that this was such an absurd request, simply because I didn't want my first time to be an act of violence.

Spreading my legs farther apart, I clutched Bradley's arms and pulled him closer as he slowly slid inside me.

Okay, now this didn't feel so good. Fuck, it hurt. He was going so slow as if he were terrified to break me.

Clenching my eyes shut, I held my breath.

"Just breathe, Dem," he whispered as I released the breath of air I was holding, and before I knew it, he was completely inside me. Slowly pushing in and out, he leaned in and kissed me, distracting me from the initial uncomfortable sensation before finally, it started to feel pleasurable.

This moment was the first time in my entire life that I was happy.

"You're so beautiful, Demi," he moaned into my

neck. "Are you okay? Do you want me to stop?"

"I've never been better, Bradley." I closed my eyes and memorized this feeling and this entire experience.

I dug my nails into his back as warmth washed over me and my toes curled. Letting out a small cry, my back arched as Bradley finished.

"Wow…" I breathed out as he collapsed beside me.

Immediately turning his head, he looked worried. "Are you okay?"

I bit my bottom lip, not able to conceal the laughter that escaped my lips. "You don't have to keep asking me that. I'm better than okay." I paused. "Bradley, thank you for giving me the most beautiful moment and now memory of my life."

His eyes glistened slightly. "I wish I could give you even more beautiful memories, Demi."

"I'm sorry you had to do this after everything that you just saw Daisy go through." I felt ashamed for being selfish and even asking this of Bradley.

"I didn't have to do anything, Demi. I wanted to. What you don't realize is that you, too, gave me the most beautiful memory of my life. A memory I'll now hold on to every time I feel like I can't wake up to another day in flames." Bradley kissed me once more. And the reason I knew it was our final kiss is because he closed his eyes and whispered against my lips, "One last memory I'll forever cherish."

CHAPTER FORTY

I SNUCK BACK into my room and hid my new sneakers and birth control packets at the bottom of my closet. Three months of protection. That's all the time I had to escape and seek help from someone, not just for myself but for the rest of the girls.

The door slid open behind me and I quickly shut the closet doors.

"Baby…" His voice sliced through my body like a million daggers.

I stood and felt my blood go cold.

"I didn't see you at the reception, but Mother told me I should let you be. What you had to withstand wasn't what you deserve. My love, I am so sorry." He moved toward me as I backed away from him.

"Don't touch me, Conrad." I put my hands up and looked at him with disgust.

"What did you just say?" Conrad's voice shifted and he stormed up to me, wrapping his hand around my throat and slamming my head into the cabinet.

"Conrad!" I choked out.

"You little disobedient brat! You're mine to touch anytime I'd like. And you know what… I think I'm sick and tired of waiting." He took his second hand and shoved it into my panties.

"No…" I forced out as he rammed his finger inside me.

His grip tightened around my neck as I gagged harder. "Con—" I gasped for air that wasn't there.

"Conrad!" Mrs. Ivory's voice echoed behind us. Releasing his hands, I hunched over and wheezed loudly while rubbing my neck.

"Oh, my goodness, I don't know what has gotten into you. Go to your room. This is no way to treat your bride." She forced him out of the bedroom and shut the door behind him.

"Demi, my darling daughter-in-law." She enhanced her Southern drawl for dramatic effect. "Stand up, sweetheart. I've brought you something." She helped me up and handed me a gift bag.

What was this, my birthday?

I hugged myself and gulped down the air around me as I wheezed. "Come on, don't be rude. Open it, now." Mrs. Ivory demanded. My eyes felt like they were going to roll in the back of my head as I tried to steady myself.

Setting the bag down, I ripped the white tissue paper out and pulled out the contents. It was an all-white lingerie set with a dog collar and leash.

"It's what Conrad picked for your wedding night," Daphne said excitedly.

I wanted to die. I used to always think that I'd never be the girl who wanted to die after watching my sister perish. I knew how much she wanted me to live; she wanted me to live, even if it wasn't a life worth living.

"The wedding is in a week. As you can tell, Conrad is more than ready to be your husband and a father. Afterward, you will both go to St. Lucia. Don't even try anything, Demi. Because if you do, I'll make sure you watch us skin Bradley alive." Mrs. Ivory's lips curved in a menacing smile.

That's it. They had something on me, just like Trent did. He always used me as a chip to get whatever he wanted with Layla. That's what happened when you loved someone or cared about them... they became your weakness.

Bradley was my weakness. I truly cared about him and maybe, just maybe, in some twisted way, I loved him, too.

Mrs. Ivory forced me to drink the peony-infused

tea. I gagged on each sip knowing what the flowers bloomed from. *Death.* I fell asleep shortly after. Flashes of Daisy's pained face kept appearing in my dreams, and her screams echoed in the silence of my bedroom. Was that what my fate had?

———

Unfortunately, I woke up the next day. Daisy, Mason, and Bradley were in the formal living area with the Ivory family exchanging pleasantries.

I'd never felt more fear in my entire life knowing that the only person in this place on my side was leaving me. I was forced to wear a short white dress and let Becca do my hair and makeup for their departure. I was also required to look presentable for my soon-to-be husband, according to Mrs. Ivory. She told me that her son deserved a woman who cared about the way she looked.

"I'd like to work today," I said softly as I walked beside Daphne.

"Why?" she fired back.

"Bradley's leaving. Who will bring the girls food?" I answered without showing much emotion.

"We've already hired someone else to fill in both of your positions. Your only job is to make and keep my son happy, and then give us a grandson." She cocked her head to the side.

"Yes, ma'am," I replied flatly and followed her into the room.

Bradley was sitting next to his sister, but he immediately stood when I entered the room. His contact lenses were back in, and his hair had been bleached blonde again.

Conrad looked between us and stood, coming toward me, causing me to flinch.

"I can't wait for the bastard to be gone." He blew his hot, muggy breath into my ear.

Squinting at him, I kept my lips together and sat down.

Daisy looked beautiful as she was permitted to wear a touch of color. She had her blonde wig on and wore a soft yellow dress with nude pumps.

Dr. Ivory followed my line of vision. "She graduated from the program with flying colors." He mocked with a laugh, and Mason Davenport laughed with him proudly.

"She'll start speaking in a week, if you want her to. And of course, if there are any problems with your purchase, we uphold the Ivory family sixty-day guarantee." Dr. Ivory handed Mason something that looked like a receipt.

But then a pit in my stomach grew and I knew, it didn't look like a receipt. It *was* one.

"I don't foresee any issues with this custom-designed bride. Ian, Daphne, thank you both for providing this brilliant service." Mason stood and buttoned his suit jacket.

"And you, my dear, are one lucky girl to be next in line for this empire." He let his eyes graze over my entire body, which caused nausea to pool in my stomach.

"Can you believe I chose her?" Conrad sighed before looping his arm into mine.

"An Ivory man always knows what he wants," Mason snarled.

"That is true, my friend. And Demi had always been the favorite girl." Dr. Ivory came up behind me, letting his hand brush against my ass before patting my back.

Bradley's fist clenched as his jaw ticked. I shook my head slightly in hopes he'd see me, praying that he'd keep his emotions in check. The way he was looking at me shattered my strength because I knew his was barely there.

Conrad and Ian made their way to have a private conversation with Dr. Davenport, leaving Daisy standing like a statue next to her brother. I hadn't seen her make eye contact with him even once.

I didn't blame her or him. How can you look your sibling in the eyes after they've been brutally raped? How can you look at your sister, knowing a thin piece of glass separated you from possibly protecting her? How can you look at your older brother, knowing he watched you be victimized and wasn't able to save you?

How can we all continue to live like this? What did any of us do to deserve being trapped in a nightmare come true?

"Daisy, I'm so sorry." I looked into her icy eyes. She was so pale that her skin was almost translucent—the result of not seeing sunlight for god knows how long. The result of being caged in an all-white, colorless, soundless room.

Daisy tilted her head and stared at me. She parted her thin, pale-pink lips and then…

She smiled at me.

"Daisy is happy," she rasped.

Bradley's eyes widened in shock as he looked at her. "Daisy…" He reached out to touch her arm, but Conrad prevented him from doing so.

"You know no bounds with another man's wife, do you?" He swatted Bradley's hand away.

Daisy threw her arms around Conrad and hugged him tightly. Bradley's brows knitted together as he looked at the shocking interaction. A sinister and satisfied grin grew on Conrad's face as he patted her like a compliant dog.

"Bradley," I began, but immediately stopped when Conrad looked at me with fury.

"Don't worry, sweetheart. Bradley's been invited back to our nuptials, and he'll have another front row seat in watching us in the holy room."

"No." I shook my head in disbelief. The one comfort I had held on to was knowing that Bradley wouldn't witness what would surely be my own personal wedding from hell.

"Oh, baby, we've really got to teach you to be silent, don't we? Perhaps you'll learn after a few days in the cages." He brushed his fingers across my lips.

"I promise, I won't…" I stammered.

"That's what I thought." Conrad smiled proudly. "Now if you'll excuse me. I must print off the final payment information for Mason, and then they'll be off. See you at dinner, my love." Conrad forced his lips on mine.

Everyone dispersed except for Bradley and me. I took two steps forward to be closer to him, but he quickly looked up in a corner of the room.

A small camera focused directly on us.

"It's off. I snuck into the security room because I knew this would be our final goodbye."

"Don't come to the wedding," I said pleadingly.

"You know I have to, Dem." He looked down at my feet. "Did you try your shoes on?"

The simple yet completely ordinary question made me almost smile, and maybe if this situation wasn't abnormal, I'd be able to respond like a normal girl who had a crush on a guy.

"I did. They're the perfect fit. Thank you again. But I won't be able to wear them..."

Bradley looked back up at me. He didn't even need to ask why. He already knew. How could I explain where they came from?

"But I'll wear them in my room. And every time I do, I'll think of you and how I wish I could use them to run away with you." I bit my lower lip, full of nerves.

"One day, I'm going to come back for you, and we won't have to run. You can wear the highest heels and it wouldn't matter because we'll walk out of this house of horrors hand-in-hand." Bradley lifted my chin with his index finger and locked his lips onto mine.

"Demi, I really, really like you." He brushed his lips once more before pulling back.

I couldn't help the tears that fell. It was all too

much, and the thing was... I didn't think I really liked him.

I think I loved him. And not because I had lost my virginity to him, or because he bought me shoes I had only dreamt of, but because for my entire life, I had never had a home.

But if I knew what home felt like, I'd take a wild guess that it was what I felt whenever I was with Bradley.

He was home to me. And now, I was losing the only home I had ever known.

CHAPTER FORTY-ONE

THE CAR DROVE down the winding driveway, and I could see Bradley look over through the back window.

I walked back inside with Ian, Daphne, and Conrad. If a neighbor had been out walking their dog or pushing a stroller, they'd assume a beautiful family was spending quality time together. They'd probably even be envious of us donning matching, beautiful, designer clothing. A gorgeous set of two couples casually going into a sprawling estate.

But behind these giant, double doors laid a haunted house full of death and prisoners. This wasn't a house, it was a morgue.

"The house feels so much lighter, almost brighter. Wouldn't you agree, Father?" Conrad followed behind

Ian to the golden bar cart in the corner of the room. I didn't know what I was supposed to do.

"It truly does," Dr. Ivory agreed as Conrad handed him a glass of whiskey.

"You won't miss him, Ian? Bradley's been with our family for years. It'll be strange not having him around. Granted, he will return for the wedding." Daphne sighed as she sank into the accent chair and brushed her hands across her white pleated skirt.

"Of course, we'll miss him. I'm not a heartless monster, Daphne," he said with complete seriousness as he took a seat next to his wife.

"Come sit with us, Demi. Why are you standing there like the damn maid?" Conrad barked at me.

"Well, she was hired to be the maid." Ian let out a dry laugh.

"It was simply to get my bride to us. She's not the maid," Conrad fired back at his dad. Wow, he was defending me? *My hero.* I rolled my eyes as I sat with them.

"Demi, we are going to do your bridal gown fitting in the morning. Make sure you get plenty of sleep, and then you'll even get to select the bridesmaid's dresses just in case we let you have them. We're going to go to the best bridal boutique in Charlotte tomorrow," Mrs. Ivory said, delighted.

I sat up immediately. "Wait, we're going to leave the house?"

"Well, of course, we are. We have an entire girls' day planned, darling," Mrs. Ivory chirped as she smiled. "We have five days until the wedding. I always thought we'd have slightly more time, but now we know Conrad is in dire need of a woman's touch. Clearly." She glanced over at her son.

Cringing inside, I knew she was referring to the fact that Conrad had attacked Daisy and then almost did the same to me. She was implying that he needed his wife to relieve him so he wouldn't go around assaulting women in front of an audience out of spite.

"Speaking of..." Ian cleared his throat and handed a small box over to Conrad, who set his glass down.

Walking toward me with the black velvet box in his hands, Conrad dropped to one knee.

Oh no.

Mrs. Ivory gasped and flung her hand over her mouth, as if she was completely surprised by the clearly staged, gut-wrenching proposal. I didn't think I had ever thought about this moment in my life. Maybe because I knew a girl like me would never have a prince charming riding in on a white horse to save me from the fire-breathing dragons. Maybe because I always knew the only way someone would be on their knees in front of me was if he were the villain.

"Demi Rao, you have taken my breath away since the very first time I laid eyes on your photograph. I remember so clearly flipping through the pages of the..." He paused and flicked his eyes to his dad, who shook his head. "I remember all the girls were blurring together. Boring, dreadful, bland... but then you were a vision. I knew the only way I'd want to improve my bride-to-be was simply by altering your hair, and now look at you. You're perfect." Conrad cracked the box open, and I couldn't help but widen my eyes at the massive stone in front of me. It was a massive, emerald-cut diamond solitaire on a thin gold band.

"Demi, will you do me the greatest honor of my life and marry me?" Conrad flashed his pearly white teeth at me, and for a moment, I tilted my head and thought how many women in the world must dream of this moment.

I wanted to say no and slap him. I wanted to spit on his face and storm out of here. But I knew they'd hunt me down and gut me—and worse, they'd hurt him.

They'd kill Bradley and make me watch. My stomach curled as I thought of my finger having to carry the weight of this ring being from this disgusting scum of a man. But, I knew better. I knew that I was a girl without choices. I knew there weren't multiple choices here. So, I sucked in a breath of air and looked at my shaking fingers.

"Yes," I whispered so low that I hoped in some way I wouldn't hear it so I wouldn't have to think of myself as the most pathetic human in the planet.

Clapping and laughter erupted around us as Conrad yanked my hand and slid the massive stone onto my finger. Standing, he pulled me into his arms and forced a sloppy kiss across my lips.

"Say cheese!" Dr. Ivory held a camera up and took a photo. The bright flash blinded me temporarily, and as I opened my eyes again, I could see her.

My sweet sister, laying in her own blood, watching me sadly as I held a knife in my clammy hands to put her out of her misery. She'd be heartbroken that this was why she died.

But then, as I thought of my sister, while the clicking of Ian Ivory's camera sounded in the background, it occurred to me.

My sister told me to run away to Charlotte, North Carolina. She specifically made it clear that I would make it here. A sick feeling in my stomach rippled through as panic set in.

Did my sister send me into a death trap?

I looked at the Ivory family—the three were chattering away, eyeing me periodically—and suddenly, the weight of the ring on my finger felt heavier. It felt like it was burning.

But then as I looked at the large stone on my finger and my skin growing red underneath the band, I realized it didn't just feel like it was burning.

It *was* burning.

Letting out a distressed scream, I tried to tug the fitted ring off my finger as my skin began to peel and burn underneath.

"Ah!" I cried out as I finally got it off and saw a reddened circle around my finger.

"What the hell?" I was breathing heavily as Conrad slowly dragged his feet toward me.

Lifting my hand up, he smiled at the flaking skin. Pressing his lips against the new wound, he sighed. "An Ivory tradition, sweetheart. Now, we're bound together, skin-deep." He looked at me proudly... *possessively*.

"You did this on purpose?" Jerking my hand out from his, I looked over his shoulder at his attentive parents.

"Demi, darling, it's a tradition. I, too, went through it. It's actually romantic." Mrs. Ivory lifted her overly drawn-in eyebrow.

"Why don't we all head to bed? Just wrap your finger in a Band-Aid and put the ring back on. Just wash it before you do since it's still coated with hydrofluoric acid. Only a slight amount, though." Dr. Ivory put his arm around his wife as they all looked at my finger, which resembled peeling, reddened leather.

I stood there, not knowing how I wasn't even in shock. This was the least shocking thing that had happened to me here. Of course, my fiancé would attempt to burn my finger off. Conrad shoved his hand around mine and tugged me out of the room. I didn't care where he was taking me. Secretly, I was hoping he'd push me off of a cliff and put me out of my misery.

"You'll no longer be staying in the servant's quarters. You'll stay in here, and in a few short days, you'll move to my floor with me." He smiled down at me.

"Don't you have to go back to medical school soon?"

"Yes, remember? I have to go back, my love, but we have time for the wedding, a honeymoon, and plenty of… well, baby-making before I leave." Pursing his lips, he eyed me with desire. I desperately wanted to get into a shower and douse myself in soap. Bleach, even.

As soon as we turned down the monochrome hallway, I recognized it.

I was going to be staying in Bradley's suite.

"The new housekeeper did an appalling job emptying it out and sanitizing it. I didn't want any of

Bradley's filth touching you, but by tomorrow, everything will be gone. I promise, my queen." Conrad caged me in against the wall and puckered his lips.

Turning my head slightly so I wouldn't have to choke on his air, I quickly groaned in pain. "My finger is killing me." I lifted my hand between our faces.

"I'm sorry, beautiful. It's all about tradition. Go ahead and clean it up, and then get some sleep. Mother is thrilled to take you and the girls out shopping tomorrow," he crooned.

"The girls?" I flung my head back toward him.

"Yes, your bridesmaids," he added nonchalantly.

Nodding, the door slid open behind me as I walked backward inside the room that now held the one and only most beautiful memory of my life.

"Goodnight, Demilion." Conrad's lips ticked in an arrogant smile. Just as I opened my mouth to ask him how he knew the nickname Layla always called me, the door slid shut and I stumbled backward, terrified of all the secrets that seemed to be swarming around me.

The room was pitch-black, and I could have sworn I felt a presence. A sensation of someone breathing down my neck. Were they watching me in here? No, they must not have cameras in Bradley's room, considering we had sex in here. I wouldn't be breathing if they knew I had lost my virginity to him.

Turning slowly, I looked around. Shadows of furniture and a lamp, darkened reflections of paintings and frames taunted me. *Humans aren't afraid of the dark because of the lack of light; we're afraid of the dark because we fear the places our own minds will take us.*

Patting the wall, I looked for the switch until the groove brushed against my finger. Flipping it on, I fell backward, slapping my mouth to stifle the scream that escaped it.

Becca stood there, completely bald, in nothing but a stained white gown and a smile growing slowly across her face.

"Hello, Demi." She smiled even bigger.

"Becca…" I swallowed the lump in my throat as chills spread all over my body. My eyes dropped to her hand, which clutched a knife.

"I miss him so much." She did a complete spin with her thin arms wide. Her head tilted toward the ceiling as she let out a laugh.

"Brad-ley?" My voice cracked.

She immediately stopped spinning, using her heels as a way to steady herself. The eerie grin on her face melted off, turning into a darkened frown. Without her thick blonde hair and full face of makeup, she looked like a completely different person.

"He didn't want me, Demi. He left me behind. He went away and took my heart with him. He saved me, you know? I was once a caged girl..." she trailed sadly.

"Wait, you were...?" The air felt colder as Becca opened her palm and held the tip of blade against her skin. She began jamming it in slowly.

"Becca..." I took a step forward, but she shot me a look, warning me to stay back.

"Bradley was allowed to choose one girl to release. We're all such beautiful birds in a way, but he chose *me*. They needed a hair and makeup artist, anyway. You know how vain Mrs. Ivory is." Becca cut into her flesh and a trickle of blood pooled in her palm.

"He didn't choose Daisy?" I was stunned. His sister was held prisoner and being tortured psychologically, physically, and in every sense humanly possible.

"They didn't let him choose her, silly. So, he chose me. Even though I think he'd have chosen me regardless. He loved me."

"Becca, why don't you give me the knife?" I reached my hand out as she looked lost in a completely different world.

Pressing the knife even deeper into her palm, her eyes shot to mine as a smile stretched across her face. "He left me behind. He didn't choose me to be his..." she trailed with her eyes closing and tears running down her cheeks.

· · ·

"His what?" I whispered as my eyes flicked between the dripping blood and the completely deranged expression across of her pale face.

"His favorite girl."

"I don't... I don't understand?" I shook my head slowly.

"He chose you. But so did Conrad... so they sent Bradley away." My heart tightened as Becca grew closer to me. Taking a few steps back, I stumbled into the wall.

"What makes you so special, Demi?" She angled her head slightly, tugging the blade from her palm, tapping it against her hand. "You're not nearly as beautiful as me." She eyed my mid-section. "You're... kind of unpleasant, really. Muddy skin, frizzy hair and perhaps even a bit thinner than acceptable."

Hugging myself, I took a deep breath as she caged me in against the wall. Pressing the knife against my throat, her cold air blew against my face.

Sucking in, I tried to push my head away without making a difference. "You're actually fucking ugly, Demi." She pushed the blade further into my flesh. Closing my eyes, I thought about how I was actually sad to die.

I didn't think I'd be sad, considering I was living a

life that didn't feel like living at all. But no, suddenly, I realized I had held on to some sliver of hope, praying I'd get another chance at life. I think that reason was also because of Bradley. Meeting him and for the first time, feeling something for someone on a deeper level.

"It's quite funny, you were never Conrad's first choice. You were the substitute. But your promiscuous sister couldn't keep her legs closed, and well, she was no longer pure for the Ivory family." Becca clicked her tongue.

My body went cold. My eyes blurred and everything Becca said no longer sounded like a language I understood.

"My... sister? No, you don't know what you're talking about. Layla had no idea who this family was. She... she was raped by Trent."

"Did you actually see her being raped? Or is that what she told you?" Becca pursed her thin lips at me.

Blinking rapidly, I thought about how I hadn't seen Layla being raped; I'd just hear them. Hear them... having sex? But she'd always come back into the closet with me. She'd always look repulsed and heartbroken.

"She fell in love with Trent, and he loved her, but business is business. When he found out Ian Ivory was no longer buying Layla for the two million dollars he had promised him, he couldn't handle it. Layla was supposed to be his largest transaction and his way out of the Nashville slums. He couldn't believe having sex with her had wrecked him. So... he set it all up, and he put Layla up to it as well. He said if she helped him get you to go to the Ivory's house, he'd marry her." Becca paused. Leaning in, she brushed my hair from my face with her blood-stained palm. "It must really hurt to know your sister didn't want you, either." She frowned at me with insincere sadness.

"We were sold by our parents to Trent. Layla... she didn't love him. You have no idea what you're talking about," I hissed. There was no way my sister, the only human in this world who had ever loved me, wanted me, protected me, would intentionally put me in the path of harm.

But in the back of my mind, I questioned why she urged me to go to Charlotte. How everything aligned so effortlessly, so coincidentally.

"Yeah, and then you both were put in *The Virgin Bride Catalogue*." She squinted her eyes at me as if she were stunned I had no idea what this meant. "Oh, you poor, silly girl. You have no idea about anything, truly."

My brows furrowed as I looked into her red-tinged eyes. "The virgin bride catalogue?" I breathed out as Becca left only the smallest sliver of space between our faces. Putting more pressure against the knife against my neck, I flinched when she let out a small laugh.

"You're going to have such a beautiful life carrying an Ivory child, and the most amazing family's legacy." A tear escaped from Becca's eye. In one swift motion, she jerked the knife away from my neck and slashed her own.

Letting out a shriek, I grabbed her hand but was too late. She didn't think twice; she didn't make a sound. Blood sputtered out of her neck as she dropped to her knees and fell into my legs. Parting my lips, I could taste the splashes of her blood all over my mouth and face.

"Becca!" I cried out. I looked around wildly, grabbing Bradley's scarf from a hook on the wall, and frantically held it against her neck as she laid, face-down, in a growing pool of blood.

"Becca! Help! Someone!" I looked up at the ceiling and quickly remembered that Bradley said his room didn't have cameras. Running to the door, I slammed my bloodied fists while shouting for help at top of my lungs. Sliding my fingers across the panel, I couldn't get it to open. Red streaks were painted all over the smooth white as I sobbed harder.

"Please..." My voice was hoarse as I collapsed to the floor and looked at Becca. I knew she was dead. She had slit her throat completely. The puddle around her had now grown so large, it was hitting both sides of the walls.

Gagging, I clutched my knees and tugged them in, praying I could focus on my breathing or anything at all. Memories of my sister flashed in my mind. I was exhausted. And then suddenly, the light cut off, and I was all alone in the dark.

But I wasn't alone, was I?

Becca was right here with me, bleeding out. More than fearing the unknown in the darkness is that sometimes, what we already know is there is more terrifying than any place our imagination could ever take us.

FORTY-TWO

"GOOD MORNING, BEAUTIFUL!" I clenched my eyes before slowly opening them. How had I fallen asleep? Looking around, my vision was slightly hazy from the stickiness crusting my eyes.

I was in Bradley's bed, tucked in the plush bedding. Shoving the blankets off, I looked at Conrad.

"Becca!" I screeched and ran toward the hallway. Dragging my feet, I froze and my mouth parted as I stared blankly at the white floors.

"Who's Becca?" A chill shot up my spine. Conrad wrapped his arm around me from behind as I stood there in complete disbelief.

"Becca..." I turned and faced him, "the hair and makeup girl?"

His forehead cinched as he brushed his finger against my cheek. "Babe, we've never had a girl named

Becca live here, and as for hair and makeup, Mother always hires a woman named Kim. She's the one who made your hair so perfect for me." Conrad turned me around to him completely. My hair was cut even shorter into a bob and dyed even brighter blonde.

"No! You all are sick! You are liars! Just like with Misha, the girl I met the first night I was here... I saw her. She had slit her throat, just like Becca did!" I tried to shove Conrad's hands off me, but he only tightened his grip.

"Demi! Demi... you have to stop. You have to stop this now. Demi, sweetheart, you need to sit down. It's time I told you everything. The truth." Conrad kept his voice steady as he brushed my arms up and down.

They say when it rains, it pours. But that's for people who have always had balanced lives—lives that were smooth-sailing, normal, and unswerving. For me, it was always, when it pours, just don't drown. The problem with lives that were always trying to sink you below a treacherous, dangerous flood is that you never know if someone out there shining a light down at you is throwing you a life raft to save you or to simply tease you with a punctured one to prolong your suffering.

Just as Conrad was about to speak, his phone hummed in his pocket.

"It's Mother." He slid it on and answered.

"What? Of course, Mother. I'll bring... I can't believe it. It's our first return in what? Years?" Conrad rubbed his tensed face. "I'll be there soon." He nodded and looked back at me.

"Well, my love, you may as well come with me. It'll be good for you to see how we process a refund. It's time to truly learn the family business." I didn't know what he was referring to. But then again, deep down inside, I think I did. I just didn't want to believe my assumption was going to be correct.

Conrad intertwined his hand with mine and, for some reason, I didn't even think twice. I didn't even try to move my hand from his. There was no longer a point in fighting any of this. My sister had thrown me into the pits of hell; my parents had sold me like a used toy at a consignment shop. No one wanted me. No one loved me. I thought that none of those things would get to me, break me, hurt me. But now, as I looked at our hands laced together, I looked up at Conrad and realized I loved being wanted.

Even if it was being wanted by the devil himself. The Ivory family did anything and everything for one another. They put their family first. They'd never let one of them be hurt or get hurt.

That's what I was becoming. *One of them.*

And I think, maybe, I needed that.

Maybe, it was the only way I could ever survive.

———

"Death would be better!" Her voice echoed in a room I'd never been to. I clutched Conrad's hand tighter as my eyes widened in shock.

It was Officer Tate and a thin, blonde woman.

"Isabella, lower your voice," Mrs. Ivory snapped at the woman struggling to break free from Officer Tate's tight grip.

What was happening? Officer Tate's eyes met mine and suddenly, his face softened. "Well, well… someone's had a change of heart, haven't we, sweetheart?" His gaze dropped to our hands.

The woman, Isabella, began screaming again until she finally sunk her teeth into Officer Tate's hands and he shrieked out in pain.

"That's it. Time to put the bitch down." Dr. Ivory sighed and calmly walked over, tapping the syringe before plunging it into her skin.

Crying out, Isabella crumpled in Officer Tate's lap. He began petting her like a dog. "Now that's how I like 'em." He winked at me as Conrad released my hand

and took a seat, then shuffled through stacks of paperwork and a laptop.

"You're sure you'd like a refund, Tate?" He cleared his throat.

"Yeah. I know you all were kind enough to give a poor old police officer a free one in exchange for... well, privacy, but she wasn't what I was promised. I was promised a submissive, quiet wife, and this one... well, she's broken. She's suddenly found her damn voice. She won't let me piss on her when I screw her, and that's what I get off on. So now, I got a shitty wife and a whole lot of tension built up cause I'm not getting what I need." Officer Tate looked at me as I awkwardly sat and took in his disgusting words full of repulsive misogyny.

I wasn't insane. Officer Tate received a free bride from the Ivory family so he'd keep his lips sealed about the horrors going on here. And now, he was returning her?

Conrad sucked in a breath. "Well, we're going to have to mark her as damaged. We are planning to open a new shop for used models at a discounted price, but Isabella is going to have to go back into training." He rapidly typed on the laptop in front of him.

"Officer Tate, we could put her through shock and white therapy at an intensive level for a week and see if it doesn't remind her of her manners?" Dr. Ivory brushed his finger across his bottom lip.

"No. I want a new one." Officer Tate's thin, crusted lips ticked upward.

"We can't just deplete our inventory and give you free merchandise," Mrs. Ivory retorted, sounding agitated.

"We garner millions of dollars per unit. The waiting list we have extends out to another five years." Ian snapped his fingers and suddenly, two men I'd never seen before appeared. With one simple nod of his head, they lifted Isabella and carried her away.

"I'm feeling tense. I'll be back in a bit." Ian looked toward his wife, and Daphne's face grew pale as she bit her bottom lip. A pit grew inside of my stomach. He was going to rape her.

"Listen, you can either give me a new one, or you can kiss this… little business you've got goin' on goodbye." Officer Tate stood and brushed his hands on his pants.

"Here's your return receipt. We need a signature." Conrad tapped the paper he had slid over to Officer Tate. My stomach churned as I stared at everyone in the room. This was surreal. How could they live like this without feeling any form of remorse?

"When can I expect to design my next one?"

"Tate… there is a wait list. This isn't some grocery

store where we have an abundance of shiny apples to hand over to you."

"Then give me her," he snickered as he pointed at me.

"Watch your fucking mouth before you speak about my soon-to-be wife. You're looking at the next Mrs. Ivory, so lower you voice," Conrad fired off without hesitation. Looking over at him, I couldn't help but feel... thankful? Thankful that I had someone who wanted to protect me for once? What was happening to me? My chest tightened as I hated myself for even feeling this way.

Conrad's eyes met with mine and his eyes widened slightly as he recognized my emotions. Leaning in, he tilted my chin up and planted his lips against mine.

"Mmm..." I sighed against them. Wasn't Conrad a product of being raised in this madness? I could help him. I could... But then, as I looked into his eyes, I realized I didn't feel anything for Conrad. I was displacing my feelings from Bradley onto the next option—the only option. Suddenly, I realized I may be experiencing Stockholm syndrome. Was I falling for my captor? I wasn't strong enough to fight the sentiments rampaging through my body. But what scared me the most was that they weren't negative emotions, they were positive.

Swallowing the lump in my throat, I heard Mrs.

Ivory shift in her seat and when I glanced over at her, she had an enormous, proud smile on her face.

She was happy for us.

They were accepting me as one of them.

Suddenly, everything changed.

CHAPTER FORTY-THREE

I HAD GAINED a new sense of freedom. I wasn't being dropped off and picked up by Bradley anymore. I wasn't cleaning or expected to do anything. As Mrs. Ivory and Conrad bickered with Officer Tate, I stood and left the room. I fully expected someone to stop me and say something, but no one did.

This is what it'd be like from now on. I'd be able to roam the estate however I pleased. As I walked the empty halls, I thought about Becca. She was real, the blood and everything was real. But at the same time, how could they just make her disappear so easily without me knowing? How could someone have cleaned the entire area when I barely slept?

I felt lightheaded from every thought, every question, and every fear. How much easier would it be to simply fit into this life and just live? I'd have endless financial security. I'd have a husband, a family, and eventually, we'd have a child I could busy myself with. Maybe I could even gain enough of the family's trust and get my college degree. I brushed my hand against my hair. It was strange having it cut this short. I felt like an entirely new person. I was a new person.

Pausing in the middle of the hall, I realized I never truly looked at the images that were hung. Bradley always had us moving so quickly, and part of me feared even looking at anything. For some reason, I always thought these images were from Mrs. Ivory's college days or something of sorts.

But growing closer, I realized these weren't old images and happy memories from her past. The glossy, deep walnut frames held small circular images that resembled what you'd see in a sorority house. They were all blonde women with green eyes, and rather the signature black dresses you'd expect to see, they were all donning white gowns and blank expressions.

Squinting, I brushed my finger against the engraved gold plaque.

The Ivory Graduates

"Graduates? From…" My heart sank. I already knew.

Looking at the Ossis wing, I tugged the thin card out and waved it across the keypad.

It opened slowly.

Glancing over my shoulder, my heart began to race as I waited for the door to fully shut behind me before walking down the hallway.

Dr. Ivory's office door was open, trickling soft light out into the otherwise darkened hallway. I wanted to go see the caged girls, but I had to pass his office first.

Freezing in front of the door, I slapped my hands across my mouth.

Ian Ivory was leaning back in his slightly turned chair. His eyes were closed, and the secret glass wall was exposed. Blinking away tears and shock, I was breathing heavily into my palm. Officer Tate's wife, Isabella, was strapped to a pole and the two men who took her away were... abusing her.

One was raping her while the other had his hands around her throat, choking her.

Taking one step closer, I saw the massive lotion bottle, tissue box, and... Ian's hand moving up and down. He was pumping as he moaned in enjoyment. Stumbling back, I realized something.

The smell of popcorn... The popcorn machine in the corner had fresh popcorn popping. This was his form of enjoyment, like how a person goes to the movies or the way someone winds down with a book. Backing away slowly, with chills running across every part of my body, I felt numb.

Ian Ivory had to be stopped. He was the pinnacle of

it all. Conrad could be manipulated, and I knew I could change his views. The man I met the first day I worked here had good in him.

I knew what I had to do next.

I have to be the favorite girl, because that's the only way I'll never be a caged girl.

———

"It's perfect." Mrs. Ivory clutched her hands together excitedly as I stood on the small platform at a bridal boutique. It felt strange leaving the Ivory estate. We even drove past Raina's house. I hadn't heard nor seen her since the time I called the police, and I couldn't help but almost laugh at that. Now I knew why the police didn't care. Who knew how many of the police officers had gifted wives in exchange for silence and protection.

"Mrs. Ivory, will the wedding be like Daisy's?" I paused before turning to see my reflection.

"First of all, call me mother. In a few short days, you'll officially be my daughter." She smiled and immediately looked at the two women helping us, then waved them off to leave us in privacy. "Now, what do you mean?"

. . .

"Will it be with a bunch of those male… clients? And inside that room?" I held my hands together to prevent them from shaking.

"No. Absolutely not. You will both be wed in the peony garden, and no one will be there besides our family. This is a private, beautiful ceremony. I just can't believe our time is coming to an end." Daphne tugged out a small, embroidered handkerchief and dabbed at her eyes. I didn't see any tears, and I knew she was just being theatrical. Was she referring to the fact that Conrad and I were going to take her and Ian's spots?

"Look at yourself, Demi. Turn around and see why Conrad always chose you."

"But he didn't? He chose my sister…" I blew out a breath of air as Daphne's mouth dropped.

"Who… who told you that?" She looked stunned but didn't deny it.

"It doesn't matter. I wasn't the favorite girl. I was just the next best thing to Layla. But she fell for Trent, her captor. *Our* captor. She was damaged merchandise, right?" I fought back my tears and held on to the sliver of courage I managed to muster.

Mrs. Ivory stood and walked slowly toward me. *Click, click, click.* I dropped my eyes to her feet. She must have changed into those heels in the car because I would have noticed the sound.

"Turn around, you ungrateful little bitch," she

hissed at me, forcefully moving me around on the stand.

Closing my eyes tightly, I took a deep breath and slowly opened them. Drawing in a long breath of air, I began to cry. Seeing myself in a wedding gown was something I never thought would happen. I never thought I'd get married. Well, I suppose at one point in time I did. I assumed when I was a very little girl I'd marry my prince charming, but that little fantasy dissipated as quickly as the summer sun soaks up the rain on a sidewalk.

The dress was one Mrs. Ivory had brought to the bridal boutique with us. It was worn by every bride in the Ivory family for generations. We were just here for alterations and accessories.

It was a stunning, yet simple wedding gown. Fitted at the top and flared out with the thick, sheen satin material. There was no beading, design, or anything extravagant about it. Just a clean, simple, exquisite gown. Tucking my short, blonde hair behind my ears I felt overwhelmed seeing myself this way.

Mrs. Ivory's cold fingers ran down my exposed back before reaching the corset. Tugging the strings aggressively, she jerked them so hard, my upper body flung forward as I choked on my own air.

"Ow!" I slapped my hands on my abdomen as she

tightened it to the point the material was cutting into my skin and causing me to cough.

"Listen to me, you unappreciative little girl. You are going to marry Conrad. You are going to be the best wife to him. You are going to bear his child and carry on this family's name. There are two options for you, Demi." She knotted the strings into a bow and dug her nails into my arms, pulling me backward into her.

"Option one, be planted in our garden and nurtured as an Ivory family member, or be buried and used as fertilizer. Either way, you're going to bloom, sweetheart. You just have to decide how."

My eyes widened at our reflections in the mirror as a smile grew across her nude-painted lips.

"Tell me, what will it be. I need to know if we're going to need to pick up soil on the way home or not."

"Option one." I trembled as my oxygen felt like it was being cut off.

"Smart girl." Mrs. Ivory's lips brushed against my skin before she planted a kiss on my shoulder. "Now, let's pick a veil, shall we?" She clicked her tongue and slid off from the podium.

CHAPTER
FORTY-FOUR

THE REST of the time spent at the bridal boutique was abnormally... normal. I tried on multiple veils, and Daphne let me choose the one I wanted. She said my jewelry would be gifted family heirlooms, and beyond that, I had nothing else to worry about since everything would be arranged. I was getting married. Out of everything I had endured at the Ivory house, getting married seemed like the least problematic.

I had come to a full circle of accepting that this was what I had to do. The options were clear, and if I wanted to live, then it meant living a life chosen for me.

We returned to the estate, but I didn't take my eyes off the windows once. I loved watching the sunlight shimmer through the dense oak trees that lined the pathway to hell.

"Mrs—" I stared, but she quickly cut me off.

"Mother," Mrs. Ivory filled in.

Clearing my throat, I relaxed my shoulders. "Mother, I was wondering if I could invite Raina and her family to the wedding."

It pained me that Raina was in on this sickness. There was no coincidence she was driving around on the bad side of town, picking me up with her toddler son in the car.

"And her family?" Mrs. Ivory crossed her arms next to me as the driver pulled into the winding driveway.

"Yes, her husband Jax and her son Kai?" My eyebrows furrowed as she pinched her lips to the side.

"Oh, I thought someone had already told you now that you just... know all the family secrets." She tugged out a tube of the nude lipstick that was the only shade we'd been allowed to wear.

Sliding it over her lips, she smacked them together. "Sure, we'll invite them." She smiled at me maliciously. The driver opened the door for us, and we headed back inside. I glanced over my shoulder, wondering how far I'd make it if I made a dash for it? How easily they'd capture me, and how quickly they'd throw me into the colorless, soundless, torture rooms they lovingly called cages?

Once inside, Mrs. Ivory directed me to head to my

room and rest since the wedding was tomorrow evening.

"I thought it was Friday?" I looked at her stunned.

"No. Plans have changed. Your IUD will be removed today, and then tomorrow is the wedding. You and Conrad are set to leave for your honeymoon on Friday."

My heart pounded as she watched me walk toward my room—well, Bradley's old room.

I slid my card in front of the panel outside of Bradley's room. It opened immediately, and I cautiously walked in. Blinking repeatedly, I flipped the light on and looked around. Not a trace of blood. Where did they put Becca's body? The chill in the room hung over me as I unzipped the all-white jumpsuit and slid the flats off. It was the first time I hadn't worn the ridiculous platform shoes.

Opening the closet, I squatted down and tugged out the box of Nike Air Jordans that Bradley got me. I missed him so much. Sliding my feet into them, I stood and put my hands on my hips and admired them.

The greatest part of this wedding was that I'd get to see Bradley. Yet, the worst thing was also that he was going to see me marry Conrad. I didn't know much about healthy relationships; I didn't know what love was since I'd clearly never experienced it. But the emotions I felt for Bradley were something unlike any others I'd experienced.

And now, I was going to marry a monster. A monster who raped a woman in front of me. A monster who was providing return receipts for human beings. A monster I'd have to pretend everything was okay with.

Peeling back the blankets, I climbed into the bed. Closing my eyes, a tear escaped as I remembered Bradley's touch in this bed and suddenly, I realized I had to figure out a way to make myself bleed tomorrow night...

If I didn't bleed on our wedding night, he'd cage me. He'd kill me. And worst of all, he'd kill Bradley.

I fell asleep with nothing but my bra, panties, and sneakers on. Some people struggled to sleep—it was an issue with control often times—but that wasn't the case for me. In my entire life, the only place I could ever truly feel safe was in my sleep.

———

Cold fingers raked against my stomach, and I abruptly jerked upright, gasping into the darkness.

"Who's there?" I swatted at the figure in front of me.

A small lighter flicked on between our faces.

Trembling and falling backward, I saw it was Ian Ivory. I grabbed the blanket around me, drawing it up higher to cover my body.

"Please leave," I whimpered, hating the weakness my voice so easily depicted.

"Sweet daughter, I'm here to remove your IUD. Our in-house expert is off today. And tomorrow, my son must... well, soil such a perfect, pure flower." He brushed his hand against my cheek as the flicker of the flame outlined his ominous sneer.

"No. You... Conrad wouldn't want his dad to do that." I swallowed and pushed back, but I could barely move since Ian was pressing his hands against my legs.

"Nonsense. What's mine is his and what's his is... well, mine." Grabbing my ankles, he tugged me in one swift motion, causing me to cry out.

"Please! No! I'm begging you." A light turned on above us and Ian's piercing green eyes stared straight into my eyes. He was a demon.

"You know I've never tasted a brown-eyed woman before. And, come to think of it, I haven't tasted a tan-skinned woman, either. You know I'm very particular about cleanliness and purity, my beautiful Demi. White is so pure, so clean, so exquisite. There are products, you know? Products that will bleach the skin. I could lighten you up a bit; we can do the contact lenses. We can make you perfect." His nails dug deeper into my ankles as I bit my quivering bottom lip.

"Please…" I pleaded.

"You know while you and Daphne were shopping, I had someone install these." He leaned down to the side of the bed and jingled the chain.

"No. No!" I kicked at him harder until I was half off the bed and he jerked me up harder.

"Fight this and you'll pay the price, Demi!" he roared, quickly chaining my ankles to the bed.

Choking on my tears, I gripped the sheets as tears poured out and he ripped my panties off.

"This is a medical procedure, and I'm a physician." Using his nails, he pried my thighs apart as I slammed them back together once my panties hung at my ankles.

Holding a tool up, he exhaled. "Demi, please. I'm just removing your IUD for your marriage to my precious son. I'm not going to hurt you. You have to relax these… tight… muscles, or it'll hurt." His voice dropped low, which was even more terrifying than when he yelled at me.

There I was, lying in bed, chained, as my soon-to-be father-in-law stared in between my legs, panting like a dog.

He swiped his tongue across his bottom lip and mumbled something to himself. Pushing my legs upright, he jammed the speculum inside me before using the tool to yank the IUD out of my body.

I moaned as the pain of the multiple tools and tugging hurt.

Ian was still talking to himself, his eyes honed-in on my vagina.

"Just one…" I heard him whisper. And then, the fear shook through me as I realized what he was chanting.

"Just one taste…" He finished the sentence with his tongue wiggling out of his mouth. Forcing my legs closed, even as his hands kept trying to pry them open, I began to cry harder.

"Dr. Ivory, I have to be pure for Conrad," I choked out.

His eyes shot up to mine and he pulled back. "You're right, Demi. When you're back from the honeymoon, I can have you whenever I'd like. Even if you're with child." He snickered.

"You know… I forgot, but I need to do one more thing before I leave you to get your bridal sleep." He hummed and walked around to my arms. Grabbing another chain, he tightened my arm into it.

"What? Please… I think you should go get Conrad," I pleaded.

"Shh. You know I don't like women who speak!" Closing my eyes, I had to calm myself down. They say if you ever encounter a dangerous animal in life, you shouldn't react and you have to stay composed. It's the only way to survive.

Because there's no running from someone who has no problem killing you.

I kept my eyes closed and moments later, I felt something foam-like in between my legs. Opening my eyes, Ian Ivory was standing with a razor, shaving cream, and a small bowl of water.

"Let me shave you, beautiful."

My eyes widened in shock as my lips parted. "No. No. No..." But he wasn't listening. He began to hum a song that sounded religious as he dipped the razor into the bowl and began shaving me.

"Conrad's not going to like this bush." He chuckled and shook his head. Humiliation and discomfort raced through me as tears poured out of my eyes. Spreading my legs apart, he sprayed more shaving cream on my skin, but I felt his fingers pad across and rub me.

"Please stop."

But he started to hum louder as he continued to shave me and shove his fingers inside my body. I closed my eyes and tried to picture an escape, but there was nothing. I couldn't even dream up an escape.

It was just black. And lonely. And quiet.

CHAPTER FORTY-FIVE

I WOKE UP GROGGY. There was a good chance Ian Ivory had drugged me last night, but I didn't care. I had no emotion left. I was completely numb. Now, I was a corpse simply pretending to live.

It was my wedding day, and I almost laughed at the thought. My wedding day. The day women dream about since they twirled around in their first frilly dress. The day parents saved up for and planned out. The day that's supposed to be the happiest day in a lifetime was a day that felt like I was finally being served my official prison sentence.

"Demi! Get in the shower!" I rolled over and saw Mrs. Ivory standing there, watching me. "Our makeup artist, Becca, is here."

· · ·

"Becca?" I stammered and pushed myself upright in bed. It felt strange looking at Mrs. Ivory. Her husband, the man she had a child with and lived with, was assaulting me just a few hours ago.

"Yes, you know Becca. Go shower, and she'll have everything set up. Everyone's already arriving for the wedding luncheon. You overslept!" She hurried away as I stood and walked to the bathroom. I felt like a robot, doing as I was told, without a care for what was to come.

I showered, but I didn't feel the steam or water. I scrubbed my body raw, looking down at the razor burn marks left behind by the aggressive and forced shave.

I didn't cry. I didn't feel. I took my time washing myself, brushing my teeth, and blow drying my hair.

Once out, I walked into the room and saw Mrs. Ivory and a woman who was dressed exactly like Becca and looked just like her, but it was clearly not her.

"Hey Demi! So good to see you, girl!" the woman chirped and when I remained quiet, she moved closer. "Becca? Remember me?" She excitedly clapped her hands together and ushered me to the chair.

"You're not Becca," I replied flatly.

"Yes, I am." She shot a look at Mrs. Ivory, who shook her head slowly. "Anyway, let's get you all ready for your special day." I closed my eyes as the brush pricked against my forehead aggressively and she tugged it through my hair.

What felt like an eternity later, the substitute Becca spun me around in the chair and wiggled her fingers. "Ta-Da!" She clapped her palms against her cheeks and jumped up and down.

I didn't recognize the girl in front of me. I looked beautiful; I looked like a bride. My veil I chose was carefully clipped into my hair. My lips were in a deep red. "I thought we were only allowed to wear nude lipstick?" I questioned.

"This color is permitted for Ivory brides. It's infused with peonies and roses all grown in the garden." Mrs. Ivory added another layer of the sticky lipstick to my pout. I wanted to vomit as I felt it seeping into the crevices of my lips.

"Darling Demi, let's get your gown on." Mrs. Ivory's voice was soft as she smiled at me, and not in the usually mocking way, but in a clearly emotional way.

"Becca, leave us alone." She waved at her. Becca nodded and quickly shuffled away.

"You know I was once a caged girl," Mrs. Ivory started as I tugged my robe off and she helped me into my gown.

"What?" I froze.

"Yes. I was in *The Virgin Bride Catalogue* and selected

by Ian. It was so very romantic. He chose me from pages and pages of women. I came from nothing, Demi. No one sold me or trafficked me. No, I met Ian's father at a bar I used to stand in the alley of, ramming needles into my flesh to feel something. His father took me in, cleaned me up, and put me through the withdrawal and intensive-white therapy program. It changed my life. I learned that words and sounds cloud our mental states; I learned that food is a privilege. I lived off white rice and plain yogurt for six months until I earned my first sliver of a banana. I didn't hear a sound for one year. But it all taught me to keep my mouth shut until spoken to. It taught me discipline and what it entails to be the best wife and mother. That's what is wrong with our society. We let women run free and turn into dirty tramps. Men like Ian, his father, and now, Conrad, help remind us, my darling Demi, that we are not meant to live like a bird soaring through a sky alone. Those are the birds that become prey, and we are safest in the cages. We are safest when we do as we are told. Procreate, respect our men, serve their every need. We are creating the new generation of women who will raise the best men."

I slid into my dress as Daphne helped to lace it up. "You really think that? You really think that these men are helping us? That we should be submissive and tortured? That we should be raped and abused? You're despicable, you know that. And one day, you're going to die a painful death." I spewed out, not caring if she slit my throat right now.

"I already know that I'm going to die a painful death, but so will you, and so will the woman who marries your son. We are meant to be sacrificial. Please take care of Conrad, my darling Demi. He's so very special." Grabbing a glass bottle, she sprayed me, and suddenly, the scent of peonies overtook my senses.

"Oh, yes, so very special and such a fucking gentle-man. Assaulting Bradley's sister in front of him? You did so well, Daphne. Get the hell out of my face, you pathetic piece of shit. You can't even call yourself a woman. You're disgusting." I turned and tugged my gown behind me. I expected her to slap me or hit me, but she didn't.

"*Amor vincit omnia…*" Mrs. Ivory said as she left the room.

Love conquers all.

She actually thought that this was love? And what did she mean she knew we'd all die a painful death?

Walking toward the mirror, I brushed my hands against my abdomen and loosened my shoulders.

Staring at myself, I couldn't believe I was the girl in the reflection. "Demi…" his voice cut through the thoughts swirling through my mind.

"Bradley?" I turned slowly, lifting the heavy gown, and rolling my lips to prevent myself from crying.

"Wow, Dem… you are gorgeous." He let out a soft sigh. "But I still miss your black hair." He came closer to me, looking as handsome as ever. His hair was colored a darker shade of brown, and his face no longer looked as pale as it did when he was here—like the sun had finally kissed him. Had he been wearing light makeup the entire time he worked here? In such a short period of time he couldn't have naturally tanned. Shuddering I felt happiness that he was free from this death trap. Scanning his body, I smiled. He was wearing a fitted navy-blue tuxedo, and he smiled back at me.

"You don't look so bad yourself. I like the hair. And the color," I pointed out.

"Ivory weddings are the only weddings that color is permitted. And the Davenports aren't obsessed with all-white, so I got my hair back. Let me help you put your shoes on." Walking toward the closet, he tugged the Nike's out.

"Bradley, I can't wear those."

"They won't be able to see them. Besides, tonight you're going to need them." He sank to the ground in front of me and lifted my foot up.

"Why will I need them tonight?" I whispered as I watched him slide my sneakers on with care.

"Because we're going to run." He slid the other shoe on and looked up at me. Then tugging a gorgeous, vintage-looking locket out of his pocket, he clasped it around my neck.

"What is this?" I asked, looking at the gold necklace.

"Don't open it. If anything goes wrong with our plan tonight and you can't take it anymore, it's the only solution I have for you."

"I don't understand?" I rubbed at the locket.

"It's a pill. It'll be painless. But you cannot take it unless things become worse than death." His voice shook as he said the words.

"You just have to promise me you'll do whatever they ask of you. Don't fight it today, Dem. I promise to get you out of here."

"A car will pick you up after Conrad falls asleep. You'll give him a glass of whiskey that will be laced. The whiskey is a tradition after…" Bradley clenched his eyes shut for a moment and I knew he didn't want to say the rest.

"After Conrad falls asleep, a car will be waiting for you and will bring you to Charleston. When you get out and you see water and the big rocks, you'll know you're safe. I'll have the boat and we'll leave. Forever." Bradley slowly stood and cupped my elbows. "If you'll have me."

"Bradley, you're not joking, right?" I rubbed my lips together.

"No, Dem, we're going to get out from here. I promise you."

"What about Daisy?" I shook my head, knowing they'd go after her.

"She's happy with Davenport. I can't do anything else for her. She's... she's basically a living corpse. But, Dem, we have a chance to get out of this. We have a chance to finally live."

"I love you, Demi." He tilted my chin up and softly brushed his lips against mine. His soft scent of sandalwood and citrus woke something in my soul as I kissed him back.

I can feel.

"I love you too, Bradley."

"Will you run away with me?" He smiled, and for a moment, I couldn't help but grab his face and press my forehead against his.

His contacts were out, and his light brown eyes were filling with tears.

"I do, Bradley," I whispered.

All I had to do was go and marry Conrad Ivory first. Lifting the locket between my fingers, I thought how Bradley knew if he couldn't get me out, then death would be better than a life here.

CHAPTER FORTY-SIX

I CLUTCHED the bridal bouquet of peonies and realized the perfume Mrs. Ivory had sprayed on me was from this garden. These flowers they forced me to hold as per tradition were all grown over the dead bodies of the girls who didn't make the cut…

My stomach tumbled as I slowly walked down the cobblestone path and the soft music surrounded everyone. Two rows of guests were there—Bradley, Ian, Daphne, other random people I'd never seen, and then… Raina. I looked at her as she smiled at me. Did she not realize this was completely absurd?

Did she not think to call for help even though they paid her to help them?

Where were Jax and Kai?

I looked back up and finally forced myself to look at my groom.

Conrad wore a classic black tuxedo and he wiped a straggling tear away.

I wanted to violently vomit. Peonies were blooming all around us, and I couldn't help but feel the pain from the presence of countless, spirits buried under this dirt.

Innumerable, beautiful souls, brutally murdered, raped, and tortured. Countless lives ripped apart.

"My beautiful bride. My beautiful Demilion." Conrad reached his palms out.

He called me by the nickname Layla did because he wanted her all along. She was the favorite girl, while I was just the substitute. He must have spoken to her and found out that she called me that.

Forcing my hands into his, I looked and caught Bradley's eyes locked onto mine. Ian Ivory stood and walked to us.

"As a father, I can't believe this day has come. When we had Conrad, we knew we'd won the lottery as parents. When he selected his bride, I trusted he knew what he was doing. I'll never forget flipping through *The Virgin Bride Catalogue* with him. He was eighteen and well, due to unforeseen situations, we had to choose another bride for him. He found Demi and circled her photograph with a black Sharpie." Ian paused and let out a proud laugh.

I was disgusted. He chose me out of a magazine the way a child does a toy for Christmas.

"Well, here we are. The end of our journey as leaders of The Ivory estate, The Ivory Experiment, and The Ivory Rehabilitation program. I feel my father would be so very pleased that we have paired countless men with their brides. We are procreating a stronger and better future for an otherwise damaged world. Now, shall we get these lovebirds married?" He wiped his tears and began the ceremony. They actually thought that they were creating a better world and future through their patriarchal and misogynistic extremist views.

My fingers shook in Conrad's hands as Ian Ivory repeated holy vows to us. I didn't look up as I pretended it was Bradley standing before me.

"Do you promise to obey your husband for the rest of your days?" Ian proclaimed.

"I do," I whispered and slid the silver band on Conrad's finger.

Looking down at the gold band he'd added to my finger, I flinched, hoping it wasn't coated in acid again.

After a moment of no burning, I realized it wasn't. The scar from my engagement ring was still wrapped around my finger.

"You may now kiss your bride!" Dr. Ivory boasted

as Conrad gripped my waist, dipped me down, and smashed his lips against mine.

Opening my eyes, I could see Bradley, who immediately looked away.

Pulling my face from his, Conrad beamed at me.

"My gorgeous wife." He lifted our hands into the air and tugged me down the aisle with him.

I'm officially the next Mrs. Ivory.

———

The rest of the evening went by in a blur. There wasn't a crowd of people to congratulate us, there wasn't a familiar bridal party or anything joyous. Daphne decided to not let me have any bridesmaids. To be honest, it was a relief considering I didn't want to be surrounded by the caged girls.

Instead, I wished away every second of our first dance, and then ate dinner.

Peeling away from Conrad, I walked to Raina, who was sipping a glass of wine and flung her arms around me.

"Congratulations, lady! Look at you, all wifed up."

"Where's Jax and Kai?" I asked, and the smile immediately fell from her face. When she didn't answer, I voiced my suspicions. "You don't live in that house, do you? Please, tell me you didn't kidnap Kai."

Everything was piecing together as I watched her face carefully.

"No. He was a paid actor." She shrugged while polishing off her wine.

"You're not even a doctor, are you?"

"Nope, an Ivory family employee. I help make sure certain products arrive at their destination. Kind of like an Amazon delivery driver." She let out a callous laugh.

Tightening my fist, I looked at her. "You deserve to be buried here, not them," I hissed as I looked at the dirt and shook my head. I walked away from her, completely repulsed.

"Come on, Mrs. Ivory, time to do one last ceremony before the best part of the evening." Conrad laced his hand with mine.

Walking inside the house, the halls were completely silent. Everything was undistinguishable beyond the glimmer of moonlight from the windows —no movements, no voices. Our shadows danced along the walls of what felt like a mausoleum. I swore I could hear haunting pleas tear through the silence. Pleas begging for someone, anyone to free them.

Walking to the massive doors, Conrad opened

them. But just as the light seeped through, I stumbled back and began to shriek.

Ian and Daphne Ivory were laying on the floor, side-by-side, with their throats slit, and in the middle sat a table with two wineglasses full of red liquid. The pool of blood around his parents grew by the minute. Their arms were tied together above their heads.

"Conrad!" I slapped my hands across my mouth, while my heart pounded rapidly against my chest.

He didn't move, he didn't react. Reaching back, he grabbed my arm and steadied me.

"Come, my love. They sacrificed for us." Lifting the wineglasses, he handed me one.

My hands shook as my eyes darted between them both. "They... killed themselves?"

"Yes."

"How are you not—"

"This was always the plan, my love, and one day, you and I will go into the eternal heavens together for our son and his bride, too."

"To be pure even after I take your purity away tonight, we must drink this to protect our morals and souls." Clinking his glass against mine, he lifted it to his lips and began to drink. "Drink it, Demi. Now." His voice shifted, and fear rose inside me as my body felt paralyzed. "Demi!" he yelled as he licked the liquid from his lips.

Placing my mouth on the rim, I slowly sipped. The thick taste of iron burned my mouth and I immediately choked and coughed.

"Drink it, or lay dead with them!" He slapped my glass upward.

Crying into my glass, I knew he wasn't kidding. This man had zero remorse that his beloved parents were dead in front of him.

And I knew he wouldn't think twice to end my life. Drinking the rest of the liquid, I gagged and prayed it'd go down. When the glass was empty, I looked at Conrad, who raised his arms up in the air.

"I feel you, Mother and Father; now, your blood is coursing through my bride's body, too."

My stomach flipped and I immediately bent over and vomited. It was their blood. He made me drink his parent's blood, and worst of all, he drank his parents' blood, too.

CHAPTER FORTY-SEVEN

SOMEHOW, I managed to stop vomiting as my new husband calmly watched me.

He wrapped his arm around me, guiding me out of the room where his dead parents laid and where we had just sipped their blood instead of champagne on our wedding day.

I felt like I was walking through darkened tunnels until we reached a side of the house I had never seen. "This is our new bedroom, my love." We walked in and the heavy scent of peonies wrapped around me. It was sickening.

"Was this your parents' room?" I cringed as I walked inside, my wedding dress now stained with patches of vomit and blood.

"Yes, but it's ours now. We control everything. We are in charge of continuing their legacy." He began undressing and paused to turn on the T.V. Backing away, something that resembled a home video began. Squinting, I walked closer to the screen.

It was a significantly younger Ian and Daphne...

Daphne was wearing... I looked down at the dress clinging to me. It was their wedding night. Ian began undressing as Daphne peeled the dress off and walked to the bed. Flicking my eyes behind me, it was the exact same room and bed.

"What is this?" I asked Conrad, who was now under the blankets.

"Tradition," he replied. "It's a sense of good luck. Mother conceived me on their wedding night, so they must have done something right." He patted the spot next to him as I walked backward with my widened eyes on the screen.

He couldn't be serious. He was going to make us watch his parents consummate their marriage while... I couldn't handle any of this. Death had to be better. Brushing my fingers against the locket Bradley had gifted me, I contemplated opening it and swallowing the pill. I could put an end to the misery. But closing my eyes, I could see his hopeful smile. I could see the courage he had for us; I could feel the love we shared as he slid the sneakers on my feet and planned our escape. I was so close to finally being able to live for the first time in my entire life. I had to fight just a little longer.

If the plan with Bradley failed, I'd take the pill. I wouldn't live this way anymore. I couldn't help the caged girls; I couldn't make a difference on my own.

"Come to bed, my bride. Take your gown off." Conrad rubbed the empty space beside him.

I could do this; I had to do this. Taking a deep breath, I remembered another Ivory tradition. Peeling the blanket back, I saw the white towel waiting for me to lay on to ensure I'd bleed. To ensure I was pure and only Conrad's.

"I'm going to the powder room for a moment. I'm a bit nervous. First time..." I added awkwardly as Conrad nodded and pointed toward the bathroom.

Hurrying away, I looked around the bathroom, quietly opening drawers until my eye caught a pair of sharp tweezers.

Hitting my head against my palm, I shook.

"Demi, come on!" Conrad called out to me.

Taking a deep breath in and exhaling, my fingers trembled as I slowly pushed the tweezers in between my legs and inside of me. I clenched my teeth together, as I pinched tiny cuts inside.

Tugging the tweezers out, I rinsed them off and put them away as the pain seared inside me. Rushing back,

I looked at Conrad and quickly climbed into bed, laying on the white towel.

He immediately crawled over my body. "I'm going to make love to you tonight." He leaned down and bit my bottom lip, tugging it and kissing my mouth aggressively. He didn't attempt to do anything else; he just shoved himself inside me and began thrusting. It felt like sandpaper as he groaned my name. Slamming my eyes shut, I tried to escape this moment and finally, I saw it.

I saw the ocean with the rocks and a boat... with Bradley waiting for me.

I'm going to be there, soon. I'll be in the place that my mind finally can escape to. Warmth filled inside me as Conrad yelled out and slammed his hand against the headboard.

Sliding out of me, he looked down at the towel.

"My virgin." He tugged the towel from under me and proudly lifted the red-stained material like it was his trophy.

I had already started taking the birth control that Bradley gave me but it might have not been long enough to work. But it had to work. Or at least, I had to cling to the hope that this wouldn't lead to pregnancy.

"Get me the whiskey. It should be sitting on your end table, babe." I looked over and saw the glass sitting there. Was it laced?

Reaching over, I handed it to Conrad, which he drank slowly, making obnoxious noises as he swallowed it down.

"Tomorrow, I expect you to participate and not just lay there like a damn blow-up doll, Demi," Conrad hissed at me before sighing and closing his eyes.

When I didn't move or answer him, he barked, "Say, yes sir!"

"Yes, sir." I wish I had put the damn poision pill inside his whiskey, but I needed it more than him if anything happened with Bradley's plan.

I watched as he fell asleep and waited at least thirty minutes in sheer fear that he'd wake. Pathetically, I considered taking the pill and just laying here until it killed me.

I was scared to leave. I was afraid that what was out there may not be better than what was in here.

Shaking my head, I slid out of bed, quickly wiped myself clean, and looked around. I spotted Conrad's keycard and grabbed it off the nightstand.

I didn't have anything to wear, but as I walked to Daphne's closet, I saw a suitcase with my name on the tag.

Sinking to the floor, I kept pacing my eyes between Conrad and the luggage. Pulling out bikinis, lace lingerie, and designer dresses, I realized it was packed for our honeymoon.

Grabbing a few pieces, I ran to the bathroom. Tugging the white, lace mini dress on, I slid a pair of reflective sunglasses on and a giant white hat. It didn't make sense since it was night now, but it's how I wanted to be when Bradley saw me. It's how I wanted to think of the next chapter of my life.

I didn't want to think of it as an escape; I wanted to think of it as the beginning I never had. Looking in the mirror, I grabbed the mouthwash and gargled as much as I could until the alcohol burned. A tube of the deep red lipstick was on the counter, and I didn't know why, but I rolled it up and coated my lips in the sticky, matte color. It was comforting in a demented way knowing I had the choice to wear it.

Sliding out of the bathroom, I took one last look at Conrad before swiping the keycard against the panel and watched the door open.

"Goodbye, husband."

Picking up my pace, I didn't go to the front door first, I went to the Ossis wing. Sliding the keycard against every panel of every door, they all slid open and I began to scream.

"Run!" I waited a moment, peeking into the rooms. The women all laid there with their short white gowns, bald heads, and desolate eyes.

"Get up! You're free, just run! I'll call for help!" I screamed.

Silence.

They didn't even flinch. Crying, I raced into Ian's office and called 9-1-1. It was the only choice I had.

"Hello? This is an emergency. Ian and Daphne Ivory have been kidnapping girls and keeping them in their house. Officer Tate is a part of the trafficking ring, so please don't send him. Please, help these girls!" I slammed the phone down after the operator spoke and took down more information. Racing to the front of the house, I slid the card and watched as the front doors opened. I blinked repeatedly, clutching the giant white hat on my head. I waited and suddenly, car lights flashed three times.

Terrified, I walked until I got to the passenger window. "Demi, I'm Kealey, a friend of Bradley's. Please, get inside. You're safe." A beautiful young woman with sandy-blonde hair and hazel eyes smiled at me. Climbing in the car, she began to drive. I turned over my shoulder and saw the Ivory estate grow smaller and smaller.

"Here's some water." Kealey handed me a bottle. "I like your hat and sunglasses," she added kindly.

"Thanks." I felt ridiculous, but I didn't take either off. I wanted to wear them. In some way I felt safe, hidden away under the hat and sunglasses. If no one could recognize me, then they couldn't hurt me.

"We'll be in Charleston in about three hours. You

can put your seat back and rest. I promise, you're safe, Demi."

But no matter how sweet she sounded or how beautiful she was, I didn't believe her. I just didn't have a choice. I was shaking violently and looked out the window at the dark sky full of stars and a full moon.

It was over. It was finally over.

CHAPTER
FORTY-EIGHT

THREE HOURS WENT by quickly and before I knew it, a tinge of sunrise was hinting into the otherwise dark sky.

"Just walk down the dock, and you should see—"

"Colorful powder in the sky?" I offered.

"Yes. Bradley's boat will be on the right, and I'm sure he'll be out there waiting for you. Good luck, Demi." Kealey leaned in and gave me a quick hug.

"How does Bradley know you?" I asked quickly.

"I was the only caged girl who ever escaped. And I guess in a way... you are too, now." She shrugged and before I knew it, she left.

"Wait!" I called out. I needed to go. I needed to find Bradley. Walking down the well-lit dock, I smiled as soon as I saw the color shooting up in the sky. It was so beautiful. It reminded me of the Indian holiday Holi.

The festival of color and celebration of love. Everyone would be throwing colorful powder all over each other and into the sky.

"Dem?" His voice instantly calmed me.

I could hear his footsteps as he ran to me. Lifting me into his arms, he nuzzled his face in my neck.

"You're here. You made it. Dem, I'm so happy. I'm so proud of you!" I could feel moisture from his tears drip onto my skin.

"You're safe. You'll never be there again. We're safe." He showed me onto the boat and before I knew it, we were sailing. There was no time to waste since we couldn't risk the wrong person finding us.

The waves surrounding us provided solace from the otherwise cloudiness and trauma of my mind.

"Here, are you hungry? Thirsty?" He handed me a plate with a sandwich and chips and a can of soda.

"No… I'm just…" I began to cry.

"I know, I know." He wrapped his arms around me and let me cry for the next hour. I shook, I trembled, I bawled. I felt every emotion I had suppressed in order to survive. Tucking me into the bed below deck, Bradley kissed my forehead.

"Get some sleep, beautiful."

I tugged the fuzzy blanket under my chin. The rocking of the boat and the colors of the darkened wood all comforted me. Nothing was white here. My life was going to finally have color again. Closing my eyes, I let myself sleep without fear for the first time in a long time.

———

I jolted upright in panic the next morning. My body was covered in a cold sweat as I looked around. I couldn't believe I wasn't at the Ivory estate. I was actually free. I was on a boat in the middle of the ocean with Bradley.

We were both finally free. Getting out of bed, I walked over to the small bathroom and looked at myself in the mirror. My bridal makeup was mostly still intact along with my short blonde hair being perfectly curved underneath my chin with the endless hairspray holding it into place. But I was dehydrated, hungry, and felt the weight of the trauma I'd witnessed.

When I closed my eyes, I saw their faces. The caged girls. When I blinked, I saw Conrad forcing us to drink Ian and Daphne's blood. When I took a deep breath, I saw Becca laying in a pool of blood.

How would I survive? Washing my face, I tugged the lace dress off, and saw an oversized T-shirt lingering on the railing.

Pulling it over my head, I knew this was how I

would heal. Bradley's scent was embedded in the fibers of this shirt, giving me comfort. Looking around the room, I glanced at the ceiling. I could hear Bradley moving around, but I needed a few minutes alone. I needed time to just be. I laid back down for a while with my fingers laced across my chest as I hummed a song to myself. The boat rocked harder against crashing waves and I decided I needed to get up.

Opening a nightstand drawer, I sat back on the bed and tilted my head as I tugged out a beautiful, cognac leather photo album. Flipping through the pages, my heart began to race. It was small images of children.

Two little boys.

With trembling fingers, I brushed them over the faces. Shaking my head, I flipped to another page and gasped. Slapping my hand over my mouth, I shuddered in shock.

It was an image of two little boys with Daphne and Ian Ivory.

Chills grew across my arms as I continued to flip through the pages and shake my head. This had to be someone else… but the faces were unmistakable. How? He couldn't be…

He couldn't be their son.

Something fell upstairs, a loud sound echoing from above. A door opened from the top of the small set of stairs. Shoving the album back into the drawer, I forced myself up.

"Dem? You up? I made us some breakfast... well, lunch. The sun's out. Come see it!" Bradley called down.

"Dem?" I heard a footstep.

"I'm coming," I whimpered, clearing my throat and looking around the small cabin.

There was nothing I could use to protect myself. I was, again, left weak. I was always the feeble prey.

This had to be some complete misunderstanding. There was no way Bradley was one of them. He *worked* for them.

I blinked away the tears and thought about his name. I didn't even know his last name.

Gripping the thin banister, I took a few steps up and immediately pulled my sunglasses on as the warmth of the sun beat on my face.

I can feel it.

But even though the sun was warm, I still felt cold. Once up, Bradley smiled at me and pointed at the two plates on a makeshift table.

"You wear it better than I do..." He winked at me and nodded at my T-shirt.

Walking slowly, I took a seat and looked down at the rice, plain yogurt, and boiled egg, meticulously cleaned of the yolk.

My breathing hitched as I felt Bradley's eyes on me. *An all-white meal.*

"Sorry, it's all I had." He sat across from me and began to shovel the food into his mouth.

"Bradley, you know it's so interesting... I never asked you what your last name was?" I rolled my lips together as I looked up at him, thankful for the sunglasses that covered my eyes.

He clutched his fork tighter as his jaw clenched. "Why the sudden curiosity, Dem?" He jammed his fork viciously into the rice.

"Bradley..." My voice cracked as tears rolled down my cheeks. "What's your last name?" I repeated myself, pushing the plate away as my stomach flipped.

He slammed his silverware down and looked at me. "Ivory."

Sucking in a breath, I began to sob. "How..." I looked over his shoulder. There was nothing but endless ocean surrounding us. I had never felt more trapped than now.

"Ian Ivory was my father, and he raped one of the caged girls he had kept for himself. That was my mother. She ran away and got us out for years. Daisy has a different father. Eventually, Ian tracked us down and dragged us back. Daphne grew envious because Ian let her stay out of the cage and started to have feelings for her. So, Daphne slit her throat, drank her blood, and had me and Daisy help bury her body in the peony garden." Bradley stood and walked to the rail. My body shook as he spoke. His words blurring together as my head spun.

"Bradley, where are we going?" I stood and gripped the rail behind me.

"Florida first, then the Bahamas." He clutched the rail tighter.

"You don't want to be like them, right?" I trembled as I looked down into the water.

"Dem, it's not that bad... We don't have to be as brutal. But honestly, it's true. The women... well, they are perfect wives and mothers. My little bird, you are destined to soar next to me." He sighed. Before I could say anything else, he tugged a delicate silver necklace out and clasped it around my neck. I glanced down at the pendant that sat just above the locket he'd already given me. *A diamond encrusted feather.*

"Did you know that feathers are crucial for a bird because it helps them stay hidden and to blend in with their surroundings. That way they can protect themselves from predators. My love, blending in is a good thing. It's the safest thing. We must carry on this legacy."

My heart shattered as I looked back at the man I had trusted. He didn't mean this. He was groomed to be this way; he was raised by monsters. But the thing was, when you teach a wolf to hunt and kill, he'll never lose the thirst for blood. He'll never not enjoy the thrill the hunt brings.

He'll never stop.

Nodding, I walked over to him and wrapped my arms around his waist from behind. Pressing my head into his back, I knew deep down there was probably some form of good in him—just like with Conrad. A little boy trapped and wishing he could have lived a normal life.

"Father had an entire business set up in the Bahamas. Even though we had a strained relationship, he put me as his beneficiary if anything happened. The pill you gave Conrad wasn't one that simply put him to sleep, it was strychnine. He's dead. The entire Ivory estate and financials are mine. The police will seize everything in Charlotte, but in the Bahamas, we have a completely different organization, and it's running steadily. It's time we take over, baby. You and me." He held my hands and turned, looking down at me with a smile.

"I love you, Dem." Leaning down, he kissed me. And I kissed him back, passionately, and with every-thing I had inside.

"Do you have any alcohol?" I kissed his lips one more time before brushing his face. "Let's get plastered and have sex. We deserve some fun, handsome." I pulled my sunglasses off, feeling so much peace in my heart.

The ocean breeze rippled through, picking up my hair and warming my body.

"I have champagne." Bradley smiled at me and pointed at a cooler. "I've been craving your body, badly." He dropped his hands to my hips and tugged me closer.

"I'll get the champagne, and you head down to bed," I whispered against his lips.

"Deal." Kissing my forehead, he went down the stairs and left me there. Walking to the rail, I gripped it and wondered how long it would take to drown.

Would I suffocate on the copious amount of water choking me? Would a shark feast on my body? Would my mind and body fight to float and try to survive until dehydration took over? How did one die in the ocean? How easy it must be, but so very painful? I wiped the tear that left my eye and looked out to the horizon.

I loved the sunshine, and I loved the ocean; two things I had so rarely experienced. It occurred to me that this was the first time I was seeing it.

The ocean.

I wanted to swim in it, I wanted to sunbathe, I wanted to feel sand under my feet. I wanted to do so many simple, mundane things.

But the family I was born to didn't let me, the people I was sold to weakened me, and the people who imprisoned me, well... they wrecked me. They stole the light from my life and now the only thing I could see was darkness.

I thought that was all I'd feel. But now, I could feel it. The warmth of the sun. Turning around, I opened the cooler and dug for the bottle of champagne. Next to the cooler was a tote box of cups and plates. Reaching in, I grabbed two cups and quickly popped the bottle, but as I poured the fizzy alcohol into the cups, I paused.

The desire to die was outweighed ever so slightly by the desire to live. But I didn't want to live a life chosen for me. No, that's the life I'd been living since I was born. Now, I wanted to live a life that I chose. That I created from the ground up, after being broken down, shattered, and crushed. I wanted to rise the way a phoenix does from its ashes. Brushing my fingers against my locket, I slid the chain off and looked down at it.

Popping it opened, I looked at the tiny white pill.

It didn't feel right, but it didn't feel wrong, either. It felt necessary and sometimes, necessary is the right thing to do.

Sliding the pill into one of the cups, I waited and watched as it dissolved completely.

"Dem?" he called out as my hands shook. I lifted both cups and walked down the steps to the bedroom.

"Sorry, I was soaking up the sun. It's been a while." I forced a smile out. Bradley was under the blankets, shirtless and grinning back at me.

"Come here, baby. After we get to the Bahamas, you can soak up the sun for a bit, but I do ask you go through the white-therapy program for a few weeks. Just to… help you be prepared to be my wife and the mother of our son." Bradley opened his arms to me. "Put the cups down. I want to make love to you."

The words triggered fear, anxiety, and panic in my body. They were the same words Conrad had said to me last night. They were two of the same. I placed the cups down and climbed into bed. Wrapping me in his arms, he began kissing my neck.

"You don't want to do a toast first?" I feigned disappointment.

"I know this isn't easy for you, making love after my brother… probably hurt you last night. Let's have that drink. It'll help loosen you up for me." He didn't even sound like the same man I had grown to love.

Moving over, I looked at the cups from a different angle and realized I didn't make note of which was which.

Fuck…

My heart raced as my mouth went dry.

"Dem, grab it, please." He nudged me.

It was ironic in a way. Maybe this was the only way to know if I was even worthy of living in such a destroyed world.

Grabbing the cups, I handed one to Bradley and looked into his eyes.

"Here's to the favorite girl." He let out a dry laugh before tapping my cup and tossing back the entire cup of champagne.

Looking down into my cup, I shook it around. "Drink it," Bradley ordered, sounding annoyed.

"Here's to the last Ivory." I smiled at him and drank every last drop.

Bradley's forehead creased as his eyes grew smaller.

"What do you mean..." He clutched his abdomen with one hand and his forehead with the other. "Demi..." He coughed.

I was shaking with nervousness, but I didn't feel any different. Was he feeling something?

Leaning in toward me, he yanked my necklace and opened it. "You... bitch," he wheezed.

I ran out of the bed and jogged up the stairs as quickly as I could. Looking around, my heart was pounding as I hugged myself. My eyes caught on the bright orange vest. Grabbing it, I put it on my shaking body and prayed. I didn't know who I was praying to or what I was praying for, but I prayed that if anyone, anything was out there, that they'd help me. That they'd protect me for the first time in my life.

Footsteps echoed behind me and suddenly, there was Bradley. His eyes were tinged red with sweat building across of his forehead.

"We're going to die together." Lifting a knife, he wobbled toward me. I walked backward to the rail and slid away. Bradley's eyes began to shut and before I knew it, he was close enough to the rail that I jumped on him, and with all my might, I shoved him over the rail, but he didn't go down alone.

He took me with him, wildly waving the knife in the air as we fell. He eventually met my flesh as we both slammed into the dark, thrashing waves.

Screaming, I saw my arm was bleeding profusely. I was still hooked to the boat by the chain attached to the life vest. Bradley grabbed at the chain, trying to unhook me, and I wiggled to stay out of his grasp. I didn't know how to swim, so I knew I'd drown instantly. I'd panic and forget how to even float.

Slapping his hands away, he stabbed the blade into my arm again so hard, I pulled back. The blade was semi-lodged into my flesh, and he let go.

He was growing weaker as I grabbed the knife from

my arm with screams I didn't recognize leaving my body. I looked at Bradley as he began to float.

Blinking slowly, he whispered, "You were always my favorite girl..."

Just before a tall wave slammed into us both, I whispered back, "And you were always my favorite Ivory. There's just no room for Jack. And there never was." Tears fell from my eyes as I watched the wave take him under and into the depths of the ocean.

Grabbing onto the boat with all the strength I had left, I pulled myself up until my nails dug into the side, and I could see the small steel ladder. Clawing at it, I tugged it down and climbed up.

Falling onto the deck, I clutched myself and cried. The warmth of the sun beat down on my drenched, bleeding body. I wondered if the sun had the strength to soak up all my shed tears one day?

Will I ever stop crying? Will I ever stop feeling pain?

————

Eventually, I did stop crying.

Eventually, I did have the strength to stand up, find a flare gun, and shoot it into the sky for help.

Eventually, I wrapped my wounds, ate, hydrated, and waited. Rocking back and forth as I hugged my knees to my chest. I chanted to myself while thinking about everything in my life. My mind was shattered just like me. Maybe one day, these chapters of my life would become a memory. Or maybe, these chapters were setting the stage for who I'd always be.

Eventually, another boat came. And when they came, I tugged on the big, white hat and my reflective sunglasses, and then climbed into a true safe haven and grinned. I was standing there in my white lace dress full of hope.

"Where are you headed, honey?" A kind man asked with concern.

"The Bahamas." I brushed my hands against my pants before sitting down.

"Would you like to eat anything, sweetie?" the older lady on the boat asked me as she cleaned my wounds.

I smiled back at her. "Do you have any plain white rice and yogurt?"

Because, after all, I was the favorite girl.

AUTHOR'S NOTE

Dear reader,

Thank you from the bottom of my heart for taking the time to read my novel. It is my darkest novel, yet. Every book I write I try to embed very real subject matters that plague the world we live in. The Favorite Girl is no different. In this book, I wanted to craft a fictional world of terror that still encompassed the horrors that actually happen. Personally, nothing scares me more than knowing there are 'real-life' monsters out there. I hope that you enjoyed Demi's story and while I do think she's out there sailing away. I do wonder what is next for her. I think with trauma at that level, I couldn't possible wrap her story up in a big, pink bow. It would be an injustice to her. She escaped, though! I think that she has a long road of healing and learning and perhaps we will see her in one of my future books to check in on her as I do with other characters from time to time.

I hope you know it means the world to me that you read my words. Reviews are a wonderful gift for authors and if you enjoyed The Favorite Girl, I'd be so grateful if you took the time to leave one on Amazon and Goodreads!

Thank you again for reading and I wish you all love, joy and happiness!

XO,

Monica

ALSO BY MONICA ARYA

ABOUT THE AUTHOR

Monica Arya is a bestselling and award-winning author of multiple novels. She is a multi-genre author, writing both thrillers and romance. Monica resides in North Carolina with her husband, two beautiful children and golden doodle. She loves to connect with readers and you can find her on social media @monicaaryaauthor or www.monicaarya.com

Facebook reader group: Monica Arya's Misfits

ACKNOWLEDGMENTS

To my children, Mila and Ari. You both were babies when I started this journey and have been my greatest cheerleaders. Whether it was holding you in my arms as I typed, opening those first copies together or just telling me never to give up. I feel so blessed that out of all the roles in my life being your mommy is my favorite. I love you both forever and always. My moon and stars, you brighten up any darkness.

To my husband, I've loved you for more of my life than not and to say I am so thankful for you is the greatest understatement. But thank you for being mine and nothing like then men in my thrillers but everything like the dream book boyfriend. I love you so much, babe!

To my family, I love you all! Thank you for always being interested in my books even though they make for awkward holiday dinners between all the slicing and spicing I write.

To my dear friend who is a sister to me, Paige. Thank you for being the 'village', for Panica and

Manica, for soul sister spirals and all the laughter, tears and more. I love you to the moon and Saturn.

To my sweetest Marcie, who has supported me from the beginning, who gets my 'unhinged' and celebrates it with me. Thank you for being a beautiful human inside and out. I feel so blessed to call you a dear friend and love you more than words!

To my girl, Joselin but also my 'Joss', thank you for being you. For always understanding so much of the behind the scenes of life and for the pick-up right where we left off vibes always. I love you!

Special thank you to Swati MH, Silvia C., Stephanie R., Jackie, Kori, Christina C., Elise, Kealey, Jessica M., Caroline, Gabby, Erin, Amanda, Allyson, Kelly, Jessica W., Cristina, Janeida F., Lisa W., Lauren F., Sarah P., Lindsey S., Linda M., and Katie L. You are all so wonderful and bring so much joy to my life. XOXO

To my rockstar ARC and street team - I can't believe I am so lucky to celebrate each book with you all. Thank you, thank you, and THANK YOU for everything. The posts, the messages, the reviews, the joy each of you gift me is something I'll cherish forever.

To my beloved readers, without you all there would be no purpose of books. Thank you for taking the chance on ME! The posts, recommendations, reviews and everything in between are things that I truly cherish forever. I am forever grateful beyond words for each of you!